FLICKER AND MIST

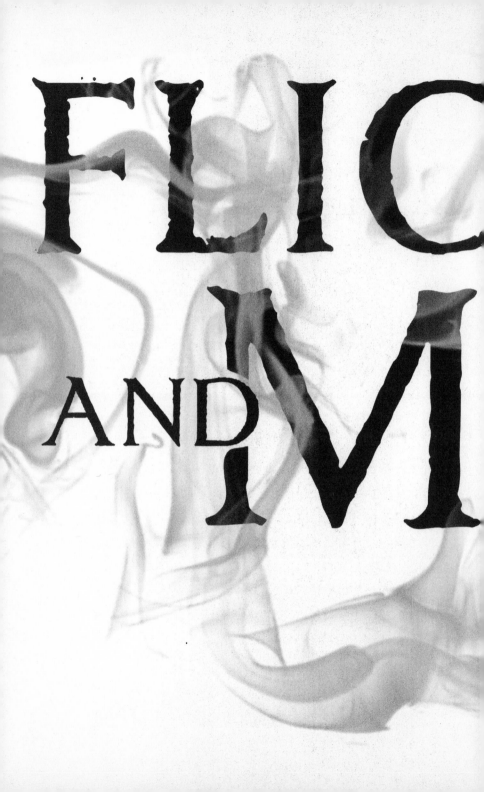

FLIC
AND M
AND

KERIST

A NOVEL BY MARY G. THOMPSON

CLARION BOOKS
HOUGHTON MIFFLIN HARCOURT
BOSTON NEW YORK

Clarion Books

3 Park Avenue

New York, New York 10016

Copyright © 2017 by Mary G. Thompson

All rights reserved. For information about permission to reproduce selections from this book, write to trade.permissions@hmhco.com or to Permissions, Houghton Mifflin Harcourt Publishing Company, 3 Park Avenue, 19th Floor, New York, New York 10016.

Clarion Books is an imprint of Houghton Mifflin Harcourt Publishing Company.

www.hmhco.com

The text was set in FreightText Book.

Design by Lisa Vega

Map illustration by Jennifer Thermes

Library of Congress Cataloging-in-Publication Data

Names: Thompson, Mary G. (Mary Gloria), 1978- author.

Title: Flicker and mist / Mary G. Thompson.

Description: Boston ; New York : Clarion Books, Houghton Mifflin Harcourt, [2016] | Summary: "In a story rich in intrigue, adventure, danger, and romance, a mixed-race teen heroine must decide which part of her heritage to claim: her privileged status, or her ability to become invisible for which her kin are being persecuted"— Provided by publisher.

Identifiers: LCCN 2016001078 | ISBN 9780544648401 (hardback)

Subjects: | CYAC: Fantasy. | Invisibility—Fiction. | Persecution--Fiction. | Racially mixed people--Fiction. | Love--Fiction.

Classification: LCC PZ7.T37169 Fl 2016 | DDC [Fic]—dc23

LC record available at https://lccn.loc.gov/2016001078

Manufactured in the United States of America

DOC 10 9 8 7 6 5 4 3 2 1

4500636864

for Amber Hyppolite

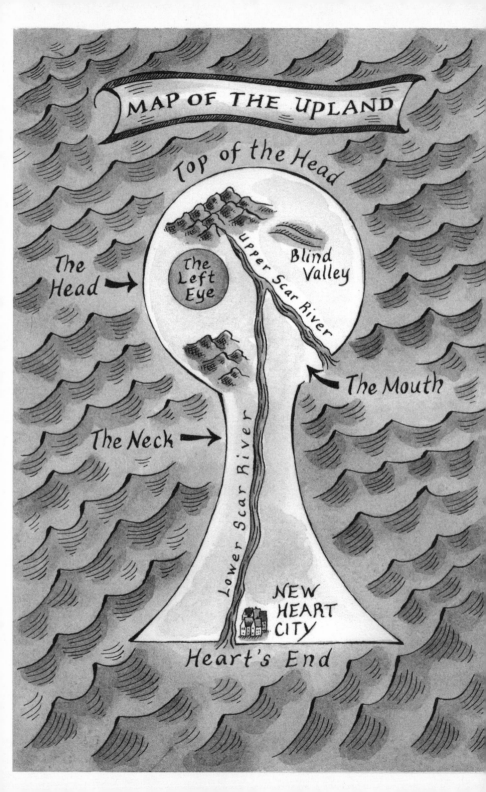

ONE

HAVING THE ABILITY SHOULD HAVE BEEN FUN. IN another world, a child who could become invisible might play pranks on her parents, might sneak around with friends, might go ride the beasts in the dead of night. In another world, the Ability might have brought freedom and joy. But I was not born in another world, I was born in the Upland, where the Ability was used as a weapon of war.

I didn't know the Ability existed until the day I learned I had it, when I was five years old. I woke up from a nightmare and began to cry, and my father came into my room, but when he turned on the light, he couldn't see me. In that way, he learned not only about me but also about my mother. She had sworn that she was an ordinary Leftie, that she had no blood of the Flicker Men, but she had lied.

My mother cried in silence. My father pounded his fist on the table.

"She has the Ability, Rhonda. *You* have the Ability!" my father yelled.

My mother said nothing.

"You lied to me. You entered the city. You had a child."

"I never wanted a child," my mother said. Her voice was soft, and for the first time I could recall in my short life, it wavered.

"You never thought to tell me why not? When I pushed for a family, you couldn't tell me this might occur?"

"I hoped it wouldn't," my mother said. "She's only one-sixteenth Flicker."

"You lied!" my father raged. He turned his back to her, faced a window with the curtain closed. After this day, it would remain so.

"Would you have loved me if I hadn't?"

My mother's words hung in the air. She and my father didn't know I was peeking around the corner of the hallway. I don't think they remembered me at all. One thing I always knew was true was that my parents loved each other. Often their eyes would meet and they seemed to float upward, leaving me below. They spoke their own language, using only their eyes—his dark brown and hers pale gray-blue.

"Rhonda ..." The rage had left my father's voice. He

remained looking at the window. "What am I supposed to do now?"

"I'm the same woman, Donray," my mother said. "Myra is the same child."

"You know the Flicker Laws," he said. "The penalty for a Flickerkin caught outside the Left Eye is Judgment by the Waters." I didn't know then what that meant. I thought the Waters judged us always, that in the scheme of life, they rewarded good children and punished bad ones. I didn't understand that when citizens committed the worst of crimes, like murder or treason or being a Flickerkin outside the Eye, the Council would toss the criminals over the cliff's edge, into the ocean, and the Waters would save them or let them drown.

"I do not intend to be caught," my mother said.

"What of Myra?" my father asked. "How can a child control this?"

"I will teach her," my mother said. "Children who suppress the Ability may go their whole lives without flickering. We have caught it in time."

"You must go back to the Eye," my father said. "You must take her and leave."

"No."

My father turned around. Tears were rolling down his face. I jumped back into the hallway. I had never seen anything like that before. "It is not safe here," he said. "I am only one vote on

3

the Council. Some Members will not care that you are my wife or that she is my daughter. They will throw you to the Waters."

"I will not leave you," my mother said. "No."

I heard sobs from both of them. I didn't see what they did, if they embraced or merely stared at each other, eyes meeting, floating in their own space. But I didn't hear another word, and we did not leave. No one ever spoke of us leaving again.

So they taught me in secret about the Flicker Men: that they were a race who were like humans but with differences, that they had come to the Upland many generations ago and lived in the Left Eye with my mother's people, who were called Lefties, that there had been a war, and that the Flicker Men had left with a cycle of the oceans and never returned. And that these Flicker Men could become invisible and had left this Ability with many of their mixed-blood descendants, who were called Flickerkin. This was before I knew what it meant to be a Leftie, to have lighter skin than the Plats and curlier hair, to be shorter than Plat women and to have more curves. I didn't know that Plat men and Leftie women did not marry, that my parents had bought the necessary papers with my father's money. Back then, I thought I might like to be invisible.

"Momma, how do I do it?" I asked.

"You must never do it," she said. She said it quietly, but with that look, with that tone that scared me more than someone else's mother shouting. She held me by the shoulders and looked at me with cold, hard eyes. "If you cause yourself to flicker, the Ability will take control. You will be required to suppress it at every moment. I will help you to never flicker again. You must never *try* to flicker. Do you hear me, Myra?" She shook me.

"Yes, Momma," I said.

"There are known Flickerkin in the Eye who have never flickered even once, and others like you, who accidentally flicker once but never again. If you do not trigger your Ability, you will be safe."

I didn't understand what she meant to keep me safe from. I only knew that I must protect myself from her cold, quiet anger.

"Yes, Momma," I said again.

"Good," she said. She ran a hand through my hair and kissed my cheek. "You will not be like me."

My father was with me every night after that. We would read together and play games, following a Leftie practice designed to help children control nightmares. I suppose my mother knew that if she were the one to help me, she might scare me more. The nightmares stopped, and I didn't flicker. We didn't speak of that awful night, and after a while, it was almost as if it hadn't happened.

So it was that between the ages of five and sixteen, I lived like any other child of a Council Member. I can't say that some didn't see me as half Leftie or take long looks at me as I walked past. But after all the years of being normal, I no longer worried about flickering. I worried about ordinary things such as young men and friendships. And, of course, the annual athletic contest called the Games. In the summer of my sixteenth year, I wanted nothing more than to ride Hoof, my purebred wetbeast, and win the ride in front of all the citizens of the Upland.

From *THE DECLARATION OF PEACE*

By Order of the Council of the Upland, approved by the
Deputy to the Waters, may they hear us: . . . while these
Flickerkin remain atop the Left Eye, they shall live peacefully
without any interference, but they shall not participate in the
mining of prezine. It is further prohibited for any person,
having knowledge of the Ability, to harbor, abet, or assist any
Flickerkin found outside the Left Eye. Any violation of this
section shall be punishable as the Waters judge.

———◆———

TWO

"TRY THIS ONE," PORTI SAID, PULLING A FINE BURgundy gown off the rack. "The color is perfect for your skin tone." Its skirt swished and swirled as she passed it through the air toward me.

"Porti," I said, exasperated, "you know this won't fit me." We stood in front of a long row of ladies' dresses, every single one of them made for a lady like Porti—tall and thin, with no appreciable parts sticking out this way and that. How she had managed to drag me down to the Drachmans' cloth shop in the hours before a party I wasn't sure. It was simply that Porti was Porti, and ever since she had ridden into New Heart City one year ago—literally ridden, winning the ladies' ride at the Games and stealing my title—she had used her insufferably friendly heart to convince everyone to do anything.

"Myra, these Lefties are the best clothmakers in the city, masters at alterations," Porti said. She looked up at Mr. Drachman, who rented the shop with his wife. Lefties, as noncitizens, could not actually own property in New Heart City. His pale blue eyes smiled at us, and he nodded, but he said nothing. I had never heard Mr. Drachman say more than a few words. "See, he can have it ready before nightfall," Porti interpreted. She held the dress in front of me. "Look at the neckline. If this doesn't reel Caster in, nothing will."

"Porti!" My cheeks began to fill with color, a phenomenon inescapable and mortifying, especially in front of the silent shopkeeper.

She leaned in to me and whispered. "I have it on good authority that tonight's the night. Let's not give him the option to lose his nerve."

"Who told you that?" I whispered back. "Orphos? Have you actually spoken to him, then?" Anyone could tell that Orphos and Porti were mad for each other. Porti had stopped speaking to him or looking at him or acknowledging him in any way. Yet somehow her aggressive indifference only made Orphos more insistent upon gaining her attention, and the whole city more sure that they would be together forever. I didn't understand her behavior at all. If Caster Ripkin, the Deputy's son, were to make clear that he wished to be more than my friend, I would leap into his arms with no games whatsoever, color in my cheeks or no.

"Well, he's Caster's best friend, isn't he?" Porti said.

"Tell me you didn't ask him straight out." I covered my face with one hand. If Orphos were to tell Caster that Porti had asked . . .

"It's all fine," she said. "He likes you. Word is he's liked you for years."

"Years?" I whispered. "We've only become friends since you arrived." It was true, but I wished I hadn't said it. There were many with whom I had grown up, with whom I had attended school for my whole life, with whom I had made small talk at obligatory state occasions and been grouped for countless official photos, who had been blamelessly polite to me but never warm, who had never invited me to their parties or spoken to me as if I was one of them—not until Porti had taken me under her wing. And I was a native of New Heart City. I was the daughter of a Council Member. She had been the daughter of no one, an orphan raised by beast ranchers far away in the Head, until she won the ride in last year's Games and was taken in by Council Member Anga Solis. And of course, she was one hundred percent Plat, tall and thin with dark, straight hair and eyes three shades darker brown than mine.

"A gentleman need not be friends with a lady to admire her bosom," said Porti, as Mr. Drachman approached with his tape measure and pins. He waved his arm at the dressing room. His face was stoic, but his eyes sparkled. I hoped he wouldn't tell his son, Nolan, what he had overheard. I didn't need all the children of the Leftie workers gossiping about me in addition to their furtive looks. I didn't like the attention they paid me already, as if perhaps they thought I was of their kind. But I was a citizen of New Heart City, something Lefties could never be. I had a paper that proved it, signed by the last Deputy himself. Legally, I was a Plat.

"Thank you, Mr. Drachman," I said, taking the dress from Porti. As I pulled it over my head—the dress was a size too big, as required for my unusual proportions—Porti chatted at Mr. Drachman, insensible to the fact that he was not going to talk back. She also failed to understand that she was now of a class with the children of Council Members and should not be so familiar with the workers.

"I suppose Nolan will compete again this year?" Porti asked.

I imagined Mr. Drachman nodding.

"I will certainly be cheering for him," she went on. "No one else from the city has a chance, do they?" She spoke of Nolan's prowess at the stone throw, which required strength most common in Lefties. Most of the serious competitors would be Plats from near Porti's home—those used to hard work. But a few Lefties would compete, Nolan among them. He had placed third last year, a surprising loss. In the Leftie community, it was whispered that he had been cheated, that the gameskeeper had given him a stone two grades too heavy. My mother certainly believed it. I didn't wish to think of this, though. It reminded me that I had lost the ride to Porti, though no one had cheated me.

"I'm ready," I called. I stood awkwardly as Mr. Drachman pinned the cloth. By the time I was done, Porti had already paid for her purchase—a delicate pink gown off the rack without a single alteration—and was chatting with Mrs. Drachman, a friendly woman as pale as her husband and with the same roly-poly shape.

"Oh yes," Mrs. Drachman said. "He's improving by the minute. We hope to have a champion in the family this year." She beamed with pride.

"I'm sure you will," said Porti.

"I too," I said, thankful to be back in my ordinary dress, though of course I wished I were dressed to ride. I wished, as always, that I were in fact riding. My beast, Hoof, would never put me through the indignity of being pinned for a gown to prepare for a party at which I would sport the palest face, the lightest brown hair that wouldn't straighten, and the sole substantial bosom among the guests.

As glad as I was to be invited now, parties were nothing compared to being on the back of a horned purebred wetbeast, flying at a speed no human could manage, leaping over walls, swimming through the deep moat of the arena. Feeling the weight and the warmth of my beloved Hoof underneath me while we flew as one.

"Ah, there she goes," said Porti. "Off on a beast." She smiled conspiratorially at Mrs. Drachman.

"Sorry," I said. I would train again tomorrow, as I did every day. But until I was on Hoof's back, I would be squirming inside my gown, always with one part of my mind on her and on the upcoming Games. They were held once a year and featured every important sport. The winners were lauded and interviewed on the radio and received large cash prizes, but I cared nothing for that. What I wanted was to win, for myself and Hoof to be known as the best rider and beast in all of the Upland. This year would be my year. Last year, Porti had beaten us by only a horn.

And perhaps Caster would win the men's, and we could stand on the winners' podium together. The picture of him and me standing side by side filled my head. I would be wearing my riding clothes, my pants and boots, with my curly hair gloriously windswept and my cheeks flushed. He would take my hand, and we would raise our joined hands together—no, he was tall even for a Plat, he would have to lean down awkwardly to do that and my arm would be pulled out of its socket. He would not take my hand, but we would raise our arms together—the crowd would cheer; my beast would stomp her feet to join in the celebration. My mother would smile and clap, and my father would yell his head off.

"I think not," said Porti, winking at Mrs. Drachman. "Nice Boy and I won't let that happen."

"Perhaps I was thinking of *you* winning," I said. "Because I am a good and generous friend." But we both knew that was not true. If either of us was generous, it was Porti. And even she was not generous enough to wish a victory for any woman but herself.

Porti laughed. "I'm sure that was it."

"May the best woman win," Mrs. Drachman said, taking my bills. She winked at me. "We'll deliver the gown to Member Solis's apartment?"

"Thank you," I said. As we left the shop, I poked Porti in the arm. "Now all the Lefties will be gossiping about me."

"Let's not worry about what he or she or whoever says," said Porti. "Let's make sure they have something to say." She shook her practically nonexistent bosom and smacked her lips in a grotesque imitation of a kiss. "Oh, Caster," she cooed. "Caster *Ripkin*."

"Orphos?" I teased. "Orphos who? Oh, *that* Orphos?" I batted my eyelashes and fluffed my hair.

She knocked into me with one shoulder. "Oh, stop."

"It's only fair," I said.

"I just want you both to be happy," she said.

"What will make me happy will be to win the ride," I said. "That's what's important. You know"—I glanced at her slyly—"Member Solis will most certainly pay your way into University, whether you place first or second. There's no need to compete so hard."

"And your father, *Member Hailfast,* will pay your way whether you ride or sit on the sidelines in a fluffy gown."

"Perhaps I'll just sit and cheer on my man," I said, pretending to fan myself like a fancy lady. We both laughed. Porti would enjoy the fluffy gown, but nothing would make either of us sit on the sidelines. That was one reason we got on so well. Porti knew what truly mattered.

"The next question, of course," she said, "is what will you wear to the winners' ball? You'll want to look extra beautiful while celebrating second place." She grinned at me and then took off at a run, trailing her wrapped new gown behind her. I followed.

"You arrogant scallywag!" I cried. We were both wearing ladies' boots with two inches of heel and dresses that fluttered around our legs, but we didn't let that stop us. We dodged work-beasts pulling carts and leaped puddles from a recent summer rainstorm. We passed from the merchant quarter through the low-lying apartments to the State Complex, where the families of the Council Members lived in larger, fancier apartments. We raced through the courtyard that separated our two homes and reached the door of her apartment together, panting and muddy and feeling grand.

From *A HISTORY OF THE UPLAND*

These Flicker Men landed on the north end of the plateau, at the top of the region called the Head. Their footprints were masked by the fall rain, and their ships were as invisible as they were. Stories of ghosts appearing and disappearing spread from village to village, stories of food stolen out of kitchens, crops cut from fields. For many months they were a fable, a supernatural curse upon the Head. Until one day, in the high plateau-upon-a-plateau called the Left Eye, a man materialized out of nowhere.

THREE

I T WASN'T REALLY PORTI'S APARTMENT, OF COURSE; IT was the apartment of Council Member Anga Solis, her new foster mother. Member Solis was always on the lookout for the best athletes from the far reaches of the Upland, whom she could sweep up and bring into New Heart City society. It wasn't just any champion who made the cut. The lucky winners of instant entrée into the elite had to be smart enough to make it at New Heart City University, poised and articulate enough to converse with the Council and their associates, and of course, Plat. Member Solis claimed she took on these charges as a solemn duty to the state. Those who were admired by the people must be appropriate objects of admiration; it would not do for the winner of the women's ride to go back to shoveling beast manure. In reality, I suspected she wished to relive her glory days, when she herself had won the ride.

Member Solis's habit of adopting the best athletes was the main reason Porti had begun to ride the beasts she raised. She had dreamed of New Heart City and the University and the life she now had. To her, gowns and ladies' shoes and extravagant parties and state politics were new and exciting, not the uncomfortable tedium they were to me. She had been raised in coveralls and work boots; I had been raised with money and privilege. Yet I wouldn't have been invited to tonight's party if not for her.

Member Solis greeted us at the door. She was also a fixture on the New Heart City social scene and loved hosting parties for the entire population of elite children. She had to show off her entitlement to the finest apartment in the State Complex, aside from that of the Deputy, since she was the longest-serving Member of the Council.

"Good afternoon, Member Solis," I said.

She stared down at me. She was short for a Plat, not much taller than I was, yet she had a way of looking at you as if she gazed from a great height. "Hello, Myra," she said. We were not familiar enough for first names. Most people treated me as a Plat, at least to my face, but Member Solis had no such courtesy. She was even worse to my mother. My mind churned with unwise replies.

"Miss Hailfast!" Member Solis's eight-year-old daughter,

Bricca, raced out from behind her mother and grabbed my hand, pulling me inside. "Have you bought a gown for tonight?"

"Yes," I said, glad for the rescue. "Miss Portianna Vale picked it out, so of course it's perfect." I couldn't help but smile when I was around Bricca. She entirely made up for her mother's rudeness. Like Porti, she was interested in both riding and ladies' fashion. Someday, she would be the darling of the whole city and a champion besides.

We went up to Porti's room, the only one occupied by a foster child at the moment. It was more lavish than my own room, with velvet curtains and an elegant four-poster bed. The closet was filled with gowns. Porti still lit up when she walked in.

"Miss Hailfast, are we going to dance tonight?" Bricca asked.

"You will be with your friends," said Porti. "You'd find the things we do boring."

"I wouldn't," Bricca said. She stuck her head into Porti's closet and riffled through the gowns. "Which one are you wearing?"

"This one," Porti said, pulling the new gown from its wrapping.

Bricca ran over to it and slid her hand along the delicate fabric. "Ooh, can I have one like it?"

"I'm sure you can," said Porti. "Now leave us while we dress. We'll see you a little later."

"See you tonight, Miss Hailfast!" Bricca raced over and hugged me. Then she grinned up at me and ran from the room.

Porti and I laughed.

"You're lucky," I said. "It's like having a sister."

"Perhaps you'll still get one," Porti said.

My mother's voice filled my head, her words evoking the terror of that long-ago night. *I never wanted a child.* I understood that she worried about producing another child with the Ability who might reveal us all, but the words still stung. I shook my head, my good mood fading. But then I thought of Porti, and how her parents hadn't lived to produce another child, and I felt ashamed of my selfishness. At least the three of us were together.

"Your father would be proud to see you," I said.

"Yes, he would." She pulled on the gown she had just bought. "Perhaps he will be here this year."

We didn't speak of her real father, who was dead, but of the man who had raised her on the beast ranch. She didn't say much about him except that he had pushed her to ride, to take the opportunity to come to New Heart City. I knew there was something she couldn't tell me about why he didn't come to watch, something more than simply having beasts to care for.

"One can be proud from a distance," I said.

She sat down on the bed. "We joke and poke each other," she said. "But I hope you know it isn't a game to me. This is my future. It's true that Member Solis will pay my way to University if I place second, but I want to win for my father. I want to win so I can tell him it was all worth it—me being here and him being there."

"I know," I said. And why did I want to win? My reasons seemed smaller. I didn't need the prize to support myself, nor did my parents care whether I won, apart from what happiness it would give me.

"But, Myra," Porti continued, "if you win, that will be all right too. The Waters won't flood the Upland because I carry the second ribbon. Nor will I be sent back to the Head to shovel beast dung. My father will still be proud. Your parents will love you, Caster will still want you, and Orphos will pursue me like a starving man pursues a scrap—all whether either of us wins or not."

"Yes," I said. As usual, Porti had hit on what was important. Though that might change in the moment, she always knew what the moment took.

She wrapped her arms around me. "Promise that no matter what happens, we'll remain friends."

"Of course," I said. "You know I'd be nothing without you."

"Nonsense."

"You are the reason for all my friendships," I said.

"They only needed a chance to see you for who you are," she said, letting me go.

Later that afternoon, there was a knock on the door. A servant stood holding the burgundy dress that the Drachmans had altered for me. Porti seized it and pulled it over my head.

"By the Waters," I said. "Was the neckline always this indecent? My father will be livid."

"Since when does your father attend our parties?"

"But Member Solis—" Surely that woman would be the first to gossip about me. She and my father butted heads on every issue. She would probably take the opportunity to make some comment on my Leftie features. *Doesn't she look just like her mother?* I imagined her saying.

A bell rang in the distance.

"Perhaps that's Caster now," said Porti, pushing me toward the door.

"Perhaps it's Orphos," I countered.

"Come," said Porti, flipping her long, dark, perfectly straight hair. "Whoever it is, the party is beginning!"

Soon the apartment was full of the children of the elite citizens of New Heart City: the Council Members, those who worked for the Council, and the senior guardsmen. There were some as young as Bricca, playing together in the sitting room, and even some who had already begun at University. I weaved my way among them, trailing behind Porti as she played hostess, sometimes blocked by the mass of tall people around me. There were no other pale faces, no one who had so much as a drop of Leftie blood—except Issa, Bricca's nanny, who stayed well out of sight.

So far as I knew, there were no others in the entire Upland who had one Plat parent and one Leftie. A marriage between the races was as unheard of as a beast with four horns. The law didn't prohibit it, but there was no need for an official ban. People believed that my parents would not be together after they died, in the land beyond the oceans, where the Waters kept the races separate. Both Plats and Lefties believed this, even the Leftie priest who had married my parents. My mother had told me that this priest took my father's money and signed the papers but refused to actually perform the ceremony, saying they were sure to be split apart at death. They had truly married themselves, at the edge of a cliff, high up in the mists of the Left Eye. What all this meant for me, since I couldn't separate my two halves, was unclear.

Until Porti had ridden into the social scene with me on her coattails, people had treated me with distant politeness, as if the Waters would disapprove of their coming too close. By the miracle of her personality, it was now as if people our age were forgetting. Sometimes I would hear a snickering comment about Lefties—how their faces were pale and their hair curly or their bodies thick—as if they didn't notice they were insulting my mother. *I* couldn't forget, though, especially at times like this when people were packed together and I stood out like a beacon.

I was separated from Porti for a few minutes, and when I found her again, she was in conversation with Caster Ripkin. He leaned down to hear her speak, his soft, nearly black hair falling into his eyes. The outline of his profile was sharp and strong. He wore a black suit of expensive, shimmering fabric—it must have cost his father a small fortune.

"Four inches this month," said Caster, half shouting over the party's din.

"Goodness," said Porti. "Really?" They looked perfect together, both tall and thin and with sharp angles to their features. That feeling rose in me before I could suppress it—which was ridiculous, knowing that Porti was pushing *me* toward him as hard as possible.

"At four testing sites," said Caster.

I slipped on a wet spot on the floor as I approached.

"Why, hello, Myra!" Caster caught me as I narrowly missed knocking Porti's fruit punch into her gown.

"Sorry," I said. "Hello. Sorry." I couldn't help but notice that his hand was still on my arm.

Caster laughed. "I should be so lucky again." He grinned down at me. Was he looking where Porti hoped he would look? *Do not blush*, I commanded myself. *Do not blush*.

"Oh, look at the time," said Porti, though she carried no timepiece. She grinned at me and slid away through the crowd. Suddenly, I was no longer jealous and wished she would come back and take his ear. It was easy to talk to Caster at school, but here, in the dark, in a fancy, indecent gown, I found that my tongue was wrapped around itself.

"I was just telling Porti about the latest survey," Caster said. "My father says they measured four inches."

"This month?" I asked, thankful he had picked a topic to speak on.

"Yes," said Caster. "He is reporting to the Council as we speak. The oceans are really rising now. It might be a high cycle beginning early—and coming fast."

The oceans that surrounded the Upland had been low since the end of the war, when the last of the Flicker Men had left, back when my grandmother was just born. And before that, we had had four generations of low water. It was too soon for another cycle.

"A whim of the Waters," I said. I frowned. This was not idle party talk. If the oceans rose, they might stop at the top of what were now high cliffs, creating warm waves lapping sandy shores. Or the water might cascade over the edge of the plateau and flood the Upland, taking all of us with it—as *The Book of the Waters* threatened, should we defy them. And if the oceans rose enough to support ships, they might carry the invisible people back from their faraway lands, people who might hold a grudge over how they were chased off all those many years ago.

We stood in silence for a few seconds, contemplating this. And deep down, below what I knew I should be feeling, a twinge of excitement rose up. If they did come across the oceans, then I could meet them, these strange, exotic, invisible people who didn't have to hide. I shook my head. My mother had warned me against even thinking about the Ability. If I were to make any effort to become invisible, I would trigger something deep inside me, and then I might be undone by almost anything: strong emotions, injuries, surprises. She herself, having used her Ability all her life until she met my father, had to hold every emotion back. But I would never try to become invisible. Perhaps I had destroyed the Ability for good.

"Myra," Caster said, "are you all right?"

"I'm sorry," I said. "It's a shock—the oceans rising."

Caster leaned down to me. "Perhaps we could build ships of our own, see what else is out there. Find out why the oceans rise and fall as they do."

"Caster Ripkin!" I exclaimed. "By the Waters!" To travel on the Waters was a great sin. But I had thought the very same thing myself. If only we could find out what caused the oceans to rise.

"Do you really believe the oceans have minds inside them,

Myra? I don't. I think it's all nonsense created by ancients who had no care for knowledge—and held now by those who fear invisible people who are long gone. I think we should explore the world while we have the chance."

"I can't believe I'm hearing this from the son of the Deputy to the Waters," I said. "Blasphemy." His face was close to mine now, him leaning down and me stretching up. To speak of ships was sacrilege. The Waters would rise up faster upon hearing themselves disrespected. And Caster's father was supposed to be doing their work.

"Come," Caster said, and he took my hand. It was a perfectly natural gesture, not awkward at all, as I'd imagined it would be. He was very tall, yes, but he was no giant. Why did I make him even larger in my imagination? His hand didn't awkwardly envelop mine, but fit as if he had taken my hand a hundred times. After this year of friendship, did it mean something? He led me through the crowd, using his height to make way through the people, heading for the sitting room. He pushed through the door, and we were suddenly free of the crowd, only to find ourselves in a room full of children watching a photobox production. They stared at us as we came in, all except Bricca, who smiled and waved at me.

I waved back.

One of the boys whistled. I couldn't stop myself from blushing. This was one more problem with my pale skin. It showed emotions that a full Plat could have kept hidden. But Caster didn't seem to notice.

"Ah, the future leaders of the Upland," Caster said, leading me around the kids, who were lying on pillows on the floor.

"It's the halfsie rider," a boy said. It was a little boy, maybe eight years old, among the youngest in the room.

"Shush," said Bricca. "That's not nice."

"Thank you, Bricca, but it's all right," I said, blushing more. It was only a child who didn't know better. I shouldn't let it bother me. Yet Caster seemed to loom taller, and I seemed to shrink away.

"A rare beauty," said Caster. "The luckiest woman in New Heart City."

"Aren't you afraid of the Waters?" the boy asked.

"The Waters have no care for how a person looks," said Caster. "It's no crime to be a beauty." He winked at me.

The boy stared up at us. He was too afraid of Caster to contradict him. But I could read his thoughts as if he had spoken. The Waters wished the races to be separate. They did not wish me to exist.

"Have a good night, children," said Caster, a slight edge to his voice. I gave Bricca the best smile I could manage, and Caster led me through another door, into a hall that led to the stairs up to the family's private rooms. Mercifully, the hall was empty. "I'm sorry about that," Caster said.

"It's all right," I said. "I don't hear it often."

"Because it isn't true," said Caster. "The boy will learn that."

I pulled my hand away. Why did the boy have to say it now? I could stand an occasional reminder, as long as I had my friends. But I didn't want Caster to be reminded that I was different, that I would never be tall or have straight hair or look as a lady should in the fashions Porti loved to play with. That if he were to choose me, he would face the stares as well.

But he took my hand again and pulled me to him.

I think I stopped breathing.

"Myra, I meant what I said. You're beautiful." He ran a hand over my hair. "There's no other girl like you." He leaned down toward me as he spoke.

"I . . . thank you," I said.

He kissed me. It was a short peck, but he didn't stand back up to his full height. He looked at me, as if asking a question. I stood on my tiptoes and kissed him, and he nearly lifted me off the ground, and we kissed for real. When he let me go, the hall was spinning. It was as if pinpricks radiated from my heart. I couldn't see his face clearly; I couldn't think.

"Are you all right?" he asked, catching me by both arms.

"Yes," I said. My vision cleared a little. That was twice I'd fallen into him tonight. I was supposed to be an athlete, not a swooning damsel. But I didn't pull away.

"Perhaps you've been training too hard."

I smiled up at him. He had said exactly the right thing. "Perhaps you surprised me."

"Does a man take a lady into a dark hallway for conversation about the oceans?" he said, putting a hand on my waist.

I giggled.

He kissed me again, this time pulling me even closer. I closed my eyes and felt it. All I knew was that he was kissing me, really kissing me, and I stood on my tiptoes, trying not to force him to bend down too far, trying to be as tall as I could. We fit together somehow, despite the height difference that I'd fretted so much about. This was the moment I'd waited for. I didn't want it to stop, and when he lifted his head, I wasn't sure what to do. Should I pull him back down to me, or would that be too much?

He ran his hand over my hair again. "Myra, I would like for us . . . for you and me . . . well . . ."

I had never seen him stammer. Could it be that Caster Ripkin was nervous—that I made him so? But I was too nervous myself to do anything more than stare up at him.

"Can we be together?" he asked.

I was shocked into silence. *Yes,* I thought. *Yes!* But my mouth wouldn't move.

"I don't mean to pressure you," he said. "I've felt lately . . . at least I've thought . . . that you wanted the same thing."

"Yes," I said finally, my brain working again. "Of course I do."

He broke into a wide grin, and so did I. We stared at each other, able to do nothing but smile.

A crash came from the sitting room behind us, then screams.

Caster shook his head wryly. "These kids should be in their beds by now." He pushed the door open. "What is going—by the Waters, what *is* going on?"

I leaned around him and saw a picture of chaos. Three kids were hopping on the couch, and the rest were racing around the room as if being chased. The photobox player was flat on its face, its glass broken in pieces.

As I entered, Bricca rushed over to me and wrapped her arms around my waist.

"Bricca, what happened?" I asked.

"I don't know," she said. "The photobox player fell."

Porti raced in through the other door, followed by Orphos. Her hair was in disarray and her faced flushed, as though she had been dancing her heart out the moment before. Orphos wiped sweat off his brow as he took in the scene. Perhaps they had been dancing together. Behind them, the faces of other partygoers peered in.

"Stop this!" Porti cried.

The kids did not stop.

"He's got me!" a boy screamed—the same boy who had called me a halfsie. He was flattened against the wall nearest me, acting as if he were trying to wriggle out of a man's grasp.

I gently passed Bricca to Caster and walked toward the boy. "What's got you?" I asked. I figured the best way to end the chaos would be to play along and let the game run its course.

"*He* does!" the boy cried.

I took his hand. "It's all right," I said. "There's no one there." The boy looked so frightened, I was no longer sure he was playing a game. "See, no one is holding you but me. Shall we take a walk?" I stepped back, pulling him with me. Tears were streaming down his face. But he followed me. We walked across the room, toward Porti. The other kids were calming now, no longer racing around but standing restlessly.

Porti came over to us. "Jet, have you had a scare?" she asked. "Come, I'll call your nanny to walk you home." She took the boy's hand, and with her other hand she took Bricca's from Caster.

"There *was* somebody," Jet said. "He had me. But when Miss Hailfast the rider came, he let me go." He looked up at me. "I hope you win this year," he said.

"Thank you, Jet," I said. "I'll watch for you in the stands." I thanked the Waters he had not called me halfsie again. I would have hated to have Porti and Orphos hear that too. I wished they hadn't heard the boy's claim that he had been held by an unseen man. There had been a panic over just such nonsense when I was a child, though I didn't learn about it until later. All the Lefties in the city had been tested for the Ability—and the test amounted to torture, my mother said. She herself had been subjected to it. How she had passed, she didn't tell me.

Porti, Bricca, and Jet disappeared, and so did the others at the door, except Orphos, who came in and clasped hands with Caster. "Playing with the kids, were you?" he asked.

Caster grinned. "Maybe."

I blushed. By the Waters, why could I not stop doing that? "All right," I said, to defuse the awkwardness. "Who can tell me what brought this on?" I kneeled before the photobox player and lifted it, hoping that no one would see how my hands shook. I didn't know if it was the boy's claim or Caster's kiss.

Orphos leaned down to help me. "Must have been some game," he said, winking.

"Oh, stop," I said.

"Portianna insulted my attire only three times and ignored my request for a dance twice," he said. "I find myself hopeful."

"Were you not dancing just now?" I asked.

"Yes, but only *near* each other," he replied. "Her persistence in not looking at me makes me quite happy."

"Or delusional," Caster put in, taking my end of the photobox player from me.

Orphos laughed. "She'll come around, won't she, Myra?"

"Yes," I said. "I'm sure she will." They got the photobox player standing, and we began picking up the glass so the children wouldn't step on it and hurt themselves.

"See?" said Orphos. "Myra has the inside word."

Caster raised his hands in an expression of surrender. "Whatever you say, friend. It's your dip." By which he meant that Porti would be the end of him, a dip in the oceans being a synonym for Judgment by the Waters. This was not all bad, if you believed. It was thought that the soul of a person who died in the ocean would be redeemed.

Orphos, who was shorter than Caster yet still towered above me, only laughed.

A girl of about ten, the daughter of an assistant to Porti's guardian, tugged at my arm. "Miss Hailfast, we didn't do it," she said. "There was a man here, like Jet said." She looked around at Caster and Orphos. "There *was*."

"What makes you think that?" asked Caster.

"He knocked the photobox player over," said the girl. "We were all just watching."

"Where is this man?" I asked, attempting to make a joke of it. "Where did he go?"

"How could I know?" said the girl. "He was a Flickerkin."

My blood ran cold. If all the children believed this, the rumor would be out in no time.

"Did this supposed Flickerkin speak?" asked Caster.

"No," said the girl. "But I heard him running. He ran after us."

"It *was* someone, Mr. Ripkin," a boy said.

"Nonsense," said Caster. "One of you must have run behind the photobox player and knocked it over. Now, who did it?" He looked around the room. No one said anything.

Porti came back in, accompanied by three of the nannies, who had been socializing in the kitchen, waiting to bring their charges home.

"Come on," said Porti. "It's past everyone's bedtime."

The kids filed out, some looking back nervously at the photobox player. After the previous chaos, they were strangely subdued. I had no doubt they believed someone had been there. And they would all tell their parents.

"Are you all right, Myra?" Porti asked. "You look like you've seen a spirit."

"It's just . . ." I didn't want to say it, but these were my best friends in the world. If I couldn't tell them a part of the truth, whom could I tell? "The children believe they were attacked by a Flickerkin. What if there's another panic?" I couldn't look at Caster, nor could I mention his father by name. "They might begin testing Lefties again."

"They won't test you," said Orphos.

I winced. He had heard me in the word *Lefties.* I was thinking of my mother. But I didn't know for sure that Orphos was right. I was legally a Plat, yes, but the Ability was passed through the blood and not the law. Perhaps my father had protected me once, but I was no longer a child.

"Maybe not," I said.

"It's all nonsense," said Caster, putting his arm around me. "Everyone will see it's just wild children who've watched too many programs on the photobox. I'll bet it was that boy Jet himself who knocked it over. Besides, there are sensors over every exit." The sensors sent out invisible beams that were supposed to hurt Flickerkin and make them visible, detecting spies. Like everything that took power, they were made from prezine, mined in the Eye. Though they did nothing to anyone visible, I didn't like to think of them. I liked to think of our kiss in the hallway and feel the warmth of Caster's body next to me now.

Orphos put his arm around Porti. "If there are any Flickerkin, I'll protect you," he said.

"Or I'll protect you," she replied. But she didn't cast his arm off. They looked at each other for a second, and then Porti pulled away.

Caster kissed me on the lips—right there in front of our friends. I was sure my entire body was blushing now.

"Aha!" Porti squealed. "This calls for a toast!" And we went back to the party, the four of us. The music was still going, and the people were still dancing, and I had Caster with me, for all to see. I tried to put the incident with the children out of my mind, and we danced, Caster and I together, closely, Porti and Orphos near each other, never quite able to be apart.

From *A HISTORY OF THE UPLAND*

The Flicker Men settled among the people of the Left Eye. They taught the Lefties to mine for prezine and sell the results to the plateau below. Thanks to prezine, the entire Upland advanced. Every home had electricity, and communication across distances became possible. The trade in prezine brought the peoples of the Plateau and the Eye together, and a government was formed in Heart City, near Heart's End. But the extraordinary metal was scarce, and some in the Eye did not wish to share what the Waters had given them.

From *THE DECLARATION OF PEACE*

Prezine, being necessary to the lives of all people, shall belong to all people of the Upland. The Council shall manage the distribution of prezine for the benefit of all. There shall be no money exchanged, except that the Council shall pay fair wages to those deserving.

———◆———

FOUR

MY FATHER HAD BEEN AWAY FROM HOME OFTEN of late, sometimes staying with the Council from dawn until well after I'd gone to bed. After he returned from his ambassadorship in the Left Eye, with my mother and my baby self in tow, my grandfather became ill, and so my father took his seat on the Council. The seats passed by heredity to the son or daughter of the Member's choice, so long as that person was of age. Some Council Members, including Anga Solis, had attempted to block him because of my mother, but the majority would not discard the law. This didn't mean he was popular, however. My father didn't officially support autonomy for the Eye or any loosening of the Flicker Laws—a fact that caused many fights between my parents—but he did advocate reducing the triple taxation imposed on Lefties in New Heart City. No one else on the Council supported that.

He had to thrust himself into every corner of the Council's business, leaving no issue untouched and attending all meetings. If he let them vote without him, they would most certainly undermine his position at every turn. It didn't help that the ocean monitors had been showing rises of inches per month, and all those who knew were much alarmed.

So it was that the morning after Porti's party, I woke to find my father gone and my mother at the dining table. She sat with her long, tightly curled white-blond hair flowing free, grimly listening to the radio.

"By my count, that's four reports," said the interviewer, an overweening man who went by the name of Sky.

"Four incidents of speculation," said the Deputy. I would have recognized his deep, raspy voice anywhere. "An incident with excited children at a party, after those children should have been in bed, is by no means definitive proof that we have a problem with invisible attackers. Quite the contrary, it's likely to be all in their imagination."

"But the other three reports were not by children, were they?" Sky asked. "There was a shopkeeper who reported items going missing from a locked shop, a woman who was tripped in the market by unseen feet, and—most disturbing, I think—a workbeast found dead in the street this morning."

I sat down heavily in my chair, my thoughts of breakfast abandoned. A dead beast?

"Is it not true that a beast was found dead?" Sky asked.

"It is true," said the Deputy. "But animals, unfortunately, perish often of perfectly explainable causes. There is no reason to believe a Flickerkin is involved."

"But this beast was locked in a stall last night. How does a beast perish in the main street, all the way across the city from its stables?"

"Perhaps the beast's keeper was not as diligent as he reported," said the Deputy. "I can assure you, the Guard is investigating the incident, and I'll report the truth of the matter to the public when I learn it. My advice to the city is: don't panic. There is no evidence of invisible invaders. The city has been free of them since the end of the uprising, more than sixty years ago. The gates are monitored by sensors, and all those of Leftie blood in the city have been tested. There are no Flickerkin here by law, and the law is enforced."

"All right," said Sky, not sounding impressed. "You heard it from the Deputy himself, folks. Don't panic. All's right with the Waters. Speaking of the oceans, I've heard a rumor that some new tests have shown disturbing—"

My mother shut off the radio with an abrupt tap. She didn't change her expression, but the truth of it was in her tight control. The story had made her ravenously angry.

"Momma—"

"Listen to him pretend to be on the side of calm," she interrupted, her voice even. "He only wants to seem more reasonable when he *finally* bows to *evidence* and begins testing."

"Everyone has been tested," I said.

"There is testing and then there's testing," she said. "The Deputy's father was in office the last time. The younger Ripkin pressed for deeper and longer shocks then but was overruled."

I sat, paralyzed. I knew a little of the method of testing, but my mother had never gone into gruesome detail.

"There are no Flickerkin left outside the Eye, but that will mean nothing once a few more paranoid citizens hear rats in the night," she continued. "Rats who just happen to scurry when the citizens of the Eye demand their rights." Neither of us commented on the fact that there *were* Flickerkin in New Heart City—us. Sometimes we could almost believe our lie.

"Momma, what's going on in the Eye?" I asked. I knew my mother kept in contact with my grandmother by voicebox, but they spoke only in the Leftie language. My mother had taught me a few words and phrases when I was a child, but she had stopped teaching me after the testing. She felt forced to keep me apart from her past, and I wasn't sure she would even answer me.

My mother paused for a few seconds, but then she spoke. "There is agitation among the prezine miners," she said, "and during the protests, one of the miners displayed a dagger." All weapons of any kind had been banned in the Upland since the war, when invisible Flickerkin had murdered Plats with concealed daggers, and Plats, in turn, had murdered Lefties with swords. The guardsmen were not armed now, and even kitchen knives were assigned to licensed cooks. To brandish a dagger was an offense suitable for Judgment by the Waters. My mother owned one, though, something I wasn't supposed to know. One day as a child I had been snooping and found it in a locked case inside her bedside drawer. The key had been easy enough to find with her apartment keys. I had never asked her about it, never wanted to admit I had gone through her things, or to confront why my mother had something that I had been taught was evil.

"What are they going to do to him?" I asked.

"I haven't heard word yet," she said. "News is slow, and my mother fears to speak over the voicebox. Even if they don't dip him, we all know the miners are dangerously overworked. The Waters apparently forbid putting Plats in harm's way but allow them all the prezine. 'For the benefit of all,' they said in their Declaration of Peace. But 'all' meant Plats and always will."

"Are things that bad?"

"The Plats have been demanding more," my mother said, "and they won't say why. They take so much prezine that power relays in the Eye go unrepaired. Does that ever happen in New

44

Heart City?" She waved an arm at our fully lit apartment. "The people of the Eye protest, and so the Deputy takes it out on Lefties here in the city."

My mother hated the Deputy, in large part because of the testing he had pushed for when I was a child, and she took little care to hide it. But there had to be some good in him. Otherwise, how could he have a son who not only didn't hate Lefties, but believed I was beautiful? Thinking of Caster made me smile, and my mother noticed.

"You find something amusing in this, Myra?" she asked. But her voice was easier now. The anger, which would have been barely visible to anyone but our family, had passed.

"It's Caster Ripkin," I said. "He's not like his father." My smile broadened.

"Caster Ripkin?" She raised an eyebrow.

"He *isn't* like the Deputy, Momma," I said. "Look at them together sometime. One radiates gloom and the other sunshine."

"Sunshine?" The corners of her mouth turned up, just a little. She shook her head.

I blushed. I couldn't tell my mother the full extent.

"We won't tell your father just yet," she said. "His heart couldn't take it, I fear."

"Just yet?" I said. "I don't know when would be a good time!"

"After the wedding," my mother said. "Perhaps after a few children."

We both laughed. I laughed heartily; my mother chuckled from the corner of her mouth. But she grew serious again. "You must remember, though, Myra. Caster Ripkin is still the Deputy's son. He may seem more different from his father than he is."

"He *is* different," I said.

"Maybe," she said. "But you must be careful. Do not share your secrets with this boy."

"Momma, I would never."

She raised an eyebrow. *You are a silly girl,* the eyebrow said. *You will fall all over this boy and forget everything.*

"Really, Momma. I'm not a fool." He wouldn't like me if he knew, I thought. Being half Leftie was one thing, being Flickerkin another. He would see me as a freak and, worse, a traitor. "Besides, it has never happened since. I might not be like you at all."

"One has the Ability or one does not," she said.

"I'm the only one like me," I said. "You don't know."

"Why should you be the one exception?" she asked.

"Because I'm a Plat," I said.

She stared at me.

"I'm sorry, Momma," I said. "But I am."

"*Ti,*" she said. *Yes.*

"Why is that wrong, when Poppa is one and you love us?"

"It's not wrong, *kopan*," she said. *Dearest.* "It's only that I wish you could know my people."

I didn't know what to say to that. She thought of her home often, and missed it. I would hear her singing softly in words I didn't understand, staring at our closed curtains as if she were seeing something far off. And when she spoke to my grandmother, her face would lighten as if a great burden had been lifted. Yet to protect me, she had to keep me apart. She had to keep me from being made an outsider, as she was.

She didn't have friends here among the Council community, and it wasn't proper for a Council Member's wife to have too much contact with the Leftie workers. In a way, she was one of a kind even more than I. To fill the silence, I switched the radio on again.

Sky was speaking with the captain of the Guard. They were discussing preparations for the upcoming Games, when the city would be flooded with people from around the Upland.

". . . but rest assured, we will be testing all those of Leftie appearance as they pass through the gates," the captain said, and my mother immediately turned it off again. We ate our breakfast in silence, my mother's mood having settled into a simmer.

"*Pracksima*," I said after a while. *Let it pass.*

"*Ti*," she replied. *Yes.* "*Gi gos hen kin.*" *But these are my kin.*

"They make it so difficult for Lefties, as though they are all under suspicion. They tax them triple, watch their movements, limit their jobs, anything to try to force them all back to the Eye. But all the Lefties here are too young to remember the war. They aren't Flickerkin and don't wish to fight. They wish only to work and have good lives."

"Are you ever sorry you came here, Momma?" I asked.

She smiled a little. "No, *kopan*. You and your father are my best life."

"But we could have lived in the Eye," I said. I had never been to the Eye, apart from having been born there. I wished to go someday, to see where my mother came from, but I had no wish to live there. The people were miners and farmers. They were said to be poor, their lives hard. I wished to take my father's place on the Council, if they would let me. A man married to a Leftie was one thing, a half-Leftie another. But I would fight for my right to be a Member. And of course, there were no beasts in the Eye. They couldn't climb the steep cliffs to reach it, and the Lefties had never imported them via their great elevating machine. They had other animals for their work—small, lithe creatures barely larger than men. A place without beasts was no place for me.

"*Ti*. But I chose my path. I married a Plat from New Heart City. It was always understood that we would live here."

And she didn't go back to visit because she feared being

tested at the gate. When we had first entered, testing at the gate had not yet begun. My father assured her that since she had been tested before, she would be exempt, but she didn't believe it. She couldn't take the risk of being discovered.

"Are you not training this morning?" my mother asked.

"Yes, of course," I said, getting up from the table. "I'm glad we're here in New Heart City, or I would never have learned how to ride a beast, or met Caster or Porti."

"Me too, *kopan*," she said. "Go now, before you miss your arena time." But I could see that the Deputy's words, and her secret, were still weighing on her. I wished she could have friends and a life here the way I could now, but she had never been accepted or made an effort to fit in. She was full-blooded Leftie, and her accent and her walk and all about her spoke of her difference.

"I'll see you tonight," I said, and then I was changing into my riding clothes, trying to put my mother's fears out of my mind.

From *A HISTORY OF THE UPLAND*

The mechanism by which the oceans advance and recede is among the greatest mysteries of our plateau. As long as people have kept records, the oceans have come and gone in cycles of fifty to one hundred years. But there is evidence that in ancient times, there were instances of advances and recessions that came blindingly fast.

From *THE BOOK OF THE WATERS*

The Waters return according to their Judgment; let no man or woman live against them.

FIVE

ON A NORMAL DAY I WOULD HAVE HAD ALL THE time in the world to ride, but with the Games approaching in only a week, my time in the official arena was short. I could still ride outside the walls, racing through the plains that surrounded the city until they turned into forests too thick for a beast to run in easily. But that was recreation, and this was sport. This was for the win I had dreamed about since I first laid eyes on my beast, Hoof.

She was pawing the door of her stall when I arrived. Her two long, healthy white horns pointed over her luminous brown-haired head, dotted with the black spots of a purebred wetbeast. She could run and she could swim and she could jump like no other beast in competition. And more than that, she was my friend, the one creature in the world whose love was unconditional, who would carry me from here through the arena and all across the plateau if I were to ask.

"Hello, Hoofy," I said, opening the door and sliding into her pen. I patted her head, and she mooed softly. "You act as though you have not just been for a romp around the grazing field, but I know they took you there."

She nuzzled my neck gently with one horn.

"Yes, we'll be going for a true ride now. It's our turn to practice the full course. Do you like my new riding suit?" I twirled for her, showcasing the tan pants and jacket designed to withstand the water of the moat yet to move with me as easily as normal fabric. The suits were made by the Drachmans, and I had been among the first to get one. My light but robust brown riding boots were tight around my upper calves, keeping out the elements but allowing me the circulation I needed to direct Hoof. There was no outfit I felt more like myself in, and no place where I felt more like myself than right here with Hoof.

"Come," I said, and I led her out of the stall. A well-trained beast needs no rein or saddle, not with a known rider. Hoof and I had been together for so long that she understood my commands, and I knew her feelings as my own. She followed me into the walkway and then out to the wider area next to the arena, the space that would be filled with vendors and spectators during the Games. Now it was littered with remains of beast feed and droppings, and as we walked out, it was being cleaned by two stable boys. One of them nodded at me.

"Good morning, Miss Hailfast."

"Good morning," I said, leading Hoof to the set of portable stairs I needed to reach her back. It was humiliating to be unable to mount one's beast without help. Indeed, I could do it at a flying leap if in a hurry, but there was no need to subject either of us to that today. I stepped off the stairs and over her back, and I was on top of the world. Hoof mooed softly, showing that she was in complete agreement. And then, through the gate of the arena, Caster appeared on his beast, Monster, followed by Orphos on Shrill. Shrill gave a deep screeching hello, living up to his name. Hoof mooed back but shifted her head sideways, pointing one horn at him. I had a feeling those two had a relationship much like that of Orphos and Porti.

"I thought you were scheduled for this evening," I said, unable to contain my smile as Caster rode up. *He may seem more different from his father than he is,* I heard my mother saying. But she didn't know him. She was wrong.

"I know somebody," said Caster, winking. "We thought we might have a little competition. A friendly battle of the sexes, if you will. Since we aren't to face each other in the Games." A point that tried me, since I was convinced that a male rider had nothing over a female, nor was a male beast stronger or faster. Yet we were forced to ride separately, the ladies on a shorter course.

"Are you sure you want to risk it?" I asked. "You might find yourself on your backside."

"Perhaps the lady will slide off in the moat and splash about like a wet fowl," said Caster.

Hooves clopped on the turf behind me. "It wouldn't be fair for our sex to make the race two against one," said Porti, riding Nice Boy (who was not a boy beast, but female). Curse me, I had forgotten we shared a practice time. She smiled broadly at the three of us, looking more radiant than ever in her riding clothes. The suit—exactly like mine—showed off her rail-thin figure. We practiced together often, but now that the Games were nearer, I had been avoiding her. We had agreed to remain friends always, but it was still a competition.

"Why, the lady is right," said Caster. "Welcome to a fine humiliation, Porti."

Porti only smiled back. "Are you ready to send these two boys home?" she said to me.

"Let's do it," I said. Not adding, of course, that I intended to place first among us all. Here and in the final contest. If she was going to observe my practice, let her see that I could win.

After our warm-up, we rode into the arena to find a

smattering of spectators in the stands, as was usual for practices so near the Games. Porti's guardian, Member Solis, sat in the front row of the Council box with Bricca. The Council box was high above us, so I waved broadly—at Bricca, not her cold-fish mother.

"Ride for our honor, Miss Hailfast!" Bricca yelled down.

"Hey, what about me?" Porti asked.

"And also Miss Vale!" Bricca called.

Member Solis said nothing but gave a small wave to all of us.

"What, you'll not root for me?" called Orphos, in mock surprise.

"Perhaps at the Games," Bricca called.

"But what if I never make it there?" he cried. "What if I die first of a broken heart?" This sent little Bricca into a fit of giggles, but Porti merely smiled.

"Ah, a smile," said Orphos. "There's hope yet." He made a tipping-the-hat gesture at Bricca.

On the far end of the stands, away from the rest of the spectators, I noticed the Drachmans. I wouldn't normally have conversed with them outside their shop, but I hadn't yet thanked them for their fine work on my suit. With the slightest twist of my body, I directed Hoof toward them.

"Good morning," I said.

"Good morning, Miss Hailfast," said Mrs. Drachman. "A fine day for a ride, isn't it?"

"Every day is a fine day for a ride," I said. "Now that I have my new clothes, I never want to take them off. I must thank you for your work. It's the finest I've seen."

"You honor us," said Mrs. Drachman. Mr. Drachman merely nodded.

I assumed they were here to watch their son practice. We were in front of the grassy mound from which the stone throw event was performed. I followed his parents' gaze to see Nolan entering the arena, rolling a cart full of practice stones behind him. He didn't look in our direction or acknowledge us but positioned himself on the mound and began warming up. I didn't know if he really had been robbed the year before, but I hoped he would win this time. He practiced daily all year round, and this made him stronger even than the Lefties who traveled from the Eye to compete, people over whom he had no physical advantage. I could admire someone who worked for his achievements.

"I hope we will stand together at the final ceremony," I said. "He will make the city proud."

"Thank you, Miss Hailfast," said Mrs. Drachman. "Between you and me, the lady from the Head stands no chance." Mr. Drachman nodded his agreement. Though he was round now, one could tell that he had once been strong and musclebound like his son, and they had the same light blue eyes, eyes like my mother's.

"Myra!" Porti waved. "Are you ready?"

"Always!" I called, and I rode over to the starting marker. Hoof pawed the turf impatiently. She was annoyed that I had stopped to chat when we could have been on the run. I patted her head. "Almost, Hoofy."

The four of us lined up at the starting point, the center of the main arena.

"Shall we do the whole course, then?" Caster asked. "Just as if it were the Games?"

"The men's course," said Porti.

"So it will be easy," I said.

"Well, then." Caster looked over at me and smirked. The whole rest of the world seemed to disappear, and I flashed back to our kiss again. "Four, three, two, go!" he cried.

We took off at a gallop; the course was arranged so that it was a sprint nearly all around. There was no need and no space for holding back. The instant we began to move, Hoof and I became one. I leaned over her back, my head over her head, between her long, beautiful white horns. Her fur melted into my skin; we breathed together. One, two, three, four, our hooves pounded. The other riders were on the edges of my vision; I saw only enough to keep from colliding. Though we were competing, they were not important. All that mattered was Hoof and me together, fast as we could go. No one could beat us if we were at our best; I was not concerned. Despite our speed, we breathed in a rhythm that came easily.

We made a tunnel through the air as we ran, pounding the grass but not jolted, powerful but smooth. We neared the edge of the arena, covered the last patch of clear grass, and dove under the padded wall that led to the moat obstacle. There was space enough for both beast and rider, but only if the two were perfectly in tune. One mistake and the rider might go flying off backwards while the beast dove forward into the moat. That had happened to us many times in practice over the years, but never in competition, and it didn't happen now. We slid under the barrier, my back an inch below the bottom, Hoof's front legs forward, her back legs pushing. I took a breath in and held it, and we slid into the moat. Our heads slipped below the water, and Hoof's powerful back legs propelled us under it.

The moat water was clear and pure, drawn from the Lower Scar River and blessed by the Deputy himself so that the Waters would not be offended by our swim. It cleaned me, sliding over my riding clothes and slicking my hair, and we rose for a breath and swam forward, rose for a breath and swam, until Hoof's front legs hit the sloping edge of the island and we lifted from the moat like the mythical mermaid on a whale, becoming again wetbeast and rider, shaking the water off and climbing the sloping hill.

We took the path through the trees at a gallop again, water flying off of us. I was ahead, but only by a little. Porti was to my left, less than a foot behind me, and I leaned even closer against Hoof, screening Porti out of my vision, until we reached the other side of the island and slid into the moat again.

A wetbeast appears too large to swim; a novice might think Hoof would sink to the bottom. But she is buoyant and graceful, and she carried me through the river water to the edge. By that time, I had three feet on Porti, and the boys were splashing another yard behind us.

After the moat obstacle came the jumps—another opportunity for Hoof to show the grace that goes with her great strength. There were four jumps, each higher than the last, with the final jump being a test of the strength of any beast. This was another spot where we had fallen in many a practice; the turf outside the approach was lined with padding for just such a blunder. We had not fallen yet this entire season, though. Falling was behind us; winning was ahead.

We pounded the turf, but Porti was not behind us—she was nearly even with us, horn to horn. We took the first jump together. Caster and Orphos gained, too, and we went over the second jump in quick succession, Porti and me together, then Caster, then Orphos.

Faster, I thought. And Hoof felt me. On the third jump, we gained inches. She flew over the wall, her legs reaching, her horns pointing, the air swooshing around us. We landed solid, ready to take the highest, final jump before the homestretch.

The tunnel of air around us was perfection: we were ready to fly. *Now*, I thought, automatically signaling Hoof with my legs.

She stopped.

I kept going, almost over Hoof's head, but I gripped with my legs and managed to stay on.

It was not just us. Beside me, Porti's beast was mooing. Porti herself was crumpled in a pile near her. Caster was clinging to his beast as I was to mine, while Orphos and Shrill were galloping in a circle. Orphos pressed his face against his beast's back, trying to calm him.

Caster and I jumped off our beasts as one and ran to Porti.

"Porti," Caster said, touching her shoulder.

"I'm all right," she said. She rolled over onto her back.

Caster lifted one of her legs. "I don't think it's broken," he said.

"Nor do I," she replied, sitting up slowly.

I watched her rise carefully. She did not appear to be badly injured. We were all taught how to take a fall. She had managed to land most advantageously on the padding. *Curse your thoughts, Myra,* I told myself. *You do not want to win because your best friend becomes a cripple.*

I reached out my hands to help her up, and she took them. She tested her weight on each foot and nodded. "Yes," she said. "Nothing's broken."

"Glad to hear it," said Orphos, who had brought poor Shrill under control. "And what, by the Waters, happened here?"

"I don't know," I said. "Hoof just stopped."

"I saw nothing," said Porti. "One second I was about to fly, the next I was on the turf."

"I didn't see anything," said Orphos, "but I heard something odd. It was as if there were too many beasts. The airflow felt like a full field."

"That's it exactly," said Caster. "It felt as if there were more of us."

"Perhaps there are invisible beasts now," I said. I meant to make a joke, but neither I nor the others laughed.

"Something was there, as sure as the ocean is wet, Myra," said Orphos. "A purebred wetbeast doesn't stop during the jump stretch for a flea."

"Perhaps not a flea," said Caster, "but there must have been something. Perhaps it was a rabbit. It could have spooked Hoof, and then she spooked the others."

"Hoof would not be spooked by a rabbit!" I cried. "She is unflappable."

"Myra's right," said Orphos. "It was more than a rabbit."

Porti climbed back onto her beast. With her height, she needed no assistance, but she was obviously sore, I noticed with guilt. Caster helped me back on Hoof, and together, the four of us passed through the gate embedded in the barrier and rode toward the finish, which was back at the starting point—the course made a large loop. But all was not as it had been. As we rode down the final stretch, Member Solis sped toward us, pulling Bricca by the hand.

"Did you see it?" Bricca cried.

"Did we see what?" I asked.

"There was an invisible rider!" she said.

SIX

IF HE WAS INVISIBLE, THEN HOW COULD WE SEE HIM?"
Orphos quipped.

Impossible, I thought. A beast could not become invisible; the Ability was passed by blood from our Flicker Men ancestors. The Flicker Men might have been different from humans, but they were not so different that they could mate with a wetbeast. I nearly cringed at the thought, but I didn't want to show that I knew so much about the Ability, so I said nothing.

"There was plenty to see, Mr. Staliamos," Member Solis snapped. "The turf was flying. Footprints were muddy from the moat. A voice called out something, though no one could tell what. He cut close enough to the Leftie boy to knock him over. The boy was cursing like a drunken guardsman."

I glanced over to the stone throw mound, where Nolan was lifting a stone out of his cart. He didn't look over at us or break concentration as he tossed it; a fine, possibly record-breaking toss many yards into the distance. His parents now hovered at the edge of the arena floor, looking grim.

"It's true," said Bricca. "Everyone saw it." Indeed, the remaining spectators were all watching us intently, and there were fewer than before. No doubt word of the so-called invisible rider had spread all over the city.

"Well, I guess the proof of female superiority will have to wait until another day," said Porti.

"Says the lady who landed on her face," said Orphos.

"What?" Bricca cried.

"Don't worry, I'm fine," said Porti.

"She got back up, didn't she?" I said. I had to admire that. I wouldn't have been able to mount unassisted after such a fall. "I'd like to see what you and your wild beast would have done, Orphos."

"I think we could use a nice cool-down ride. How about it, Myra?" said Porti.

"Wonderful," I said. I would much rather have continued to train, even with my greatest opponent, than deal with whatever had just happened. It might not have been an invisible beast, but it had been something. Sky would be on the radio even now, broadcasting speculation and rumor. Anyone who doubted the presence of Flickerkin would begin to believe.

My mother and father were both home when I got there, a rare sight recently. They sat at the dining table, leaning their heads together as if it were each other's thoughts they listened to and not the radio. My father was tall and thin, with dark hair only lightly streaked with gray, brown eyes, and a skin color I could achieve only when well baked by the sun. He towered over my mother even seated, and yet when they were together, they seemed as one.

I started to head for my room so I wouldn't have to hear the worst, but my father waved me over to the table.

The Deputy was speaking again. "The reports from the arena today are indeed disturbing," he said. "I don't want to say too much while the investigation is ongoing. And let me be clear. The Council does not believe that New Heart City has been invaded by a Flickerkin enemy. Such talk is premature, and I encourage all citizens to remain calm."

"*Premature,*" my mother scoffed.

"Rest assured that the Guard is conducting a thorough investigation. No one was seriously injured. It is likely that this was merely some kind of prank. But whatever happened, we will find out and punish those responsible."

"Isn't it recorded that the uprising began in much the same way?" said Sky. "Those Lefties with the Ability were the first wave of a rebellion that took the lives of hundreds of Plateau People."

"Uprising," said my mother. "Do they teach you these lies in school?"

I shrugged. They indeed taught us that the Lefties had rebelled out of greed for the prezine in their mines, wanting it all for themselves, to sell at whatever exorbitant prices they demanded. Whereas my mother had taught me that they had fought for better working conditions and for freedoms Plats took for granted. My mother had also taught me that it was the Plats who had started the war by giving a group of striking miners the dip, something the Plat government denied.

". . . violent actions," the Deputy was saying. "Whereas by all indications today's incident was not violent but merely disruptive. There are so many differences between the two events that we should not even be speaking of them together."

"How long is this investigation going to take?" Sky asked. "How can we, the citizens of New Heart City, be sure of our safety?"

"We are taking precautions," said the Deputy. "Though, as I said, we find it highly unlikely that there was a Flickerkin rider on an invisible beast, we have taken steps to deploy more sensors. These sensors, as most of you know, emit a pulse of light that is invisible to the naked eye and yet, when it intercepts the body of a Flickerkin, makes the Flickerkin visible. Per the terms of peace, we are not able to molest any Flickerkin who remain in the Eye; therefore we have been unable to test these sensors on real Flickerkin . . ."

"*People,*" my mother said. "You *say* you have not tortured *people.*"

". . . will be deployed at all entrances to the arena, as well as in other undisclosed locations."

My father turned the radio off. "You have nothing to worry about, Rhondalynn," he said. "The sensors can harm a Flickerkin only when he or she is invisible. It will have no effect on you or Myra."

"And since it will not affect *us,* we shouldn't be worried," said my mother.

"I didn't say that," my father said. "But you will be safe. If there were secret Flickerkin here in the city, we would want to know about it. They would be risking the peace for all."

"This is why the Plats are taking even the prezine from the power relays in the Eye," my mother said. "They wish to build more sensors. And for what?"

"Have you not heard of the latest depth surveys?" my father asked.

"A few inches," she said.

"For now," said my father. "Who knows how soon the oceans may carry ships?"

"What ships?" my mother asked. "Why would the Flicker Men come back to this island abandoned by the Waters?"

My father shook his head, stopped by my mother's blasphemy.

"Poppa," I said, "are you saying the Deputy is afraid the Flicker Men might come back? And we're using prezine to build some kind of sensor to fight them?"

"Yes," said my father. "That's exactly what I'm saying. And that's why the Deputy doesn't want people to panic."

"Are you saying there might really *be* Flickerkin here? Something for them to panic about?" My mother and I were the only ones in the city. They had both assured me of this since I was a small child.

"It's unlikely," said my father. "They've stayed in the Eye for all these years. But this disturbance today is hard to explain."

"What did you see?" my mother asked. "Don't evade the question." As always, she saw right through me. I hadn't intended to say a word. The last thing I needed was for her to fear that I'd be thrown from Hoof and forbid me to ride—or attempt to forbid me.

"I only saw the disturbance after," I said. "Bricca was upset. Member Solis was convinced it was an invisible rider."

"It wouldn't take much to convince *her*," my mother said.

"But there are no invisible beasts," I said.

"Of course not," said my mother. "There are no beasts of any kind in the Eye."

"Caster's father doesn't want to believe it," I said.

My mother shook her head. I knew what she thought: that the Deputy was merely waiting for the panic to spread so that he would be "forced" to believe and begin the testing. But I didn't know what to think. Caster was so accepting, thought me beautiful *because* I was different. From whom did he learn that?

"I must go back," my father said. "There is much to do to get the new sensors in place. Don't worry. All this will pass soon —you'll see." He gave my mother a quick kiss, and she smiled, a weary little smile.

"Will I see you tonight?" she asked.

"I don't know," he said. "Most likely late. Good night, Myra." He leaned down and kissed me on the top of my head. "You look as if you had a good ride, despite the trouble."

"Yes," I said. I didn't want to admit that I could think of no reasonable explanation for what had happened. If even I couldn't think of one, then people like Sky, who wished to stir up a panic, would succeed.

But it meant nothing to me, I told myself. I hadn't flickered since I was a child. I intended never to flicker again.

I continued toward my room to bathe and change. I was about to call Caster on the voicebox, because I couldn't stop thinking about our kiss and his smile this morning, but I picked up the receiver to find Porti calling me. This happened inordinately often, but usually I was attempting to call her, too. And she was bursting to talk about our ride.

"What do you think happened?" she asked. "What could spook our beasts like that?"

"I don't know," I said.

"Do you think it's possible? An invisible rider on an invisible beast?"

"My mother says it's nonsense," I said.

"If a man can flicker, why not a beast?" said Porti.

"Because it's passed by blood," I said.

"We're related to the animals, aren't we? Haven't we evolved from the fishes?"

"But why would one of them ride around and disrupt our practice?" I asked.

"Perhaps to make us crazy," she said. "Perhaps they have a grievance." She paused. "Does your mother know any Flickerkin? I mean, did she, back in the Eye?"

"Of course she did," I said. "She told me they like to keep to themselves, that they weren't the ones who started the whole uprising anyway. They aren't miners and never were because the Council won't let them near prezine." I was saying too much. But it was reasonable for me to know this. My mother could have told me because she was from the Eye and happened to know it.

"I wonder what will happen," she said.

"My mother thinks they're going to start testing Lefties again, which means torturing them to make sure they can't flicker," I said. "My father says she's safe because she's been tested before, but she doesn't believe it, and she fears for me."

"How could they test you? You're considered a Plat."

"I don't know if that's enough," I said. The words fell from my mouth like stones. What good would my piece of paper do me when it came to a panic? A Deputy's signature couldn't change my blood.

"Well, you would pass any test," she said.

"Of course," I said. The lie was easy because I had been telling it my whole life. It might as well have been true. With half of my mind, I fully believed it. "But she fears they'll hurt me."

"She's just being a worried mother," said Porti. "Member Solis warned me to stay away from Lefties. As if I even know any apart from the Drachmans."

I let that pass. I was glad she had forgotten my blood so quickly. But why did Member Solis think Porti had to worry about ordinary people like Nolan and his clothmaker parents? They were obviously not Flickerkin. Nolan himself had been knocked over during his training. Did the other Council Members fear ordinary Lefties too?

"What?" Porti called to someone in the apartment. "It's Myra! . . . What? All right, I'm coming!" Then, into the receiver: "I have to go. Next time I see you I want to hear *everything* that's happened with Caster!" And then she hung up. Why had Member Solis called her away? What did Porti have to do on a Saturday after training?

I picked up the receiver again to call Caster, but no one answered. So it was not until Monday that I saw him again. And by then there had been more strange incidents, and the City was spinning into a full panic.

From *A HISTORY OF THE UPLAND*

And when the uprising began, the Flicker Men supported their Leftie friends. They infiltrated Heart City, bringing daggers concealed on their persons. They and their mixed-race children, the Flickerkin, killed many Plateau People, leaving the sand at the edge of the oceans covered with blood. It was only when the oceans began to recede that the Flicker Men, fearing that they would become trapped on the plateau, took to their ships and fled the Upland.

From *THE BOOK OF THE WATERS*

Thus, the uprising was defeated by the Waters. They watch over us and protect us always.

SEVEN

SOMEONE INVISIBLE PUSHED HIS WAY THROUGH THE market, knocking people aside and overturning a fruit stand.

Four workbeasts were found wandering, having been let loose from their stalls in the dark of night.

A man's bag jumped out of his hand and didn't drop to the ground for seven yards.

Doors all over the city were heard opening and closing by themselves.

Footsteps were everywhere. Noises abounded.

My mother said it was nonsense, or else being staged by the Deputy to justify testing.

My father didn't come home except to sleep.

Sky blasted the city with theories about what the Flickerkin wanted. Did they wish to start another uprising? Were they here to disrupt the Games? Was it a prelude to an invasion from across the oceans?

Monday morning as I was getting ready for school, he was saying this: "It has also come to light in the last few days, coincidentally, that the oceans are rising at an alarming rate—four inches over the past month. Could these two phenomena be related?"

"Well, quite possibly they could," said the guest, an old man who taught at the University. "We don't know what is happening across the oceans. What have the Flicker Men been doing since they left our shores? People who have no respect for the Waters—who ride across them as if they were roads—may be capable of anything."

"Could these people—whoever is causing this—be Flicker Men invaders and not Flickerkin from the Left Eye?"

"Well, I believe the oceans are still far too low to carry ships," said the professor. "But might the Lefties be in contact with the Flicker Men? Voicebox technology does not preclude that. We have allowed them to keep some prezine in the Eye— far too much, in my opinion. There are reports of power relays being stripped."

I headed for the door, attempting to avoid my mother. She had been in one of her quiet, suppressive moods all weekend, and I didn't want to hear her reaction to this theory. But as I opened the door, I couldn't help but overhear her mutter, "Too much prezine? They have *none!*" I didn't see how they could have *none*; it was only that the Plats took *most* of it. I didn't know how much you would need to run a voicebox powerful enough to reach the Flicker Men, who lived unimaginably far away across vast oceans, but surely—I stopped myself. How could I be thinking as if the professor were right? Lefties were already in danger of being tortured. Things could only get worse for these people who, whether I liked it or not, were my kin.

I dwelled on this as I went to meet Porti in the courtyard. Today I felt every difference between myself and my Plat friend. I was squirming inside my dress, feeling the brush of my unruly curls against my face. *I should not be ashamed of my Leftie half,* I told myself. I was as proud of my mother as I was of my father. But I didn't want to look different. I wanted to look as Porti did rushing toward me, her swooshing skirt billowing around her, emphasizing her tiny waist.

She started right in commenting on ladies' fashions as we walked to school, oblivious to my discomfort, or perhaps choosing to ignore it and act as if nothing were wrong.

"I don't think the swooshing skirts will last," she said, ruffling hers with both hands. "They're too busy. I think we'll give them up before the end of summer."

"It looks fine on you," I said.

"What does your mother say?" she asked, knowing I feared I couldn't wear the style.

"She had three of them made special for herself," I said.

"What about you?" She eyed my plain, straight skirt. Like my mother, I was more comfortable in pants, but I could wear them only when I was riding. Pants on women were the Leftie fashion, out of favor in New Heart City. My mother had taught me that we stood out enough even in gowns.

I shrugged.

"I know what you're thinking," she said, "but you can have some made special, too. I bet your mother looks great in them."

"You just said they were too busy," I pointed out. "Despite that fact that you're wearing one this morning."

"Yes, but *for the style*," she said. She grinned at me and inclined her head toward a lady walking away from us who was swooshing so energetically that it was almost absurd.

"I'll think about it," I said, thinking that the swooshing would only make my hips look bigger.

At that moment, Caster passed in front of us with Orphos and another friend, Gregor, also the son of a Council Member. Caster stood a few inches taller than both of them and walked in the middle, clearly the focus of attention. I couldn't believe that he had been kissing me on Friday night, that he had asked me to be seen with him. As he passed us, he smiled and gave a little wave.

I waved back, and they went ahead of us into the building.

"Ah," Porti sighed loudly.

I poked her. "He could have heard you."

"The battle is won," she said, winking.

I couldn't stop myself from grinning as we took our seats on the right side of the room, in the front with the other children who had some connection to the Council. The privileged were not officially required to sit separately from the workers; that was just how it was. We all took the same lessons, as education for all was mandated by the Council. Nevertheless, some children of workers didn't go to school, since they were needed in their parents' shops. Nolan sometimes didn't show up because he, like his parents, was an expert clothmaker, and his skills were often needed during busy times. But today he was here, sitting alone in the back. As the only Leftie in our year, he was often alone, usually quiet. Today was the first time I had really noticed that. I had to stop myself from looking in his direction, from acknowledging that we had a kinship. I didn't want the others to suddenly decide that perhaps I belonged in the back of the room with him.

Our teacher, Mrs. Invar, cleared her throat. "We are going to have a special lesson this morning," she said. "There has been much news over the weekend about the Flickerkin and their ancestry and potential danger to the citizens of the city. So we are going to discuss this important issue."

I sat up straight in my seat, startled. We had learned about the Left Eye, and about the uprising, while studying the geography of the Upland. But that lesson was taught to younger students. I found myself looking down at my lap, hoping that Mrs. Invar would stop talking.

"The region of the Upland that we generally refer to as the Left Eye, as you have already learned, sits high above the rest of the plateau," Mrs. Invar began. "Many thousands of years ago, Uplanders seeking refuge from an incursion of ocean water climbed the cliffs and settled at the top, where they were isolated from the rest of the population and evolved their *unique physical characteristics*." Perhaps Mrs. Invar did not mean to put such emphasis on those words, but I heard it that way. My cheeks burned, and I hoped that the warmth was only on the inside. Although she was paler than I, my mother never let herself blush. She would have chastised me to no end for allowing myself to be bothered by my teacher's words.

"It was during another major incursion that the Flicker Men arrived on their invisible ships," Mrs. Invar continued. "While the Plateau dwellers dealt with them only at a distance, distrustful of their Ability, the people of the Left Eye welcomed the Flicker Men into their lives. The Flicker Men, too, so they told us, came from a high country. They taught the Lefties new farming methods that increased their crops, and how to mine deep without cutting wide." It seemed that Mrs. Invar conspicuously did *not* look at me as she spoke. But I told myself I was inventing it. She had never treated me differently before.

"During this time, most of the Flicker Men left our shores, but some remained, even forming families with the people of the Eye." She tapped the board behind her, which then displayed a scientific diagram, including drawings of pairs of people. The Lefties were depicted as human-shaped, the Flicker Men as plain circles. "The Ability that allowed the Flicker Men to become invisible came from something in the blood." I watched with a mixture of horror and fascination as Mrs. Invar, who normally did not teach us science (that was reserved for our special lessons with the chief scientific advisor to the Council) continued to explain that the exact cause of invisibility was unknown, but the Ability could propagate itself through generations of intermixing with human blood. "Thus," she concluded, "a person with only a small amount of Flicker blood may have the ability to instantaneously dissolve."

"*Dissolve* isn't the right word," said a voice from the back.

The whole class turned to stare at Nolan, who sat rigid, his white blond hair rising in unruly curls that accentuated his solemn face.

"Oh?" said Mrs. Invar. "Nolan, would you care to explain?"

"A person who can flicker doesn't dissolve; they only make it so you can't see them. They're still there, as solid as you are."

"Well, yes," said Mrs. Invar. "That's true. A Flickerkin is still solid."

"A Flickerkin is still human," said Nolan.

Everyone stared at him in silence. I remained as quiet as possible, trying to keep the color from my cheeks. No one was staring at me, but I feared they would. Then Nolan broke his gaze from the teacher's and looked at me. His blue eyes met mine. *My eyes are brown,* I thought. I was only half Leftie, while he was full. I was nothing like him. He looked away, and the kids turned back around in their seats, some of them glancing at me. It was as if Nolan had torn away a curtain with his eyes, ripping my Plat features from my skin and leaving only the Leftie.

"The Flicker Men were very closely related to humans," said Mrs. Invar. "Scientists theorize that the two races diverged about three hundred thousand years ago, the last time the oceans were in full recession. This allowed our ancestors to reach the Upland without boats. And here we evolved into modern humans." Mrs. Invar did not directly express her opinion about whether Flickerkin, those Lefties with some Flicker blood, were human or not, but the implication was clear. We were *very closely related* to *modern humans,* which meant not human at all.

Porti didn't know I was a Flickerkin, but she had seen Nolan look at me. She too must have seen me anew. But when lunchtime came, she treated me no differently, and I pretended nothing had happened. As Porti and I entered the courtyard and approached the benches with the cold luncheon prepared by the Council's kitchen, I studiously avoided looking anywhere near Nolan, who sat with the few Lefties from the other classes.

"Smile," Porti whispered, poking me.

Caster waved us over, and as bidden, a smile spread across my face. We sat across from him as he slathered his bread with honey.

"Weird lesson this morning," said Caster.

"Better than learning about the history of the Head, *again*," said Orphos, sitting next to Caster. "Pigs, pigs, beasts, pigs." He winked at Porti.

She tossed her napkin at him.

Orphos caught it and held it dramatically to his heart, closing his eyes.

Caster grinned at me knowingly.

"I like learning about pigs," I said. I also liked learning about inherited traits. No one in the world was more interested than I in how I could have the Ability, despite being at most one-sixteenth Flicker. But it was too dangerous for me to express an interest. It was better that, in public, I learn about every part of the Upland besides the Eye, every culture except my mother's. What I learned from my mother had to stay between us.

"My father's working on installing the sensors," said Gregor, on the other side of Caster. His father was the Council Member in charge of the Guard, though the day-to-day operations of the city police force were run by another. Gregor's father was an engineer by trade, who personally worked on much of the Council's technology. He probably knew more about these sensors than anyone in the Upland. I was dying to know what Gregor knew but was afraid to ask.

"Do you think they will work?" Porti asked.

"My father thinks so," said Gregor. "But of course we have no test subject."

I knew what my mother would say to that, how her eyes would burn even as her cheeks remained free of flush.

"Who cares if it works?" said Caster. "There aren't any Flickerkin to catch."

"Is that what your father said?" Porti asked.

"No," said Caster. "He's starting to buy this nonsense." He shook his head.

"But you were right there," said Porti. "Something knocked me off my beast."

"Some animal, mostly likely," Caster said. "The simplest explanation is usually the best—didn't we learn that in our science lesson?"

"You're right," I said. "It's only a panic."

"Well, better safe than sorry," said Gregor.

"I hope there are Flickerkin," said Porti. "I'd like to meet one. What does one wear when one is invisible?"

Caster and I exchanged an eye roll. Leave it to Porti to bring up fashion at every possible occasion.

"I'd rather talk about the Games," said Caster. "It's shaping up to be a good contest."

"The best in years," I said. Leave it to Caster to say the right thing, to bring up something that would make me smile.

"It's too bad they separate the men and the women," Caster said. "I'd like to see who'd come out on top. Since our personal contest was cut short."

"I'm not afraid to try again," I said.

"Oooh," said Orphos and Porti together.

"I think that's a challenge," said Orphos. "You're not going to let that pass, are you, *Caster Ripkin?*"

Caster laughed. "I wouldn't want to unseat a lady."

"Oooh," Orphos and Porti cried again.

"*You're* not going to let *that* pass, are you?" said Porti, poking me.

"*I* wouldn't end up on the ground," I said.

Caster grinned. "After the Games. Just in case you do win. I wouldn't want to ride injured."

"A wise choice," I said. "After the Games, then." We smiled

at each other, and as our eyes made contact, I nearly stopped breathing. If only there were not others around us.

The bell clanged from the school building, signaling the end of the lunch period. I almost jumped out of my seat. As we walked back to school, Porti giggled in my ear. "Did you see? While he threatened to unseat you, he examined your bosom."

"Porti!" I whispered back. I too had noticed, and now I was blushing.

She poked me. "Prude."

"I? You still haven't even kissed Orphos!" I whispered. But then we could talk no more, because class started again.

Mrs. Invar moved on to a literature lesson, and my mind drifted to Caster's smile as he mentioned the Games, and to his eyes indeed—though not too obviously—examining my bosom, and then to the Games themselves. There were many events, from footraces to strength contests to games of purely mental skill. But both Caster and I cared about only the ride.

Last year, when I had placed second among all the women in the Upland, my mother had cheered for me, a rare moment of forgetting to always be still. This year, Hoof and I would make her even more proud. I glanced at Caster, who was doodling on his paper while Mrs. Invar talked about symbolism in a book I feared neither of us had finished reading. I again pictured us on the winners' podium together. Perhaps he would not only take my hand, but he would put his arm around me. Perhaps he would even kiss me, in front of the photoboxes, in front of the entire world.

As I pictured this scene, the door from the courtyard burst open and two guardsmen walked into the room. Their boots pounded against the bare wood floor. I recognized them from the streets. I knew the Guard as nice men who settled disputes over prices. Crime was rare, serious crime even rarer. One of these two was Brach, who was about ten years older than I.

"Nolan Drachman." Brach looked right at Nolan, who had returned to his place in the back. It was not a question.

Nolan looked calmly at the guardsman. "Yes?"

"You must come."

"Must I?" Nolan asked. He remained seated.

"You are required in the office of the Deputy," said Brach.

The students looked at one another. Caster seemed just as surprised as the rest. He raised an eyebrow at me and shrugged. Nolan, however, was prepared.

"Today's lesson was no coincidence," he said. He directed his gaze at Brach but spoke loudly, to all of us.

"You must come," said Brach.

Nolan rose slowly from his seat. "May I ask why I, the son of two clothmakers, am being summoned to meet with the Deputy to the Waters?"

"His Excellency does not share his reasons with us," said Brach.

"How many other Lefties have you brought in today?" Nolan asked.

My chest tightened. The morning's lesson spun through my head. *Very closely related.* I caught a glimpse of my light brown hair, lying in a telltale curl against my shoulder. But surely Nolan must be wrong. Surely he had committed some crime. Or perhaps the Deputy wanted to commend him for his fine work in his parents' shop.

"Where are my parents?" Nolan asked.

Both guardsmen stepped forward.

"Tell me exactly where my parents are and what you have done to them, and I'll come," Nolan said. His face was still a picture of calmness, but his fists were clenched, his muscular body taut. No wonder they had sent more than one wispy Plat to take him.

"I know nothing of them," said Brach. But anyone could tell it was a lie. The man was used to wrangling a fair trade out of a fruitseller, not placating boys.

Nolan dissolved into thin air. There was no sound, no warning. One second he was there, and the next second he was not.

The room burst into noise.

"Blessed Waters!" Porti said.

"Did he just—"

"No!" That was Orphos, whose mouth hung all the way open.

The guardsmen looked around them as if they couldn't understand what had just happened. The door opened of its own accord and then slammed shut. They stood frozen for one more second, and then Brach cried, "After him!" His companion pulled the door open, and they both raced off into the courtyard.

But I was wrong to think that Nolan had dissolved. He had said it himself: He had still been there. Another Flickerkin in New Heart City. What had been happening was not paranoia but real; at least, that is what everyone would believe. My throat closed upon itself; my breathing stopped. We were going to be tested—my mother, every Leftie in New Heart City, even me.

From *A HISTORY OF THE UPLAND*

Heart City was destroyed, but the Plateau People rebuilt it, and New Heart City became the center of a renewed union. The daggers that had killed so many Plateau People were outlawed, and so also were the swords used by the Plateau People to kill Lefties. A new era of peace began, and continues.

From *THE DECLARATION OF PEACE*

People of the Left Eye may reside upon the Plateau as permitted by the Regulations of the Regions: the Head, the Neck, and New Heart City. But no Region shall suffer the residence of Flickerkin.

EIGHT

I CAME HOME TO FIND MY PARENTS IN THE MIDDLE OF A raging fight.

"Myra!" my father exclaimed as I walked in the door. "Why did you not come straight home?"

"I did," I said. "School has just ended."

"You waited until school ended?" my mother asked, her voice calm and cold. Whatever ire had been directed at my father was now directed at me.

"What did you wish?" I asked. "Should I have run out screaming 'I'm next'? Would that not have been suspicious?"

"Myra, we must leave the city," my mother said.

"Leave?" The weight of the stares of both my parents together nearly pushed me backwards through the door again. I needed to go to the stables, to ride, to prepare for the Games.

"The Council voted this morning to test Leftie workers," my father said. "You and your mother are not workers, so the order doesn't apply to you."

My mother snorted. "It doesn't apply to us *for now*. A nice manipulation by Ripkin."

"Rhonda, the Deputy himself voted against it. Why would he—"

My mother interrupted, turning to me. "They have jailed the clothmakers, and now their stupid boy has made a spectacle of himself. You didn't act if you knew him, did you? Tell me you didn't even look."

"I looked as everyone else did," I said. "Only that."

"A stupid boy," my mother repeated.

"Did he have no right to escape jail?" I wasn't friends with Nolan, but I didn't like my mother's tone—as if his display somehow reflected back on me, though I had done nothing.

"They will vote soon to test us," my mother said. "We must leave. Tonight."

"Rhondalynn, we need not be so hasty," my father said. "You have been tested before and passed."

"So have the Drachmans," my mother said. "And what of Myra? We spared her when the Deputy's father gave the orders, but with this Ripkin—"

"He voted against it, Rhonda."

"He is playing a game," my mother said. Her voice grew

quiet and filled with ice. "It is Ripkin who has the power. And he is now *forced* to act."

"He has assured me that he will not support testing you," said my father.

"Oh, he has *assured* you?" my mother scoffed.

"I can't leave before the Games!" I cried. I couldn't leave at all. My friends were here, and Caster, and my home. But the Games were everything, and less than a week away now. This was supposed to be the run-up to the best day of my life—the day I would win the ride. And I couldn't leave Hoof. There were no beasts in the Eye. I tried to hold my emotion back, but it boiled inside me. I couldn't miss the Games. I couldn't leave Hoof. I couldn't believe that this would happen.

"Let us think," said my father. "Why take the Games from Myra when she has worked so hard? If the Waters are against us, then we will leave when the Games are done. They will not finish testing before then. But, Rhondalynn, I don't believe they will test you. These incidents are the product of hysterical imagination; the Guard will find no other Flickerkin, and things will all go back to normal."

"You are naïve," my mother said. "You see the good in all people. But there is no good in Nelston Ripkin. He carries the hate of his grandfather and great-grandfather before him—it was a Ripkin who gave our miners the dip to start the war, but you forget that."

"Rhonda, there have been no executions for thirty years. They have deported Flickerkin; that is all."

"And who ordered the last execution? Ripkin's father, the best of the lot!"

I couldn't stand there and listen to them argue. My mother had her fears and would not give them up. My father had been outvoted and would be again. Perhaps my mother was right to fear. But we were not to be tested yet. I was to have my Games, and I didn't want to think beyond that. I changed in a hurry and sped back out past them.

"Myra!" my mother called as I passed her.

"Let her go," my father said. "She will be fine today."

"Donray—"

I closed the door on my mother's next objection. If she was right, then I would lose everything. But surely my father was right. Surely now that testing had begun, the people would see how wrong it was. Caster would see. Before I realized consciously what I was doing, I found myself heading not toward Hoof's stable but toward Monster's, and I found Caster there with him, brushing the giant beast's glossy black coat.

He turned to me with a smile, and then the smile faded. "Myra, what's happened?"

Of course I couldn't hide it. I put my hand to my cheek, as if I could wipe the flush away. "It's the testing," I said. "My mother says it's torture. She thinks they'll do it to us."

"To you?" He wrapped me in his arms. My face pressed against his chest. "You have nothing to fear from it."

"They will test us until they are sure," I said. "What if it hurts me and I can't ride?" I couldn't, of course, share my true fear. I couldn't share that my mother wanted to leave the city. To say it would be admitting guilt.

"My father won't do that," Caster said. He unwrapped his arms from me a little and leaned down to kiss me. I stood on my tiptoes, and we connected, and now I felt a whole different kind of flush. He ran his hand through my hair, which was pulled into a ponytail but sprang out from the back, impossible to contain. "Myra, you are safe. You are not a Leftie. It's only Lefties who are being tested—Leftie workers."

"My mother thinks it will come to us," I said.

"You are a Member's family," said Caster. "How could you be suspect?" But then he frowned. "My father began the testing with the expectation that they would find nothing and calm fears. But now that they've found a family of Flickerkin, I don't know what will happen."

"They'll torture every Leftie worker in the city," I said. "How can my mother and I sit and be happy even if we aren't tested?" *I shouldn't be saying this to Caster Ripkin,* I thought.

"You're right," he said. "It's terrible. I've told my father what I think about it. He says he agrees but is forced to calm the people's fears."

I winced at this confirmation of my mother's words. As the Deputy, he couldn't be forced to do anything. At the very least, he could hold off implementing the Council's vote.

Caster wrapped me in his arms again. "Perhaps Nolan was the one playing those pranks. He might come back and confess, and this will all be over."

"Nolan and his parents were in the arena that day," I said. "Fully visible."

"Then they'll find the real culprit soon," said Caster. "Before the Games."

"Yes," I said. We were now talking as if, indeed, the strange occurrences were caused by Flickerkin. Now that the clothmakers had been arrested and Nolan was on the run, there would only be more stories, more panic. "I must ride," I said. "I can't stand here."

"Ah, that's my lady!" Caster said. "Perhaps I can give you a ride to your beast's stable?" Before I could answer, he had picked me up by the waist and lifted me onto Monster's back. The beast mooed a greeting.

"Hello, Monster," I said, thinking only of Caster's hands on my waist.

He climbed on in front of me, and I wrapped my arms around him and pressed my head into his back. This was how things were supposed to be, after a lifetime of wishing for it.

"Find Hoof," Caster said softly. We passed through the stables slowly, savoring the minutes. Riders rode together infrequently, and I had never been this way with a boy, our bodies pressed together, and on top of a beast, the one place in the world that made me truly happy. I was not going to give this up.

When I returned home, my mother and father had ended their argument, and he had gone back to the Council. I came quietly to the dining table, ready to hear my mother's anger at how I had walked out the door. But her anger had been replaced with a truer calm.

"Your father and I have come to an agreement," she said. "We will stay at least until the Games are over. You have worked too hard and come too far for me to take this away from you."

"Thank you, Momma," I said. I didn't wish to ask about after the Games. This was one fight I had won, and I would take my victory.

"But I will not rely on Ripkin's assurances. We must prepare you for the test." She held up a set of two rings. They were thin and delicate, bronze-colored, and looked like a large pair of hoop earrings, but they were connected by a long, thin chain of ordinary metal. I didn't understand.

"These cuffs are made of prezine," she said.

"Prezine?" I had rarely seen the metal naked. It was always

hidden inside things, too precious for people to wear. It took all we had to power the city. My mother must have gotten hers from her relatives in the Eye, and at great cost.

"This is how they do the test," she said. "Hold out your hands."

"What are you going to do?" I asked.

"I am going to put the cuffs on you and shock you to see how much you can endure." She said this without flinching. "If you flicker, we will leave the city at once. If you pass my test, then we will stay for the Games."

"What does it take to pass?" I asked. The cuffs were small and looked harmless. But my mother had used the word *torture*. And now she wanted to do it to me.

"The last Deputy stopped at ten shocks," she said. "His son was a close advisor at the time. He argued for at least fifteen."

"Will it weaken me?" I asked.

"No," she said. "It will strengthen you. You must learn to endure. Don't you want to stay? To ride your beast, to be with this boy?"

"Yes," I said. There was no arguing with this. "But not the day before the Games. All right?"

She nodded. "All right, Myra. But every day until then." She snapped the cuffs around my wrists. They felt cold, and there was a slight buzzing, as if electricity was already flowing through them. I didn't like it. I squirmed in my seat.

My mother gave a little smile. "Good girl. It's bad for us to have prezine next to the skin. It prevents the flicker."

"Prevents? I thought it was supposed to cause it."

"By itself, it prevents," she said. "With stimulation, it causes." She held a thin rod of prezine in one hand, the length of an arm from wrist to elbow. At its top, it mixed with some other metal, something black and shiny, and the part she touched was cased in wood. "I touch this to the cuffs, and you will feel a shock, all right?"

I said nothing. It was not all right.

She shocked me.

I screamed.

She shocked me again.

Again, I screamed. Sweat poured down my face. How could such delicate cuffs cause this?

"It's all right to scream a little," my mother said. "If you don't, it will look like you practiced. But holding back the scream is part of maintaining control. You can maintain control even through the pain." She shocked me again.

This time I didn't scream. Instead, I bit the inside of my lip.

"Good," she said. She reached down and unclasped the cuffs. I gasped with relief and rubbed my hands. She took one of them and rubbed it for me. "Myra, I do this because I love you. Because I don't want you to be tossed into the ocean. Because I couldn't live without you." Any other mother would have shed tears as she said this. My mother's eyes were not even wet. But I felt the pressure of her hand on mine, the control it cost her to say this.

I couldn't hold the tears back. "Momma, you torture me."

"I'm trying to make you strong," she said. "As I know you can be. When you are a mother, you will understand. You will do anything for your child." As she said this, she turned away. Perhaps her eyes were beginning to get wet. I didn't like to see this weakness that she hated, so I turned my head, too.

"You didn't even want children," I said. "I heard you say so. The night Poppa found out about us."

"I wanted to spare you this," she said, still looking away.

I was not in a mood to understand. I still felt the residue of the shocks, still sweated beneath my gown, still itched from the feel of the cold prezine. I jumped to my feet, raced to my room, and slammed the door with all my might. And then I sat on my bed, trying to stop the crying, trying to stop the anger, trying to be everything she wished me to be. Because no matter how much I hated her in that moment, I had to be like her; I had to endure or risk my life.

My mother wanted me to stay home from school, but I refused. First of all, she wished it, and I had hate brewing in my heart for her; second, I didn't want to look guilty; and third, I needed to see my friends. I needed to see Porti and Caster and feel that something in my life was still right.

"I think I'll go with something simple," Porti said. "Let my healthy flush take the place of ruffles and lace."

"What?" I asked. I was lost in my memory of last night's radio broadcast, heard during my attempt to calm myself. Nolan, whom the Deputy called "only a boy," had evaded justice. The guardsmen were deploying more sensors and assured the people that they would work, though they had never been tested on real Flickerkin (an assertion my mother didn't believe—she thought the Deputy had tortured many). More strange happenings had been called in, which Sky was only too happy to repeat. He had urged citizens to lock their doors, to be vigilant about the sound of footsteps and strange breezes. Why would Nolan choose to walk around inside people's homes at night, turning lights on and off? I wondered. It was dangerous nonsense.

"Or do you think I should go with something bejeweled? Because others will be doing simple and I will wish to be the center of attention?" Porti was speaking of what she would wear to the winners' ball, I realized.

"Orphos will like the simple," I said.

"Hmm, maybe. What are you wearing?"

"I don't know, Porti," I said shortly, almost snapping. "I just want to win." My arms were sore from the shocks, and my heart was sore from recalling who had given them. I couldn't take this idle talk of dresses and balls.

"Gregor!" Porti called, flouncing away from me, as she would do when I had offended her.

"Porti," I began. But I didn't have the heart to go on. I went into school by myself while she chatted with Gregor, who happened to be standing right next to Orphos. I couldn't endure these games when *the* Games were so near. What I wanted was to sleep and recover and forget about all that had happened.

Nolan's chair was conspicuously empty. Mrs. Invar didn't speak of him, nor did anyone else. We all kept up the appearance of a normal schoolday. Overtly, there was only the restlessness of knowing that school would be canceled for the rest of the week in preparation for the Games. But there was a silence underneath it, perhaps a fear. Did they worry that Nolan would come into their homes? That all the beasts would be let loose to roam the streets?

Caster walked me home that afternoon, not Porti as usual. He kissed me in the courtyard, melting away the tension of the day. "I'll see you at the arena," he said, giving me one last kiss.

"Soon," I said.

But when I walked in the door, I knew it would not be soon at all.

From *THE REGULATIONS OF NEW HEART CITY:*
PARTICULAR TO THOSE PEOPLE OF THE
UPLAND WHO RESIDE THEREIN

Each Citizen of New Heart City shall receive living quarters as described:

For Citizens, one bedroom for each man, woman, couple, or child.

For people of the Left Eye, half the quarters allotted Citizens.

For Members of the Council, additional quarters as befits length of service.

NINE

MY FATHER WAS STANDING AT THE WINDOW, staring through a tiny gap between the curtains. As I closed the door, he turned to me. He seemed thinner, grayer, as if he had aged ten years in a single day.

"They took her," he said.

I froze in place, unable to speak. I had never seen such a look on my father's face. His eyes were red, his skin blotchy. He clenched his fists so tightly that the skin on his hands was almost white.

"She was right, Myra," he said. "We should have left in the night."

"But the Deputy said . . . Caster . . ." I clutched my schoolbooks to my chest as if they could protect my heart. *They took her.*

"The Council held another vote early in the morning before I arrived," he said. "All those with a drop of Leftie blood must be tested."

"But she could pass," I said. My blood pounded in my ears. She was an expert at fooling everyone. She must have passed.

"And so they came for her before I heard of it. The Deputy himself performed the test." He unballed his fist and clenched it again. The assurances meant nothing; Momma had been right.

"But she can endure it," I said. She would not have screamed. She would not have cried.

"I went to his office just as it ended," my father continued. "She was sitting as calm as could be, and they were reviewing the photobox reel—the Deputy and the guardsman Brach."

"The photobox?"

"She didn't flicker during the test," he said. "But they recorded it, in case something should appear that could be seen only if played back slowly."

I waited.

"There was a finger," he said. "The littlest finger could be seen to flicker." A tear rolled down his face. "I insisted on seeing it, of course. I ranted and raved, claimed to know nothing. But the finger was gone."

"Where have they taken her?" I asked. But even as I did so, I still couldn't believe it was real. Perhaps my parents were playing a trick on me, to convince me that this was serious and I should practice well.

"He gave her seventeen shocks, Myra. *Seventeen*. She didn't flicker but a finger."

It was not a trick. They wouldn't do that. Momma, perhaps, but not Poppa. "Where is she?" I asked. I should have dissolved into sobs. That was what Momma would have expected of me. But I didn't. I felt as if I were not there in the room, as if I were looking down on my crying father from a great height.

"She went away with perfect calm, saying we knew nothing about her, that you didn't have it." He wiped his eyes. "To the jail, Myra. Behind bars."

"But what will they do?" I knew what the law said. Punishable as the Waters judge. That meant a cold dip.

My father shook his head. "The Council may suspend the Judgment. In the past they have deported Flickerkin back to the Eye." My father suddenly broke from the window and sped past me. He locked the bolt on the door and set the chain. He turned to me and grabbed me by both my shoulders, towering over me. "You could be tested at any moment." I crashed back into reality, into my body, looking up at my father from far below.

"Poppa, I can't pass," I said. "I can't do it." My tears threatened to well up now. How could I have control that even she didn't have? How could I possibly endure seventeen shocks? Momma had given me only three.

He shook me. "You can do it. It's not only how you react, it's what they want to see. She is a Leftie, but you are only half. They have known you all your life, watched you grow up with their own children. They will want you to pass."

"They have taken Momma!" I cried. "They don't care about me." I put my hand to my face, my pale face, surrounded by hair that bounced and curled.

"What matters is the test," my father said. "If they don't know you have the Ability, then you are safe."

"I can't even do it," I said. "If I wanted to spy, if I wanted to hurt anyone, I couldn't."

"Of course you can't flicker," my father said. "It was only a fluke. You're only the tiniest bit Flickerkin. We will keep practicing, and you'll be fine." But his grip on my shoulders was too tight, his voice too controlled. He knew as well as I did that the Ability was not something that came and went like a child's obstinate refusal to eat anything but cheese sandwiches. I had been scared many times since that day eleven years ago, and I had screamed and shouted and cried and laughed for eleven years without triggering a single episode—but it all meant nothing in the face of the Deputy's test. Those children my mother spoke of who had never flickered in their lives had not been tortured.

My father turned me around and pushed me into their bedroom, where a chair was set up. My mother had practiced here, I realized. She must have done it after she tested me. I had been so angry with her that I hadn't thought about that, about what she must have suffered. He reached into the closet and removed a box designed to hold a men's pocket timepiece. I had seen the box many times and never known what it held.

"I'm sorry," he said as he took out the cuffs.

I sat down in the chair. My mother had endured this seventeen times at full strength. I had no right to complain. I set my hands on the chair's arms. "It's all right," I said.

"You've never flickered," said my father, holding the triggering rod in his left hand.

"I know," I said. But even if I never flickered, with too many shocks I might confess. We both knew that although I might be physically strong enough to win the ride, I would never be as mentally strong as my mother.

Each time my father touched the rod to the cuffs, I took the shock. I took it four times, five, six. I didn't flicker, but I screamed. I would never be able to sit there and endure it with only a fake scream or two. Seven. We took a short break. Eight. I held my scream. Nine.

"Stop," I whispered. Tears rolled down my face. I had made it to nine, but that was all I could take.

My father wiped his own tears away, then ripped the cuffs

off of my arms. "I should have stopped before now," he said. "What kind of a father—"

"No," I said. "No, this is right."

He attempted to put the cuffs back in their box, but the chain between them wouldn't fold correctly, and he threw the cuffs and the box onto the bed. "You haven't flickered. Perhaps you can't."

I said nothing. I just wanted to sleep.

"Perhaps they will stop early. They'll see that you're more like me than like her."

"Poppa . . ." I was so weak that I could no longer sit up straight. He turned, saw me slumping, and caught me before I fell out of the chair. He lifted me up and set me down on the bed, brushing the cuffs and the box away. I curled around my mother's pillow, a huge green thing with lace ruffles. *The lace was made by Nolan's parents*, I thought suddenly. Who were in jail for nothing except hiding their ancestry, as we had hidden ours. "I should have done what he did," I said. "Nolan. I should have flickered and run." Except I didn't know how to flicker. I couldn't have done it to save my life.

"No," said my father. "You won't run. To attempt to leave the city now would be damning. We'll get your mother released. She poses no danger to anyone. The rest of the Council will see that."

I didn't have the strength to think about the politics, to

guess what would happen in the future. But I couldn't believe that he was right, that freeing my mother could be as easy as waiting. "Poppa, why did you even go there?" I asked.

"What do you mean, sweetheart?"

"The Left Eye," I said. "Nobody goes there except the Guard."

"Somebody had to," he said. "How can we maintain the prezine mines if we don't have an ambassador?" He kissed my cheek. "Besides, I thought the girls were pretty." I tried to imagine what it must have been like for him to see all those pale people, to see my mother for the first time, stepping out of the Left Eye mist. She must have seemed so exotic.

She had lied. From the beginning, she had claimed to be as human as he was.

"I'm sorry," I said.

"What do you have to be sorry for?" he asked.

"I'm not human. I can't pass."

"You have my blood and your mother's strength," he said. "You can take a beast over the high wall and back through the moat. You are capable of winning the ride. You can do this, too."

"I don't have her strength," I said.

"You will find it."

I don't know if he said anything else, because I fell asleep there on my parents' bed, cradling my mother's pillow.

I dreamed of riding my beast through the grain fields of the Neck, golden spires waving over my head, my cheek pressed against Hoof's back.

The summons came in the morning: a cold call on the voice-box from the Captain of the Guard. They let my father accompany me to the Deputy's chamber, a last nod to his position as a Council Member. But they made him leave me at the door to the outer chamber, and I passed alone between two guardsmen, the same two who had attempted to take Nolan. They both looked more severe now, hardened by the day that had gone by. They wouldn't be so foolish as to let another target escape. I didn't fail to notice the sensors above the door. They appeared as small, bronze-colored prezine eyes, complete with black pupils. Perhaps that was where the invisible beam of light came from.

My father gave me a practiced, nonchalant smile. "See you in a few minutes," he said from the hall.

"Of course," I said. This was all just a terrible inconvenience. It meant nothing to me that my mother had been taken away to jail. I had nothing to do with any of it. I stepped forward of my own accord into the Deputy's office, because I wouldn't let myself be pushed by anyone. I could feel them following me, though, their shadows hanging over my head, their boots heavy on the lush carpet.

The Deputy sat behind his desk, reading a paper that I recognized as the daily State Complex report. It was a briefing for all the Council Members that contained word of the crops in the Neck, the mining in the Eye, the condition of the ranches and roads through the back country of the Head, the commerce in the market. He was reading it as if this were a day like any other. Or he was hiding, unwilling to look my father in the eye.

You have played cards with my mother, I wanted to say. *You have eaten at our table. You have ridden throughout the Upland with my father for weeks at a time, sharing a campsite. You have sat on the Council together for ten years.* Instead I looked down at him and said, "Good morning, Your Excellency. May the Waters hear me." I nearly choked on the words. I no longer believed in the slightest that I could speak to the Waters through this man.

He set down his paper and stood up slowly, easily, as if this were nothing. He was barely shorter than his son, and he had the same deep brown eyes and sharp jawline, the same straight, narrow nose. "Ah, Miss Hailfast. Thank you for coming," he said. He smiled, and the resemblance to Caster shattered. The Deputy's smile was not easy and disarming, though perhaps that was what he intended. Because of the intention behind it, the smile was lifeless, as were the eyes.

"Shall I sit here?" I asked, inclining my head toward the chair on my side of the desk. Without waiting for an answer, I sat.

"Of course," said the Deputy. "We'll get this unpleasant business taken care of."

"My mother never told either of us," I said. This was technically true, since my father had learned the truth by failing to see me.

"Must have been quite a shock," the Deputy said. He took a pair of prezine cuffs from a box on the edge of his fine desk. A *shock* indeed.

The guardsmen stood straight and silent on either side of the door to the office, between the outside and me. More sensors lined the doorway.

"Yes," I said, forcing emotion into my voice. "I can't believe she lied to me."

"Terrible," he said. "Hold still." He clamped one of the cuffs around my left wrist. It was smoother than the contraband cuffs I'd practiced with. I could only feel the slightest cold against my skin, and that low buzz, which I was sure someone who was not a Flickerkin would not feel.

I looked up at him, tears filling my eyes. "I'm not like her," I said. "I would know, wouldn't I? It would have happened sometime?"

Let him believe you are scared not of failing the test but of being one of these horrible things, my father had said.

Horrible things? I'd asked.

The way he sees it, my father said.

But he hadn't known about my mother. If he had, he wouldn't have brought her back to New Heart City. He wouldn't have married her, and I would never have been born.

"I'm sure you would know," the Deputy said. "This is only a formality." He clamped the other cuff closed. Then he stepped to one side, and for the first time I saw the photobox, standing in front of the office window. There was no sign to indicate whether it was recording. "Now, this will hurt, but only for a second." He tapped the side of one cuff with his triggering rod.

The shock flowed through me, and I screamed a little. But that was the fake scream, the scream of a girl who hadn't practiced.

"Very good." He tapped me again.

I gasped.

Again.

Again.

It was easier than it had been last night. Either my father had turned up the intensity to prepare me, or the Deputy was going easy.

Again.

No, he was not going easy. The shock resonated when it was gone, shaking itself free from my body. Was this what it felt like to have one's molecular structure rearranged? Was this the beginning?

Again.

I could endure this.

Again.

Tears rolled down my face, and my hands gripped the chair. My mother had not given in to the pain this way. She had endured. I pressed the tip of my pinky finger into the chair's wood. The finger that had betrayed her was still visible.

Again.

More tears. I couldn't wipe my face, so they ran down my cheeks onto my blouse.

"Ah, Myra, don't cry," said the Deputy. "It's all over. We need only review the film."

Over? He had shocked me only eight times. I didn't dare to say anything that might change his mind. I simply let the tears flow. Maybe there was some sympathy, after all, behind those cold eyes.

The Deputy waved Brach over. Together, they stood behind the photobox and looked at something I couldn't see.

I closed my eyes, unable to watch. My chest heaved. If emotion could cause me to flicker, then I was done for. I couldn't control myself to save my life. How could I be so weak?

One cuff clicked open, then the other.

"Thank you for coming, Myra," said the Deputy.

I opened my eyes. He was gazing down at me, his expression calculatingly pleasant. Was he letting me go?

"You're a brave girl," he said.

I gripped the chair as I stood up, then raised a hand to wipe my face. *I need to say something,* I thought. But all my calm platitudes, my nonchalant small talk, had disappeared with my resolve not to feel pain.

"It looks as if my son was right," said the Deputy. "He swore up and down that Miss Hailfast could never be a Flickerkin *or* a liar."

"Tell him thank you," I said. "And have a good day." I lifted my head, wiped my face one more time, and moved slowly, carefully, between the guardsmen. I left the Deputy's office and passed out in my father's arms.

From *THE REGULATIONS OF NEW HEART CITY:*
PARTICULAR TO THOSE PEOPLE OF THE
UPLAND WHO RESIDE THEREIN

All residents of New Heart City ages nineteen and older shall pay, as tax, one-sixth of their production to the Council, to be used for the benefit of all. Except that people of the Left Eye, being noncitizens, shall pay, as tax, one-half of their production.

———❖———

TEN

I SLEPT ALL THAT DAY AND NIGHT, DRAINED FROM MY EN-
counters with the cuffs. I dreamed of my mother, as she
was when I was young. Once we were alone in our apartment, just the three of us, she would take down her hair and let
the blond corkscrew curls fall around her shoulders. My father
always said he saw those curls before he saw the rest of her, that
he was already in love before he saw her face. In the dream, she
was straightening my long dress, telling me to hold still while
she pinned it for alterations.

You're a true Leftie, she said, smiling around the pins in her
mouth. *We'd all rather wear pants.* Then she said something in
the Leftie language that I couldn't understand.

I woke in my own bed to find my father sitting by my side.
As soon as I opened my eyes, he broke into a smile.

"You passed," he said.

"Yes." I tried to smile back at him. I should have been ecstatic, or at least relieved. I truly had not believed that I would pass. I had believed that I would be taken away. But now that I was out of danger, my mother's situation weighed on me. It had been two nights and a day since they had taken her, and we had heard nothing. We had done nothing. "Poppa, how are we going to get her out?"

He patted my hand. "I have a meeting with the Council now. There's no evidence that your mother has done anything with her Ability. I'm hopeful that they will release her, to leave for the Eye if nothing else. Now that you are cleared, we can leave without betraying anything."

"To leave for the Eye?" Yes, it was better than jail. But I still didn't want to go.

"A last resort," my father said. "We won't leave until the Games are over; after all this, we owe you that."

"Do you really think he'll let her go?" I asked, pushing myself up in bed. My father spoke of the Council, but it was the Deputy who had the power. My mother had been right.

"She has done nothing except falsely swear her ancestry upon entry," he said. "There is no reason for the Waters not to show mercy."

"Not the Waters," I said, "the Deputy."

"He is the Deputy to the Waters," my father said. "They

speak through him." He could not still believe that, I thought. But I didn't feel like challenging the entire foundation of our culture. I only cared about what would happen to us.

"The radio said that the clothmakers could get the dip," I said.

"Nonsense," my father said. "They'll be expelled too. It's only the boy who's in trouble because he has fled."

"If it's nonsense, why am I hiding?" I asked. "Should I go turn myself in?"

"Perhaps it isn't total nonsense," my father admitted. "Nothing in this world is certain. There is even still a chance that you can have your life here, that they will let her come home—if not now, then once the panic has died down."

The Council would have to change the law for that to happen, to repeal the total ban on Flickerkin outside the Eye. But I didn't say that to him. He was clinging to hope.

"Oh, Myra," he said. He wrapped his arms around me. "I went to Ripkin and asked him not to test you. I told him I'd do anything to spare you from this."

"You did?" I wiped my face.

"While you were sleeping the night before last, I went to him. I told him that you don't have the Ability, that I would have seen it in you."

And he had tested me anyway. This man who had known me my whole life, who had shared our table and much else.

Perhaps he had gone easy on me because of Caster, but he had still tortured me. He had put my father through the humiliation of begging.

My father looked down at the ground, no doubt thinking the same thing. And now he would have to go to the full Council and do more begging, as if he were not one of them but a poor supplicant from the upper Head.

"Go to your meeting," I said. "See if you can help Momma. If nothing else, we need to see her."

"I will," he said, patting my hand. "You get your rest."

"I'd rather go to the stables," I said. "Even with all this, I mean to win. I am cleared of suspicion now," I added, in case he wished to stop me.

"Don't push yourself too hard," he said. "You don't want to be worn out for competition tomorrow."

I nodded, grateful that he was letting me go. The Games were tomorrow. I had much training to catch up on.

"I'll come find you if I learn anything." He kissed my forehead and then left the room.

I got out of bed slowly, sore and tired from the shocks. But I still meant to win. Now it was not only to make my mother proud, but to prove that there was nothing wrong with being half Leftie. And if the truth ever came out, all Plats would know that a dreaded Flickerkin had beaten them.

. . .

I moped my way down to the stables, pondering our situation. Why did the Deputy and, it seemed, most of the people, hate Flickerkin? Few of them had been alive in the days when the Flicker Men still lived among the Lefties, when they had secretly infiltrated the old Heart City. If anyone related to them had been killed in the Leftie uprising (or as my mother called it, the war), it would have been their grandparents or great-grandparents. The Eye had been integrated back into the Upland government as a dependent state for more than sixty years. The Flicker Men had left, and the Eye had been quiet. Lefties were farmers and miners, regular people who did nothing to offend anyone.

Certainly my mother had done nothing. I had done nothing. I had never even been to the Eye since I was a baby. I couldn't have told you the name of the Leftie leader or how he was chosen or what he stood for. I wasn't connected to the Lefties except by my *unique physical characteristics.*

I stewed on all this until I reached the stables, where I found Hoof chewing on hay and stomping, restless from the break in training.

"I'm sorry, Hoof," I said as I brushed her wide back. "I didn't mean to neglect you."

She snorted, eyeing me as if she wasn't buying the apology.

"I was tied up," I said. "Cuffed, actually. But we've both been kept indoors for too long. Let's make it a good practice.

The kind that will intimidate the whole field. There will be even more spectators today. Maybe they'll be waiting for my mother's daughter to fall."

Hoof spat the last of the hay out of her mouth. Of course she couldn't understand the words I was saying, nor the reasons why I now needed to perform well more than ever. But she had been with me since she was born and I was a child—hence the simple name that had stuck despite my mother's protestations—and she knew when I was upset. She always did what she could to help me, and I her.

"You're ready to go, too; I can see that," I said. I pushed open the gate to her stall and led her out. There were many others in the stable, mostly trainers and stable boys bustling about in preparation for the last training day. Most of the beasts were still in their stalls, because many of the riders would rest in the morning and train only lightly in the afternoon. They subscribed to my father's theory about saving themselves for competition. I, however, believed that one could not ride too much, and I had been out of the arena for two days. I had to get back in the swing of things or I would stumble tomorrow.

Funny how everyone was going about as if nothing had happened, as if there were not three Flickerkin in the jail at this very moment, as if all the Lefties in the city were not being tortured by the Deputy simply to stop a panic. As I led Hoof down the passage between the stalls, I glimpsed a flyer hanging on a notice board. It was a picture of Nolan, the same one that had been circulating since his disappearance. It had been taken at last year's Games. He was holding his ribbon above his head in a pose of triumph, but the look on his face was only half a smile. Perhaps that was because he thought he'd been cheated out of first place—a rumor I now believed more than ever. Someone had scrawled the word *Leftie* across his face.

Before I had formed the intention to do it, I reached up and tore the picture down from the board.

"What are you doing?" Porti said from behind me.

I whipped around. But I couldn't conceal the picture balled in my fist. "Someone wrote *Leftie* on it. It has nothing to with him being a Leftie. He's a Flickerkin."

She stared at me for a second. "I suppose the picture won't help much, since no one can see him."

I opened my hand and let the picture fall to the ground. "I suppose not."

"I came to find you," she said. "You wouldn't answer my calls. I heard—"

"It's a lie," I said.

"Your mother—"

"Unfairly accused," I said. "She didn't flicker. She doesn't."

"Why do they think so?"

"They say they saw a finger," I said. "But it was a trick of the light. It's a vendetta against all Lefties, just because of what we look like. Because we're different." I said it with strength, showing the anger I felt. Perhaps it was true. Perhaps she had actually passed, and we believed she flickered only because we knew about her. We ought to be fighting the test results. Perhaps my father was doing that with the Council now. But I doubted it. He was too honest. More honest than I. And I had just declared myself to be a Leftie, something I had never done out loud before. Something I did not believe. I wished to take back the words, but it was too late.

"What about you?" she asked. "Are they going to test you?"

"They have," I said.

Hoof snorted and pawed the ground.

"They have! Well, you obviously passed. But what was it like? What did they do?"

"They shocked me until I passed out," I said. "All to prove I'm the same person I was before."

"Shocked you! How—"

"We must go," I said, gripping Hoof's collar. "She's been cooped up, and I need the practice." I didn't mean to snap at Porti, but there was something about the slim silhouette of her riding clothes, her nearly black hair tied in a twist. Something unfair about the way she stood there, fresh and fully prepared for the Games, wondering what had been done to me.

"Myra!"

I turned around. "I'm sorry," I said. "It's been hard."

"Of course." She took a breath as if she was going to step toward me, but she didn't.

Tears welled up behind my eyes. But I couldn't break down now, here in front of my competitors. "I have to ride."

She ran forward and threw her arms around me. "I can't believe they did this to you," she said. "You aren't even a Leftie."

"I know," I said. But I thought, *What does she mean, not even a Leftie?* Did she mean that I wasn't poor like them, or that I wasn't a sneaky, suspected spy? I pushed her gently away. "I really do have to ride."

"I too," she said. "We will make it a good show—prove we both deserve to be here—the Council Member's daughter and the poor orphan from the Head." Leave it to Porti to find some way to make it seem as if we were in this together, even when her success depended upon my failure.

"We both deserve it," I said. I glanced at the crumpled paper next to my boot on the ground. Nolan, the workers' son, also deserved to have his fair chance.

"Do not let this defeat you, Myra," she said, hugging me again. "*You* are still the same person. One of the best riders in the Upland. My best friend."

"Thank you," I said. It was exactly what I needed to hear. Before the test, I had been poised to win, and after the test, I had the same skill. I would be strong.

"Call me tonight," she said. "We still must discuss our

attire for the winners' ball." She flashed me a smile as she walked away. I recalled last year's ball, when we had only just met, and I had been bitter over my loss. I had hardly spoken to her. This year, things would be different. I would aspire to be more generous, whether I won or not.

She *was* my best friend—the only friend who had spoken to me since my mother was arrested. Not that we had been answering our voicebox. My father didn't want us to speak rashly. And where was Caster? Was he one of those rings we had left unanswered? But all my friends' parents probably supported the testing. Their parents were on the Council or close to it. My friends probably heard day in and day out how dangerous Lefties were, and they now counted me among them.

Just then I realized that the stepladder I relied on to climb onto Hoof's back was missing. I looked around the edge of the arena and the wall of the stable, but it wasn't there. I was the only one known to use it; could it be a coincidence that it was suddenly gone? Someone had to know where it was.

"Excuse me," I said to a stable boy passing by, but he didn't stop. "Excuse me," I said to a woman pulling a cart full of stones. But she didn't stop either. "Anyone?" I called out to the four people passing by me, but all only glanced at me and kept walking.

"Does the lady need assistance?" said a voice from the other side of Hoof. I looked around to see Caster smiling down at me from atop Monster. A part of me wanted to leap up to him, if I could have made it. But instead, my face began to burn. I didn't want him to see that someone had stolen my ladder, but I had no other option than to accept his help.

"My stepladder seems to be missing," I said. "Would you mind giving me a boost?"

Caster dismounted smoothly, not missing a beat. He pulled me into him and kissed me. "Ah, we need to train, don't we?" he said with a laugh.

"Sometime today," I said. I let the smile happen. He didn't hate me because of my mother. He wasn't treating me differently. I could almost have given up on training and stayed right there with him all day. As I stood on my tiptoes to kiss him again, I was vaguely aware of the people around us; they stared. But that was all right.

"I'd be honored to boost the lady," Caster said, kneeling with an exaggerated flourish.

I stepped into his clasped hands and vaulted onto Hoof's back.

He stood, and now that I was mounted, I looked down on him from above.

"Thank you," I said. *For not hating me.* But there would be time to say all that later, when we were in the winners' circle together.

"Anytime." He grinned and gave a little bow, and in his eyes there was something else, something that seemed to be telling me I would get through this.

I returned his gaze, trying not to betray all my emotions.

"It's a good thing the men and women don't compete," he said. "So I'm allowed to hope you win."

"A fair point," I said. "You can count on me to cheer the loudest for you—until our rematch, of course." The thought of our coming competition made me smile a true smile. I gave Hoof a light nudge. "On, girl!"

I wanted nothing more than to race out to the main course and do a full run, to blast the spectators with the fact that I was still here. Perhaps someone had stolen my ladder, but I didn't need it; I had at least two friends. I would show everyone that I was the one to be feared tomorrow. But I held myself back. Hoof needed to warm up before going full speed, and so did I. I couldn't afford for either of us to be injured. So I rode into the warm-up arena, which was a circular stadium behind the main complex. There were only a few places for spectators there, and only a few other riders. We took off at a slow trot.

"That's it, Hoofy," I said. I tried to slow my anticipation, to let myself feel the connection with my beast. Her coarse head hair flattened in the breeze and her ears perked up as we made one pass around the arena, then another. One more pass and she was trotting steadily, no longer suffering from her confinement.

"Are we ready, then?" I asked her, squeezing my knees together, giving her the signal that I was ready.

Her heart beat faster and her ears flattened. That was a yes.

"On, then!" I guided her out of the practice arena and to the entrance of the main complex. There was no one at the starting block except an official gatekeeper, whose job was to make sure only registered competitors trained in the arena. Since today was the last day of training, there were no official times; you were expected not to ride on top of others' horns. I didn't remember the gatekeeper's name, since he was from far out in the Head and only came in every year for the Games. But I recognized him and waved a greeting.

"Myra Hailfast," I said. "Second seed."

He stared at me open-mouthed.

"Don't you remember me?" I asked. "I'm sure we met last year. Besides, I'm on the list of competitors."

Hoof snorted. She was becoming restless again. Once I signaled I was ready to start, it wasn't good to wait. She might waste her strength and lose her focus.

"Miss Hailfast . . ." He trailed off and fumbled with his paper.

"The women's course is clear, isn't it?" I asked. I was required to wait until the gatekeeper gave me clearance, but I hadn't seen anyone in the moat as I rode in. Surely I had plenty of space.

He looked up. "Hasn't anyone told you?"

"Told me what, sir?" I asked, setting my hand on Hoof's head to steady her.

Her ears twitched.

"That people of the Left Eye have been taken out of competition." He looked frightened, as if I might jump off my beast. But I only sat there, trying to make sense of what he had just said.

"I am not from the Left Eye," I said. "I am a citizen of New Heart City. My father is Donray Hailfast, Member of the Council." I paused. "My father is on the Council," I said again, as if he hadn't heard me.

"You have been taken off the list," said the gatekeeper. He held up the paper, though it was too far away for me to read. "The Council Adjunct came himself with the names to remove. Yours was among them, Miss."

Where was my father when this happened? Had he been outvoted, or had they snuck around him as they had when they took my mother for testing? I stared ahead at the course. If I were to ride it, the gatekeeper couldn't stop me.

As if reading my mind, he stepped in front of Hoof. "I'm sorry, Miss Hailfast. It's not coming from me. *I* know you aren't a Leftie."

"I've been hearing that a lot lately," I said. "But still, you're not letting me ride."

Hoofbeats pounded on the turf behind me, and I turned to see Caster riding in our direction. He pulled up next to me. "I just heard," he said. His face was flushed, his eyes burning. I had never seen such a look on his face. "My father didn't tell me. I swear it."

I could still see the course, and I could have made a break for it, escaped from the gatekeeper. But what good would that do? Tomorrow I would be sidelined. I couldn't win.

"I will talk to him," Caster said. "This can't happen."

I turned to him, tears falling. "I passed his test. Did he tell you? He gave me eight shocks with a smile."

His face fell, and I felt bad. It wasn't he who had shocked me. It was only their faces that were alike.

"Of course you passed," he said.

We sat there in silence while the gatekeeper twisted his paper in his hands. Finally, I turned Hoof around. She pawed the ground in confusion. Caster rode with me silently back to the stables. We received sidelong glances from the trainers and the competitors who were just arriving. I felt more conspicuous than usual.

Everyone besides me must have known. Had Porti known but failed to tell me? No. I dismissed the thought. She would never have kept something like that from me. She would not want to win this way. Caster's father must have purposefully hidden it from him.

When we reached Hoof's stall, Caster dismounted and held up his arms. I let him lift me off my beast and set me down on the soft turf. I always wanted his arms around me, but now that his hands held my waist, I could do nothing but cry. I put my hands over my eyes, as if I could somehow hide my humiliation.

"I'm sorry," he said. "It may not help, but I don't agree with excluding Lefties. It hardly seems proportional, all this over four Flickerkin."

I should have denied that my mother was one, but I was in no shape to say anything. *She* wouldn't have cried.

He pulled me into his arms, and my face pressed against his chest.

"Finding out about your mother, it must have been terrible," he said.

I took a breath, trying to get myself together.

Caster reached down and wiped the tears from my cheek. "I told him you weren't one of them. You couldn't be."

"I know," I said. "He told me." The Deputy had stopped at eight shocks because Caster had intervened. Caster had saved me from being caught. I wished I could thank him for what he had really done for me.

"Remember, your friends know you. We're still here."

"Thank you," I said.

"Myra!" My father was coming toward us.

Caster pulled away from me. "Council Member—" he began.

"Good day, Mr. Ripkin," my father said. He looked from Caster to me. "I came as soon as I heard what they had done —during a secret meeting. Apparently someone has told you."

I nodded, wiping the rest of my tears from my face.

"It came from the Deputy," my father said. "He considers all the test results preliminary—for those who passed. He claims there's a threat to the Games." He took a long look at Caster. "It's hard to see the advantage to a rider of not being seen."

"Poppa, it's not Caster's fault," I said.

"I know." My father sighed. "Go on, Mr. Ripkin. Get your practice."

"Myra . . ." Caster put a hand on Monster's back.

"Go," I said. "I'll be all right."

"I'll come see you," he said.

"After the Games," I said. "After you win."

He nodded and jumped onto his beast. "Good day, Myra, Council Member Hailfast." He rode off, back toward the main complex.

"The Ripkin boy is too familiar," said my father.

"Poppa—" I was about to defend Caster, try to explain our compromising position as something other than what I was glad it was. I clung to that, knowing he still wanted to be with me. I wasn't just a half-Leftie; he saw me as human.

"Never mind that now," my father said. "I've gotten leave for us to see your mother."

"You have?" I made sure Hoof was safely back inside her stall. She grunted and stared at me with wide, wet eyes. "I'm sorry, Hoofy. I'll be back as soon as I can."

"Let's get to the jail before the Deputy has a change of heart," my father said. "This development with the Games is disturbing. There's no possible justification for it."

"They can't do anything to you, can they?" I asked as we walked. "You're on the Council, and you're one hundred percent Plat."

"I don't know if any of that matters now," he said. "I've harbored a Flickerkin."

Two Flickerkin, I thought. And he must have been thinking it, too, because he put a hand on my back, as if he could protect me. I wasn't sure he could protect either of us.

From *THE BOOK OF THE WATERS*

In that land beyond the oceans, the Waters shall surround the people, never receding or destroying, but filled with love. And there the people shall live forever: those of the Plateau in their own land and those of the Left Eye in theirs. Each land will be bountiful, and none shall want.

ELEVEN

THE JAIL WAS AT THE EDGE OF THE STATE COMPLEX, on the opposite side from the arena, so it was a long, dusty walk in the summer heat. I should have been riding at full speed through the course, not walking at a snail's pace through the abnormally crowded streets. It seemed that eyes followed us everywhere. I was used to being looked at; I was a most unusual sight. But I was also a familiar sight, and I had grown up here, so everyone knew me. Now the city was full of strangers from all over the Upland, and the news about the tests and the jailed Flickerkin had aroused their interest in me. It didn't help that I was wearing riding clothes and not riding.

I kept my head down, relying on my father to pay attention. He guided me with a strong hand on my back until we had passed out of the crowds and approached the jail. I had never been inside it before, obviously. Why would I have needed to go near a place that housed vandals and thieves? I couldn't even have said exactly which building the jail was in. My father led me to a nondescript door that stood out only because of the two solemn guardsmen stationed in front of it.

"Good day, Member Hailfast," said one of the guardsmen before my father could even open his mouth. The man opened the door and held out an arm, signaling for us to pass. We walked past a desk manned by another guardsman, and that made the highest concentration of the Guard I had ever seen in New Heart City. The man at the desk nodded to us politely, but my father didn't acknowledge him.

"To the left," the man behind us said. We turned the corner, and I saw my mother.

She was in a cell behind bars that crisscrossed each other. The space was not as bad as I had expected. She had a large bed with blankets taken from our apartment, an upholstered chair, and a side table on which lay a stack of books and a cup of tea. Still, she was behind bars. Her face was pale, without makeup. I had never before seen her face bare in public.

As we approached, she set down the book in her hands and stood up from the chair, a blank look on her face. Her wrists were cuffed with prezine but not bound together. The delicate cuffs might have been bracelets, but they kept her from flickering—as if flickering would help her now.

Sensors were located high up on either side of the cell. If I took another step forward, I would be caught in their invisible beams. I knew they could only affect me if I were invisible, which of course I wasn't, and yet every fiber in me wished to avoid them.

"Come forward," my mother said, reading my mind. Her blond curls were held back by a ribbon, but the tie was imperfect. Strands flew unkempt around her face.

I took a step, willing myself not to flinch beneath the sensors.

She reached a hand through the bars and took mine. "You have been crying." She didn't say it with a mother's sympathy, but as an accusation. I wasn't strong enough.

"They have prevented her from riding," my father said.

"I endured the test," I said. "I may have cried, but I endured it." My face was becoming flushed again. Leave it to my mother to make my emotions stronger while she admonished me to contain them.

"They fear invisible riders?" said my mother. "What will they fear next? I suppose if one sleeps invisibly, it might scare the mice."

I passed the test while you couldn't, I thought. *I was stronger than you were.* Why was she not relieved? But then, I told myself, she couldn't show her relief in front of the guardsmen.

"Have they treated you badly?" my father asked.

My mother waved her free hand at her cell. "A bed, a chair, and a table. Books. Food from the Council's kitchen. They escort me to a private bath. A very civilized prison."

"How are they treating Nolan's parents?" I asked.

"I know nothing of them," she said. "I suppose it's too risky to let us see one another, since there's an alleged conspiracy to overthrow the Council. We're being directed by some unknown evil force in the Left Eye." She was staring straight at the guardsman behind us. "Perhaps we're even being directed from across the oceans. We're an advance party of Flickerkin stooges preparing the land for nonhuman marauders."

"There is no such charge against you, Mrs. Hailfast," the man said.

"If there is no charge, then why am I being held?" she asked.

The guardsman shrugged. "I have my orders."

I had not articulated even to myself why the Deputy was doing this, but of course my mother, in her sarcasm, was exactly right. How else could they justify what they were doing? Someone must be spreading tales of just such a conspiracy. All because of a few strange happenings. Had nothing else strange happened during all these years of peace?

"I have spoken with the Council," my father said. "The *rest* of the Council, that is. They say they haven't taken any vote on when you will be tried or what penalty they will seek."

"Well," she said. She bit her lip as if she had more to say.

But she was too wise to rant against the Council in front of a guardsman.

"Rhondalynn," my father said, taking her other hand, "we will get you out of here, and this will pass."

"Yes," she said, looking up at him. She was only barely taller than I was, so she had to look far up. My father gazed down at her.

"I love you," he said.

Her mouth broke into the slightest smile. Perhaps there was even a bit of moisture behind her eyes. "And I you." They looked at each other for a long second, and though I was still holding on to one of her hands, it was as if I had disappeared and the two of them were alone in the jail, or in the world.

Then my mother turned to me, and the spell broke. "You must hold your head high," she told me. "Attend the Games. Sit in the Council box. Be seen."

"Momma, I can't watch it!" I hadn't had time to imagine what I would do if I couldn't ride. I hadn't *watched* the women's portion of the ride for three years.

"You can and you will," she said. "Show them that you are a citizen of the Upland. Be *visible*."

"Momma, you don't understand! How can I—"

"I understand perfectly," she said. "You are better than the rest, and you will show it by cheering on your rivals. Root for your friend Miss Vale."

"I suppose I should wear a smile," I said, letting go of her hand.

"I will be there," said my father. "We'll face it together."

"Think of something that makes you happy," said my mother, with a little bit of softness. "They will not know what it is."

Caster suddenly jumped into my mind, the feel of his hands on my waist as he lifted me off Hoof. I nearly smiled right there, but held it back. I shouldn't be smiling about anything, today or tomorrow. But maybe with my mother's advice, I could get through it. I didn't want to be the weak girl who cried. I wanted them to see that we could not be beaten.

"All right," I said.

"Good girl," my mother said.

"We must go, Member Hailfast," the guardsman said.

My father glared at him, then turned back to my mother. "We'll come again," he said. "Remember, we are doing everything we can and we love you."

"I know," she said. And they were in their own world again, smiling.

"Come," said the guardsman.

My parents' hands separated, my mother gave me a tiny sad smile, and we were walking away from her, back down the hall, past the desk, and out into the dusty street. I was sorry to have to leave her, but I was glad not to be under the sensors or staring at those bars. If not for Caster, it could have been me inside that cell. I gasped, trying not to burst into tears.

"We will get her out," my father said, putting his arm around me.

I nodded but said nothing. We walked back to our apartment in silence, because although we had vowed to help her, we did not know how.

From *THE BOOK OF THE WATERS*

And from the Plateau People the Waters created the people of
the Left Eye, and these people were also right. For the Waters
create only with reason.

TWELVE

MY FATHER WENT TO THE DEPUTY'S APARTMENT that night, but the guardsmen turned him away at the door. He came back to our apartment stone-faced, holding a paper.

"They have voted me suspended," my father said. "I am to face charges of harboring and false swearing."

"You have sworn nothing false," I said. "When Momma entered the city, you didn't know. That's the truth." It was late, but I had no thought of sleeping. I was thinking about Hoof, and about Caster, and about the sensors that had borne down on me, and about my mother's face as she told me I must sit in the Council box. I could barely process what my father was saying, but I knew that if the Council were to convict him, he would be removed. Our hereditary claim to Membership would be eliminated, and that was the least of it.

"Yes," he said. He stared out the window. Below our apartment was the wall separating those of us in the State Complex from the ordinary citizens. And beyond that, dark except for a dim street lamp, was a street still packed with visitors. "But I knew for a long time."

"What if she had told you from the beginning?"

He shook his head. "I don't know. Before you love someone, you can more easily believe the worst of them. Once I loved her, I could not." He put an arm around me, and we both looked out the window. Would we soon be on the outside, looking in? Or so far from here that the world would look completely different?

"What will we do?" I asked.

"I will make my case," my father said. "I will say that I knew nothing until the test was complete."

"A lie, Poppa?" I tried to laugh, to make light of the fact that my father was always so honest—except for this one thing.

"They may call you in to speak for me," he said.

"I can do that."

He squeezed my shoulder. "I know you can, Myra. You have your mother's strength, whether you know it or not. Tomorrow, we will go to the Games and sit in the Council box as your mother wishes. Until my case is heard, I am still a Member. And we are citizens of New Heart City." We. It was no longer only my mother and I who were in danger. We had dragged him into it. "But we also must have a plan," he said. "I will contact your grandmother and make preparations for you to travel to the Eye. I will follow with your mother when I can."

"I'm not leaving," I said. I had never met my grandmother in the Eye; she was nothing to me. And I thought of Porti, of Caster, of school, of the whole world I knew. Of my mother's strength. Of being seen. Of not giving up.

"I hope it won't come to that," said my father. "But I will make a call in the morning. They will meet us on the road if need be."

"Who is 'they'?" I asked.

"Your grandmother and her relatives," he said. "Perhaps it's time you met them anyway, learned more than a few words of the language."

"I don't want to leave."

"It may not be our choice," said my father. He sighed. "Your mother and I hoped to shield you from all this. We hoped the peace would last, and we would be a symbol for what the future could be. We hoped there would be many children like you."

"They must stop putting Lefties in jail," I said. "There aren't any spies."

"No, there aren't," my father said. "But the situation in the

Eye is worsening. There is talk of another strike, much like the one that started the war. The miner caught with a dagger has been sentenced to Judgment."

"When? Why didn't you tell me this before?" I shouldn't have raised my voice to my father, but I couldn't believe it. How could my world be tearing apart?

"I wanted to protect you," he said. "I wanted you to grow up with no worries or fears." He turned away from me. "But the plateau is too small for that."

"I must sleep. I must be fresh to play my part tomorrow," I said, and I rushed into my bedroom and slammed the door. Of course I wouldn't sleep. I lay awake trying to imagine the Left Eye, this mystical place high up off the ground, with thin rains and pale people, where they spoke a language I barely knew. I couldn't go there. It would be too strange.

The women's contest came first by tradition. This was because it wasn't considered as important as the men's. This unfair situation normally irked me, since I was convinced that I could beat any of them if given the chance, but today I hoped it would work to my advantage, as there would be fewer people in the Council box. I wouldn't have to fake my smile in front of so many.

The gatekeeper at the entrance to the restricted Council area stared at us as we approached.

"Member Hailfast," he said.

"My daughter and I are here for the riding," my father said.

The two stared at each other for a moment.

"Are we not on the approved list?" he asked.

"Yes," the gatekeeper stammered. "Of course you are, Member."

"Of course," said my father. "Good day." We brushed past the man and faced the surprised looks of the three Members of the Council who were already in the box.

"Donray!" said Member Solis. She was wearing the fashionable swooshing skirt with a garish bright purple bodice. A spectator's outfit, I thought meanly, before remembering that I also was wearing a skirt. A humiliating turn of events. I looked at the ground.

"Hello, Anga," said my father.

The other two Council Members, Orphos's father and Gregor's father, glanced at each other. Orphos's mother looked away.

"Please, join us," said Orphos's father. He moved aside to make room for us between himself and Member Solis.

Gregor came in from the other entrance with Porti's foster sister, Bricca. They stopped short when they saw me. Bricca glanced at her mother, who gave her a little nod. Only then did Bricca come forward, slowly, to greet me. Her normally exuberant smile was missing, replaced by caution and a failure to meet my eyes.

Gregor gave me a tight smile and looked away.

"Good day, Miss Hailfast," Bricca said. And with that, she and Gregor sat in the seats Orphos's father had just offered us. I didn't care about seats, but I couldn't believe the change in Bricca. She was afraid of me. Anga Solis must have said terrible things about me to her little girl. It was as if Bricca and her mother had dropped a bucket of ice over my head. I hadn't changed or done anything to deserve this. It wasn't right.

I didn't look at Anga Solis, or at Bricca, or at my father. I saw my mother's face, heard her voice admonishing me to be seen. But it was too much. I turned and raced out of the Council box. I ran past the surprised gatekeeper and out into the throng of people. My skirt slapped against my ankles. I was unused to walking here without my riding boots, and my ladies' boots skidded across the turf. I nearly slipped and fell into a man carrying a tray of drinks.

"Hey!" he said. And then, under his breath, "Leftie."

It seemed that all eyes followed me as I ran, without thinking, toward the stables. Most people here wouldn't know me, since many had traveled here for the Games. They saw only my short stature, my strange coloring, my bosom that I couldn't hide beneath my modest blouse. I pulled at the buttons around my neck as I ran. Now my collar choked me. If I went to the Eye,

I thought, at least I would be able to wear pants. No one would find my body worth staring at.

I skidded into the stables, past the stalls where the men's beasts stomped impatiently, past the empty stalls the women's beasts had just left. The riders would be in the practice arena now, doing their final warm-up.

Hoof stomped and growled at me when I reached her.

"Hoof, it's terrible," I said. I joined her in the stall and closed the door behind me, wrapping my arms around her body. She was too big for me to get my arms all the way around, but I laid my face against her side, let her coarse hair brush against my cheek. I confided in her about all my troubles. "Little Bricca is a different person today, as if she barely knows me. Momma is in jail for nothing. Poppa has been suspended from the Council. I'm only cleared *preliminarily*, even though I *passed* the test. We might have to leave New Heart City. Momma will be so angry at me for leaving the box."

Hoof snorted.

"And I can't ride," I said. "I've trained all year for this day. All my life!" That was the most unfair thing of all. What I had worked for had been taken away. "They tell you to *work* and then you will be happy," I said, raising my voice. "Well, I've worked. My father has worked. My mother has worked. You have worked. We have all worked, and what has it gotten us? To be shunned by our supposed friends. Forced to wear this *costume*." I tugged at my buttons, finally pulling the top two apart. I was tempted to rip my skirt off. Why had I not left some pants here in the stables?

Something poked me at the base of my skull, stinging me.

I yelped and jumped away from Hoof. Putting my hand to my neck, I whipped around but saw no one.

"And now I'm being attacked by bees," I told Hoof. "Everyone is in on it."

I felt another sting, stronger this time. My hand, which had been reaching for Hoof's back, disappeared.

I gasped and looked down at myself, but I was not there. I almost screamed but choked as my body popped back into view. It came with a burst of pain, as if I had been stung by bees all over. I grabbed Hoof, unsteady, afraid I would fall, and then stared out at the passage. There was no one there. No one had seen.

"Hoof," I said. "Hoof." What else could I say to her? I couldn't speak out loud about what had just happened. I couldn't deny it; I had flickered.

"I knew it," said a voice from the shadows.

I froze.

"Don't worry, Myra," said the voice. "Look here."

I turned toward the voice and still saw no one. But then a figure flickered into view. His blond hair was wild, his face was dirty, and his clothes looked unwashed. But there was no doubt about it—it was Nolan Drachman. He stood close to a hay bale, still in shadow. In his right hand, he held a rod like the ones the Deputy and my mother had used to trigger the prezine cuffs.

"You did this to me?" I whispered. I stomped toward him. "You did this? In plain sight?"

"Calm down, Myra," he said. "No one is here. They're all watching the riding."

"How did you do that?" I demanded. "Why?" I couldn't get past the sensation of my body *missing*. One second I had been there, and the next I had not. And I hadn't given my permission.

"There is a sensitive spot at the base of the skull," he said. "Guaranteed to make one flicker."

"But why? You had no right."

"I heard about your mother," he said. "I also heard that you had passed the test. But I *knew*. I could see it in you—my parents could, too."

"Your parents are traitors," I said.

"Because they lied?" he asked, seemingly unoffended.

"I never lied," I said. "I was a baby when I passed through the gates. It was my mother who took the oath."

"I was born here," said Nolan. "So it's our parents who are guilty."

"No," I said. "They all *had* to lie. They're not traitors. I said it because I'm angry—you've done something to me. I haven't flickered since I was a child." I said this last part in the smallest of whispers, as though Hoof might overhear and repeat it.

"Then they've taken something from you," he said. "They've taken away who you are."

"*You've* taken something," I said. "I wasn't even sure it could happen again." What if he had triggered my Ability, as my mother feared, and now I would go about flickering like a pre-zine lamp switched on and off? I didn't know how to control it.

"It's all right," he said. "I didn't hurt you. The Plats would have to know about the trigger point to use it. Even most of us don't know."

Us. "Why are you here, anyway?" I snapped. "They'll catch you."

He laughed. "Not likely." He vanished, then reappeared again. "They can't place those sensor things everywhere."

"I'm not your enemy," I said. "Or your friend. Why would you care about exposing me?"

"I'm not here to expose you," he said. "I wanted to know for sure. You may be the daughter of a Council Member, but now you can't deny that you're one of us. We need all the strength we can gather."

"One of us who?" I asked. "All the other Lefties passed the test. So it's just your family and mine."

"Maybe," he said. He knew more than he was saying. I

could see it. Had other Lefties passed the test even though they were Flickerkin? I couldn't imagine anyone being stronger than my mother. If she had failed, surely no one could pass—no one who hadn't been given leniency, as I had.

"You must leave," I said. "I can't be caught with you. My family is in enough trouble."

"Haven't you ever *wanted* to flicker?" he asked.

"No," I said. "I never want to flicker again." My mother's voice filled my head. *You must never do it.* I hadn't tried. I hadn't done it on purpose.

"Myra—"

"You had no right," I repeated.

"True enough. I'm sorry," he said. "But you wouldn't have told me. I need to know who my friends are."

"We are *not* friends. It's a shame—a shared shame." *I didn't try,* I told myself. *I must still be safe.* I looked down at my hands. There were as visible as Hoof, as the stall, as the straw. I was still there. *Momma, tell me I'm still safe,* I thought.

"I need help," he said. He ran his hand through his wild curls, and I noticed that his muscular arm seemed a little thinner. It had been less than a week, but perhaps he hadn't eaten. Despite my anger, I felt something for him. He had done no more to deserve his fate than I had mine, and he had no protection from a well-placed father or from the Deputy's son. "I can get food," he continued. "But being invisible, it's not as much help as you might think. I can still bump into people. I can't rest because someone might stumble over me." He gave a little laugh. "I can't bathe. Imagine what people would do if they found a tub of water splashing itself?"

"It's a good thing we're in the stables," I said. "You fit right in."

He laughed harder. "Yes, I suppose so. If you would let me stay here . . . Are you the only one who comes into this stall?"

"The stable boys come in," I said. "But they have a schedule. You can avoid them." What harm could it do to let him stay here, as long as nobody found out? It would be nice to have something I could *do* other than bemoan my fate. Let the Guard waste their time searching dead ends.

"Thank you, Myra," he said. "I knew you were a good person."

"If you poke me with that thing again," I said, "I'll tell the Deputy about you myself."

"Understood, Miss Hailfast," he said, and he gave a bow. As he leaned toward me, I caught a whiff of the result of all this time without a bath.

"I think I'll pass the Games by giving my beast here a good wash," I said. "I might accidentally leave a bucket behind."

He grinned. "That would be a most careless mistake." As he said it, footsteps pounded on the turf. I turned to see a stable boy hurrying down the passage. When I turned back, Nolan was gone. I took a step backwards, looking at where he had been standing. But there was nothing. Only a pair of footprints in the dirt that might have been left behind by a stable boy. From now on, I could never be sure I was alone.

A cheer from the crowd carried from the arena. The women riders must be nearing the end of the course.

Hoof snorted and pawed the ground.

I didn't want to go back out there, with everyone staring at me, knowing I had been forbidden to ride. Maybe it would be good for me to learn how to use my Ability. Then no one would see my humiliation. But if I did that, I would be allowing the Deputy and his cronies to walk over me, to shame me out of my own life. I was still the daughter of a Council Member. I was *not* going to flicker again. I turned back around to face where I thought Nolan still was.

"I have to go to the box now," I said. "I'll come back tonight."

"Tell me what fool wins the stone toss," said Nolan's voice.

"A fool carrying half the weight," I said. I had no doubt that he had been cheated last year. As had we all.

From *THE BOOK OF THE WATERS*

Of all the sins worthy of Judgment, murder is the most foul.
For what the Waters have created, only the Waters may destroy.
There shall be no laws of men that permit any death except by
Judgment.

THIRTEEN

I DIDN'T LOOK TO MY LEFT OR RIGHT AS I WALKED BACK to the Council box. If people were staring at me or whispering comments, I didn't notice. A loud cheer went up as I neared the box, and then there was wild clapping and more cheering. I resolved not to listen, tried not to guess what was going on. Then the crowd began chanting a name, and though I tried not to hear it, I couldn't help it. "Vale! Vale! Vale!" they chanted. My stomach tightened. If anyone but me was to win, it should be her. She was the best rider in the field, and she was my best friend. But I had trained to beat her. I could have beaten her.

"Miss Hailfast," said the gatekeeper. He looked only at my face, but I could have sworn he was thinking about my shoes —the ladies' boots I was stuck in.

"Is my father still in the box?" I asked.

"Yes, Miss," he said. His eyes were full of sympathy, and I couldn't take that.

"Thank you," I said sharply, breezing past him again.

"Vale! Vale! Vale!" The box had more occupants now, and all were on their feet, cheering. Even my father was cheering for her. I stood at the entrance for nearly a minute, watching them, until they began to settle.

"Myra!" My father came over to me. He put an arm around me. "Are you all right?"

"Perfect," I said. I stared at Gregor, who was now on the far side of the box, cheering. Bricca was still jumping up and down while her mother clapped in triumph.

I couldn't let on that anything had happened apart from losing control of my feelings. Even my father couldn't know about Nolan. He couldn't know that I had flickered for the first time since my childhood, either. He still held out hope that the first time was a fluke, that I wasn't burdened by my mother's lie. I slipped away from him. He would be ashamed of me if he knew.

"I'm just going to sit and watch," I said. *And don't talk to me,* my tone added.

"Myra . . ." He let me go. I sat in the empty chair farthest from Gregor, the one person my age in the box. That put me in the front corner, unable to speak to anyone but in view of everyone. That should make my mother happy. They would all see that I had come back. They would see every inch of me.

Down in the arena, Porti was receiving her first-place ribbon. Someone put a bouquet of flowers in her arms, and she stood there in her riding clothes, a towel around her neck, tall and beautiful and flushed from her ride, waving her free arm at the crowd. I watched her numbly. Was it any worse to watch from up here than it had been to watch from a foot away last year? Now I felt as if the event were on a photobox recording, as if I were not here at all. Except that my constrained feet and rebuttoned, choking blouse reminded me that I existed.

Sky was down there, interviewing the top finishers. He was an especially skinny man with hair that stuck up every which way, making him look always excited. The third- and second-place winners thanked their beasts and their parents. I tried not to listen.

"And now, Miss Portianna Vale, representing the Head!" Sky said. "How does it feel to repeat your win? I'll bet your place at the University is a lock now." He handed Porti the receiver.

"I am very happy to have proved that I still have the skills to ride the course," said Porti. Her voice was quiet, but with the amplification, it carried well. I couldn't help but hear it. "Yet this ribbon is not mine to keep."

The crowd chattered. Porti raised her voice.

"There is one rider who earned her place today but is not here," said Porti. "I rode this course with her only last week. Before our ride was cut short, she was ahead of me, and I ended up on the turf. Miss Myra Hailfast deserves this." She raised the ribbon above her head. "Myra, this is for you." She turned to Sky. "Where I come from, in the Head, there are many Lefties," she said. "They live and work among us, are taxed equally, are counted as friends. Yes, I wish to attend the University. But only if my friend Miss Hailfast is welcome on equal terms. I do not wish to live in a city where merit is tossed aside for fear." She handed the receiver and the ribbon back to Sky, who looked as if he did not know what they were. And then she dropped her flowers on the ground and walked past him, crossing the open stretch of the arena.

The crowd burst into jeers.

Porti didn't acknowledge them. She walked straight and tall until she reached the exit and disappeared from view.

In the Council box, all were silent.

I fought back tears. I hadn't been able contain my jealousy, and then she had sacrificed everything to support me. I lost the fight, and the tears streamed down my face. Where was she going? I needed to go after her, to make it up to her somehow. She had done this for me, knowing how much it would anger

Member Solis. She might have to leave the city. But now the photobox projector above the arena showed my face. I couldn't leave with all eyes on me.

I sat up as straight and tall as I could and lifted my hand to wave. Let them see me cry. I was here, being seen. That was all Momma could ask of me.

"What a statement!" Sky exclaimed, the photobox moving back to him. "I think that's a first for the Games, folks. Thank you to all the lady riders for an outstanding opening run. And now, let's introduce the men!"

I sat straight as the remaining women left the field and the men appeared. They would start and finish in front of the Council box, and the photobox projectors would let us see what happened along the course.

Now the men rode out in order of seed, the lowest seed first. All the men looked similar because all were Plat. They were all tall and thin, with dark brown hair and tanned skin. They sat up straight on their fine beasts and waved at the crowd.

Ten riders had qualified at last month's trials. Orphos came out fifth, and the box behind me erupted.

"Stal-i-amos!" Orphos's parents and Gregor shouted.

I couldn't bring myself to shout, but as I clapped for my friend, Porti entered the box. She passed in front of everyone and sat next to me.

I didn't know what to say.

"I almost didn't ride," she said. "I shouldn't even have ridden."

"No, Porti." I embraced her. "What you did—it means everything."

She wiped away a tear. "Let us cheer for the boys," she said. We stared down into the arena. I was crying, but with her next to me, I felt stronger. I was no longer alone.

In second seed, Caster rode out. He led Monster around at a prance, and I clapped, and my heart ached. I thought he smiled at me, but I couldn't be sure. In the arena everyone seemed to be looking at everyone.

The starting flag waved, and the riders were off. The men's course was a fine mix of obstacles, revamped since the day we had trained together so that the competition course would be fresh. There were races and a moat crossing to the island, and jumps of varying heights. First there was a flat-out race from the starting point to the high wall. This could be the most important leg of all, because only one rider dared take the flying leap over the wall at a time. Caster sped ahead of the rest, leaning over his beast's head.

Behind me, the Council cheered.

Caster's beast, Monster, was huge, larger than the average competitor. His horns were long and thick. They stuck out from either side of his head above his ears, coming to sharp and deadly points. His powerful legs pounded against the ground, and right before he reached the wall they propelled him into the air. On the ground the giant beast looked—and was— heavy enough to crush four men, but now he soared weightless through the air. Caster leaned flat against his beast, appearing like a hump growing from Monster's back. They cleared the wall by nearly a foot.

The crowd burst into cheers, and the large photobox projector screen above the arena switched on. We saw Caster racing away from the arena toward the lake. Two other riders took the wall and then Orphos. Everyone behind me was cheering, and I found myself caught up in the chase, leaning over the edge of the box, even though the screen was positioned so that all could see.

The rider behind Caster had nearly caught up, and they leaped into the moat side by side, Caster splashing a huge spray over the other's head. How I wanted to be out there! My hands gripped the sides of my chair. To feel the water flowing, the beating of the beast's shoulders beneath my chest. Soon they would go under—now! Caster and the beast disappeared as he and the second rider began the journey under the moat wall. With an immense shake of water, they both appeared on the other side and swam for the island. The rest of the pack was close behind. Orphos was fighting a boy from the Neck for third place.

Out of the water and dripping wet, Caster sped for the next jump, an uneven hedge topped by vicious brambles. He was beginning to pull ahead again, but the other rider surged forward and cut him off, taking the jump wildly and too short. His beast stumbled and recovered, but that allowed Caster to fly past him as Orphos pushed ahead of the Neck boy and took the leap. Orphos's beast, Shrill, landed on four feet. Then the ground exploded beneath them, spewing dirt and debris into the air. I could see neither boy nor beast.

Porti and I stood as one, craning to see anything on the screen. The crowd shouted, and people all around the arena jumped to their feet. I grabbed Porti's hand.

No noise came from the island—the photobox did not capture sound. There was only the crowd screaming as the dust cleared, and when the scene was revealed, Caster was off his beast, kneeling over someone on the ground. I couldn't see who it was. The rider who had been in second place was half standing next to his beast, hanging on for support. Caster raised his face to the photobox, and I felt as if he were looking me right in the eye.

"Dead," he mouthed.

FOURTEEN

BEHIND ME EVERYONE WAS SHOUTING, ASKING EACH other what Caster had said. Orphos's father rushed forward to the edge of the box. "Where is he?" he yelled to the arena. Orphos's mother came up next to her husband and hung on to him in tears.

Porti clung to me.

On the screen, the photobox focused on Caster, revealing the face and shoulders of the man he was kneeling over. It was Orphos. He had been torn apart, his shoulders separated from his torso. Blood covered everything.

Porti screamed—a cry of pure anguish. She let go of me and took off for the exit. This set everyone in motion. Orphos's father grabbed his wife and they ran after Porti, and Gregor ran after all of them, and the rest of the occupants of the box were all crying or yelling. I should have run after Porti, I thought. Orphos was my friend, too. But I was frozen in place, staring at the screen, watching Caster leave Orphos's body and go to the rider clinging to the beast. He steadied the other competitor and helped him to the ground. Then medics swarmed the scene, pushing Caster out of the way, and I lost sight of him. *I should run and find him*, I thought. My feet were about to move, but then I realized that it might not be good for Deputy Ripkin's son to be seen in public with a half-Leftie who had just been jeered by the entire city.

Orphos was dead.

My father stood next to me. "Are you all right?" he asked.

I wrapped my arms around his waist. "What could do this? Who?"

"We'll have to find out," he said.

"There is very good security before the Games," said Member Solis from behind us. "The entire arena is swept."

"Obviously not so well," said my father.

"Perhaps someone set an explosive after the inspection," said Member Solis.

"A trusted man?" my father asked.

"Or an invisible one," said Member Solis.

My father stiffened.

"There are no Flickerkin in New Heart City," I said.

"None at all?" said Member Solis, raising an eyebrow. "I'm

told there are three in our jail and one known to be on the loose."

"My mother is innocent," I said. "As for the boy on the loose, don't you think he's back in the Left Eye by now?" I was surprised at the easy way the lie rolled off my tongue. My parents had taught me that I should always be honest even when it pained me, in every detail except for our one secret. Now that secret was expanding, and I didn't know how much bigger it would get.

My father pulled me closer. "She's just lost her friend, Anga. Jenton has lost his son."

"And I'd like to know who's responsible," Member Solis said.

"Blaming invisible bogeymen won't help with that," said my father.

The Council Members and their associates still in the box were watching us now. Member Solis couldn't be the only one who blamed Flickerkin for what had just happened. Indeed, even I could think of no one else who would want to make such a statement, except for ordinary Lefties. After all, the government was rounding up Lefties and torturing them. They had been excluded from the Games for no reason at all.

What if Nolan had caused the explosion? I had agreed to shelter him in my beast's stall. If anyone found out that I had seen him, it wouldn't matter that I had no part. And why was I more concerned about that than about the death of my friend? What had happened to me over the last few days?

"Poppa, I think we should go," I said.

"We have no reason to leave," he said. But he must have seen something in my face, because he sighed deeply and turned to Member Solis. "Well, Anga, you've succeeded in making life unbearable for a sixteen-year-old girl—your own foster daughter's best friend." He raised his head to address everyone in the box. "We should be mourning young Mr. Staliamos, not blaming each other."

Tear-stained faces stared back at us. They were not friendly. These people were all thinking it—that Orphos had been killed by a Flickerkin.

"Poppa, come on," I said, grabbing his arm. I didn't know if they would let us leave, if they believed only that we were dirty by association or that we had a part in the murder. Not *we*, I. My father couldn't be suspected of doing it, only of harboring me. But hadn't I just run from the box? Couldn't I have gotten to the island and back in time? *No*, I thought, *I'm not wet. I would have had to swim. Surely they can see that*. But perhaps they attributed a magical drying-off power to invisible people. Perhaps they didn't care about logic at all.

I lowered my head as we set off for the exit from the box, my father's hand firmly on my shoulder. Caster's face rushed back into my mind. And Orphos's body. I pictured Orphos smiling, flirting with Porti, taking every opportunity to tease her. He was such a good-natured person. We'd all assumed they'd be together, maybe even marry someday. Porti had never admitted that she liked him, no matter how plain it was to all. Not until today, when she'd been the first to run to him, even before his parents. Tears were rolling down my face again. Orphos was dead, and Porti would never be the same.

With my head down and my eyes flooded with tears, I nearly ran smack into the Deputy. He stood blocking our way out of the Council box. Four guardsmen stood behind him.

"Excuse me, Your Excellency," said my father.

"I'm sorry, Donray," the Deputy said. The guardsman Brach made a little motion as if tipping a nonexistent hat, his sarcasm apparent.

"For what are you sorry?" my father asked coldly.

"We must take you into custody for the charges."

We both stared at him. My father kept a hand on my shoulder.

"It's for your own safety, Donray," the Deputy said. "In light of this attack, the public will not tolerate a man who has harbored a Flickerkin walking free." My mother's words flashed before me. The Deputy again pretended he was *forced* to act.

My father's hand tightened on my shoulder.

"You don't need to worry about Miss Hailfast," the Deputy said. "She will come live with me. I will personally see that she is taken care of in the manner appropriate for a Member's daughter."

My blood froze. Live with the Deputy?

"I am no threat to anyone," my father said quietly. "My daughter does not deserve to have both her parents taken away."

"I'm sorry," the Deputy said again.

"The Council can't have voted in the last five minutes," said my father.

"They have already voted on the charges, Donray," said the Deputy. "No further vote is needed."

A wall of men, the Deputy and the four guardsmen, faced us. There was no way for us to escape what they called justice. My father turned to me. "Myra, I will not let this continue. I will be back before you know it."

"Poppa, no," I said. But I could do nothing.

My father addressed Member Solis. "Anga," he said, "I would be most grateful if you would take in my daughter. It would be much help to her to be with her closest friend during this difficult time."

"I don't think Myra is good for Miss Vale," said Member Solis. "We've just seen the kind of influence she's been. I'm sorry, but I will not be able to take her." The woman's eyes were cold. She couldn't see Porti's sacrifice as a sign of her open and friendly heart. She couldn't see compassion and friendship as good qualities. It was when I looked into her hateful eyes that I regained my strength.

"I'll be fine, Poppa," I said. "The Deputy will feed and clothe me, I'm sure." I looked up at him. "He will let me visit you."

"Of course, Miss Hailfast," the Deputy said. And his eyes, I saw to my surprise, were not cold. But I didn't trust the emotion that was in them.

My father hugged me and pulled me close. "I will fix this," he whispered. "I love you."

"I love you," I whispered back. And then he stood up and stepped forward, and two guardsmen approached him. Brach took one of his arms and the second man took the other, and they cuffed his hands behind his back. My heart pounded as he walked away; my vision blurred. They had taken my mother, but I had not been alone. Then they had taken my ride, and I had endured it. Now they had taken my father. I was left with the man my mother hated most in the world, the man who had tortured us. Orphos was dead and Porti shattered. But somehow, I remained standing.

"Shall we go, then?" I said. I walked past the Deputy, between his personal bodyguards. I headed back to the State Complex, to the Deputy's apartment, and the men followed me.

FIFTEEN

THERE WAS ONE BRIGHT SPOT ABOUT BEING FORCED to live with the Deputy. Even as I walked ahead of the guardsmen, nearly blind from the stress of all that had just occurred, I was aware that I would be in the same apartment as Caster. He was one thing in my life that was still good. And he had to be dying inside, as Porti was. He had seen something that no one should ever have to see—not on the photobox, as had the rest of us, but in the flesh.

When I reached the Deputy's apartment, though, Caster wasn't there. A servant, a thin middle-aged man, regarded me glumly as he let us in.

"Good day, Your Excellency," he said to the Deputy.

"Thank you, Koren," said the Deputy. The door closed behind us, heavy and solid. The guardsmen stayed outside.

The sitting room beyond the entrance was elegant, modern, and clean. But it was silent as death.

"Miss Hailfast," the Deputy said, looking down at me with sad eyes. He didn't try to smile. "I know that this has been a most difficult day. I wish I could explain all to you, but I must attend to the situation. Koren will show you to a guest room." He turned to Koren. "Provide the lady with anything she needs."

"Yes, Your Excellency," said Koren.

"I will be back when I can, Miss Hailfast," said the Deputy. "Please rest and don't do anything rash. I promise things will begin to make sense." He gave me a little bow and ducked out the door, leaving me with the somber Koren.

"Are you hungry, Miss Hailfast?" Koren asked.

"No, thank you," I said. "I just want to lie down."

I didn't really wish to lie down, but that is what I did. I lay on a fine bed in a room decorated with expensive art and stared at the ceiling. I might be as much a prisoner as my parents; I had no idea what would happen if I tried to leave. I had said I'd take water to Nolan, but I had no hope of doing that now.

I turned on the radio, but all I heard was the news of the attack over and over, and worse, Nolan's name. The whole city believed he was responsible. If it was not Nolan, Sky said, then it was another Flickerkin, and what, really, was the difference? All who hid from view were suspect. I didn't know what to think.

Nolan had seemed to be himself, so far as I knew him, except that he had been afraid and dirty and in need of help. He had never shown any desire to hurt anyone. But then, I had never had a conversation with him before that went much beyond hello, and when they had tried to take him, he had seemed to know more than I did. He was defiant.

And why shouldn't he be?

But defying unfairness was different from killing people. Surely Nolan couldn't kill anyone, much less people he had gone to school with since childhood. The Deputy, however bad he was, still hadn't killed anyone. Or had he? A miner had been sentenced to Judgment, I remembered. Was he with the Waters now, and had someone retaliated by killing Orphos?

I should have been with Porti, preparing for the winners' ball. Though only one of us could have won, we both would have placed. We would have been honored with fine food and drinks and speeches. Porti would have been beaming in a fine gown, one that made her feel she was more than a beast rancher from the Head. The kind of gown she deserved to wear. She should have had that, and I didn't know what she had now. Member Solis had been so angry about what Porti had done for me. Perhaps I had ruined everything for her.

I decided to try to call her from the voicebox receiver in my room. I wasn't sure whether the Deputy would allow me to have a working receiver, but either I wasn't a complete prisoner or the Deputy had forgotten to cut my access.

Bricca's nanny answered. "Hello?"

"Issa? It's me, Myra," I said. "May I speak with Portianna?"

"I'm sorry, Miss Hailfast," said Issa. "She's not available." And she hung up on me.

I didn't believe for a minute that Porti wasn't home. Probably Member Solis had rounded her up, dragged her away, and locked her in her room for her sins. Porti had to be losing her mind in there, as I was here.

There was a knock on the door, and before I could answer, Caster burst in.

"Caster!" I ran to him and wrapped my arms around him.

"Myra," he said, cradling me.

"Are you all right?" we asked together.

"I couldn't get my father to say more than two words," Caster said. "How could he do this?"

"Never mind that," I said. "I can't believe what you saw."

He walked past me, rubbing a hand over his hair. "It wasn't him," he said. "It was something else. His body wasn't even his anymore."

"Do they know anything about how it happened?"

"A great deal of prezine," Caster said. "Buried and set to trigger at the weight of a hoof."

"But who? Why?"

"Nobody knows anything," Caster said. "It's all speculation. Invisible men. Disgruntled miners."

"I didn't know prezine could do that," I said. Though I might have guessed. It did everything in the city. All our lights were powered by it, all our machines.

"The method is supposed to be a secret," said Caster. "Only Gregor's father and my father are supposed to know." Knowledge of explosives was banned along with daggers and swords.

"How are his parents?" I asked. "Did you see Porti?"

"They were devastated," he said. "Shouting and crying, his mother and father both. Porti couldn't stop screaming, until Member Solis came with her servants and took her away."

"I tried to call her, but Issa hung up on me. Member Solis hates me."

"The world is all askew," Caster said. "Your father has done nothing but protect his wife." He came back and wrapped me in his arms again. "At least you're here with me."

It would have been wrong of me, but I wanted to smile. I liked the feel of his arms around me. It wasn't fair for me to like it, though, because Porti would never have Orphos's arms around her. And she had wanted that so badly.

Caster kissed me, only a peck. "My father hasn't hurt you again, has he?"

"No," I said. "He acted like he was sorry." I couldn't keep the bitterness out of my voice.

"As soon as he gets home, I'll talk to him," Caster said. "I'll do what I can to get your parents out of jail."

"Thank you," I said. "I don't think it will help. I don't know what will help."

"We'll figure it out," he said. He kissed me again. This time it lasted a little longer. I stood on my tiptoes and got lost in it. Here was one thing that helped. But I pulled away. It wasn't right.

"I have to see Porti," I said. "After all she did for me, I can't let her sit alone."

"Of course," he said. "Here." He pulled a key out of his pocket. "So you can come and go."

"Thank you," I said. I hugged him, and as much as I didn't want to, broke free and headed out. I was afraid Koren or some other servant or a guardsman would appear and stop me, but no one did.

It was dark outside. Darkness didn't normally bother me because there was little crime in the city, much less in the State Complex, but today everything was off. I walked briskly, not looking from side to side, trying not to look for hidden sensors. Every little square thing seemed to be one. Along with every-thing else that had happened, I had flickered. What if somehow they could catch me even when I was visible? What if the Deputy learned of the trigger point? What if I were to fall and hit that exact spot? I didn't know if there was some other trick that could undo me, another accident around a corner. I was a stranger to myself now. As I walked, I looked down at my body to make sure I was still there.

There was no one in the courtyard, and I easily reached Porti's door. I knocked, at first quietly, and then louder. No one answered.

"Porti, it's Myra," I called. I waved at the peephole in the door. I couldn't believe that no one was home. Even if Porti really was not there, surely Issa would be, and she couldn't turn me away from the door as easily as hanging up a receiver. I knocked again.

Slowly, the door opened a crack. It was Member Solis herself.

"I came to see if she's all right," I said.

"She'll be fine," said Member Solis.

"I'd like to talk to her," I said.

"This is a bad time." She started to close the door, but I put out my hand to stop it. I wanted to push my way in, but what would that do? She would only summon her servants to throw me out.

"Please tell her I came by. I don't want her to think I've

abandoned her. He was my friend, too." I choked on these words as the image of Orphos's body displayed on the huge screen popped into my mind. "Tell her to call me when she can."

"I will tell her," said Member Solis, and then she shut the door in my face.

I stood there on the walkway. Porti was inside, and I couldn't see her. I doubted Member Solis would tell Porti I had been there. She would let Porti believe that I had abandoned her after what she had done for me. All because of who my mother was? Because of what I looked like? The tears that had been for Orphos began falling for myself.

I didn't want to go back to the Deputy's, but I could think of no other option. There was no friend I could turn to whose parents wouldn't treat me as Member Solis had.

I walked slowly out of the building and back into the court-yard, keeping my head down. Member Solis had known me nearly all my life. She had been cold to me, and rude, but she had always allowed me in her home. Tears filled my eyes and nearly blinded me, but I pressed forward. I wished Hoof were with me. She would still love me, being too dumb to see that I was short and pale. Perhaps I would go to the stables, never mind Nolan, never mind anyone. No one could keep me from my best comfort. I determined that I'd do that, go to the stables, when an arm grabbed me around the waist from behind.

I screeched in surprise and tried to pull forward, but the arm pulled me back. I was pressed into the hard front of a man's body.

"Where are you going, Leftie?" a man's voice asked.

"Out to plant another explosive?" said a second man from behind me. In front of me, I saw only the empty courtyard. There was none of the ordinary bustle and laughter, no one but me and the two men.

Out of the corner of my eye, I caught a glimpse of part of the man's face. "Is that you, Brach?" I gasped. "I know it's you. You'll be imprisoned."

"I'd like to spend time with your Flickerbitch mother," said the other man, whose voice I couldn't place.

"Help! Help!" I screamed. I kicked Brach's shins, but he held me fast.

Then one of the men yelped, and Brach dropped me. I fell forward, landing on my hands and knees. I twisted as I rose, ready to defend myself, but there was no need. The men were occupied, fighting someone unseen.

"Run, Myra!" a man's voice called. But one of the men landed a blow on what looked like thin air, and then the other man connected. I couldn't simply run away. I ran toward Brach and kicked him as hard as I could in the back of the knee with the heel of my ladies' boot. He collapsed forward into invisible arms. The invisible man tossed him aside, then landed one more good blow to the second man's head.

"Damn it, Myra!" Nolan—for who else could it have been?—grabbed my hand. "Come!" He began to run, and I ran with him, out the side of the courtyard and into the street.

"Flicker!" he whispered urgently.

"I can't!" I said. And if I could have, I wouldn't—I'd be seen.

"Come on," he said.

I kept going, holding a solid hand I couldn't see, afraid I would trip over his feet and take us both down.

Two more guardsmen, the only people on the street, saw me and gave chase.

Nolan pulled me around the side of a building.

"Flicker," he said. His voice, his breath, were above mine.

"No!"

"We'll both be caught." The warmth of his body radiated toward me. Even so close to him, I could see nothing. He no longer smelled like a beast stall. Now he smelled of a rainstorm.

"Leave, then," I whispered. "Thank you, but I'll be fine now."

"Not after allowing yourself to be rescued by me." He shook my shoulders. "Those were guardsmen who attacked you, Myra."

The other guardsmen were coming. Their footsteps pounded on the hard turf.

"I don't know how," I said. "Go!"

"Damn it!" He let go of my hand.

The guardsmen turned the corner and found me standing calmly in the alley, facing them.

"Oh, thank the Waters," I said, stepping forward. "It was terrible!"

As I spoke, Brach and the other man who had attacked me approached. They were both bloodied, but moving well. They hadn't been seriously hurt.

"There was an invisible person," I said, bringing tears to my eyes, which was not difficult. "He attacked all of us. He would have kidnapped me if you hadn't given chase. The Waters know what would have happened then."

Brach stared at me from the shadow of the overhang. I couldn't read his expression. I could only hope that his attack on me wasn't authorized, because if it was, then I was destined to join my parents—and attacking an officer was a true crime.

"We're glad you escaped, Miss Hailfast," said Brach. He met my eyes, and I nearly gasped with relief, but I held myself steady.

"This is no time to be out, Miss," said one of the new guardsmen. "We're enforcing a curfew until the perpetrator of the explosion is found."

"I didn't mean to be out," I said. "I was only going to see Porti—Portianna Vale." At once it all rushed back to me, the look in Member Solis's eyes, the door slammed in my face. I looked at the ground.

"Let me escort you home," said Brach.

"Of course," I said. What else could I do? It was as if I could hear Nolan yelling at me, *What are you doing, Myra? Flicker and run!* But I couldn't flicker, and I had nowhere to go but back to the Deputy's. Surely Brach wouldn't attack me again after promising to protect me in front of those other guardsmen. I couldn't convince myself that I was safe, and yet I went with him. I didn't want to look at him, so I sped ahead. Perhaps I had injured him enough that I could outrun him. We were in the courtyard before he came up next to me. He put an arm around me and leaned down.

"That was a wise choice, lady Leftie," he said.

"I don't know what you mean," I said. An image of a younger Brach smiling at the child me flashed into my mind. How could a person change so much?

"That kick was not so wise," he said.

I stopped cold and pulled away. "Why attack me?" I asked. Blood flushed my cheeks, and I knew speaking my mind was unwise, but I couldn't stop myself. "What have I done? I was in the Council box, you know. Many witnesses. I've lived in New Heart City my entire life. I have no connection to the Eye whatever."

"You are the daughter of a traitor," Brach said. "A mongrel. And a friend of a fugitive Flickerkin, obviously."

"I don't know who that was," I said. "As for me, I'm a citizen of New Heart City as much as you."

"You shouldn't be," said Brach. "No Leftie should be allowed to live among us." He spat on the ground, narrowly missing my left foot. "Except to carry away our trash."

I could think of nothing to say to such hate. It was beyond argument. I could only hope that the man cared more about preserving himself than about hurting me. "It's still a crime to attack me," I said. "The Deputy himself wishes to care for me."

"For now," he said. "We'll find your Flickerkin friend and get rid of the rest of you." He put a hand on my back and turned me toward the entrance to the Deputy's building, then pushed me forward. We walked the rest of the way in silence. Hate radiated from him like a flame, and my mind sped over what he had said. How many others were there like him? Was it truly not safe for me even to walk in my own complex? How could I live in a city where this was true? Should I tell the Deputy what had happened? Would he take my side, or would he do nothing and let them have me?

Brach knocked on the door, and the Deputy himself answered immediately, as if he'd been standing right there.

"Myra!" He grabbed me and pulled me inside. "You should not have gone out alone. I don't know what my son was thinking, failing to accompany you. Thank you, Brach. You're a good man."

"Your Excellency," said Brach, bowing. Without another word, he turned and walked down the passage.

"Your Excellency," I began, the honorific sticking in my throat.

"You may call me Mr. Ripkin," he said, pulling me into the sitting room.

"Father—" Caster got up from a chair.

"Quiet, son," said the Deputy. I couldn't address him by his name. He was still the Deputy, the man who spoke with the Waters. I didn't truly believe that, and yet somehow at the same time, I did. "Sit," the Deputy said.

I sat on a large, stiff sofa.

Caster sat back down in his chair.

The Deputy remained standing. "Do you think this is a game?" He looked from one of us to the other. I didn't think he wished us to respond. "There has been an attack by persons unseen. Your friend is dead, ripped to pieces before your eyes." His eyes were no longer sad; they were ice. "We do not know who; we do not know why. We know only that someone gathered a large amount of prezine, prepared it in a way no man is supposed to learn about, and buried it in the arena. All without being seen, without triggering an alarm."

I hadn't considered what someone must have had to do to

place the explosive. I hadn't thought of anything but how the attack had affected me.

"We don't know when they might strike again, or against whom. You"—he pointed at Caster—"you leave my side without a word. And then you"—he pointed at me—"you leave this apartment alone as if all were normal."

"Father—"

"Quiet! I must keep all the citizens of the Upland safe, and I can't do that if I must worry about the two of you. I can't spare guardsmen to watch two children; we are stretched thin. You must police yourselves. By the Waters, Caster, do you not *like* this girl? What possessed you to let her go?"

"He *lets* me do nothing," I said.

"That's the Leftie way, isn't it?" the Deputy raged. "Women wear pants and mine ore, and always their first word is *no*. Your mother may have taught you how to rule a home, but she has not taught you how to survive."

"Father, that is out of line!" Caster said, standing.

The Deputy ignored him. "You were very lucky tonight," he said to me. "The Waters can't protect the foolish."

The chime of the sitting room voicebox rang through the sudden silence.

The Deputy picked up the receiver. "Ripkin."

Caster and I waited, the fight paused, both of us afraid of what news the Deputy was hearing.

"Then find them!" he yelled. "Throw them in a cell and toss the key to the rising ocean." He slammed down the receiver. Then he became quiet. "Three thugs have just beaten a Leftie garbage collector. It is not known if he will survive." He turned to me. "Now do you see why I ask you to be careful?" He shook his head and strode out of the room. In the silence that followed, Brach's attack flashed before me. I couldn't believe I was thinking this thought, but the Deputy was right. I was a fool to have believed I could simply walk through the courtyard.

"I'm sorry, Myra," Caster said. "He had no right to say that. He acts as if the great burden of leadership allows him to face the world with his ass."

"No," I said. I saw Brach's face, the hate in his eyes before he spat. "Caster, you must tell no one."

Caster sat down next to me on the sofa and took my hand. "Why? What is it?"

"Your father . . . he isn't wrong. That guardsman, Brach . . ." I was about to tell him the story, but of course I couldn't. I couldn't betray Nolan. No one could know he was still in New Heart City, much less that he was watching out for me, that he knew I could flicker. But I couldn't be completely silent. "He is full of hate," I said. "He called me a mongrel. He said all Lefties should leave the city. Spat at my feet."

"No," said Caster. "Myra, that's awful. But it doesn't make my father right. You can't live like a prisoner."

"How did Brach come to be that way?" I asked. "Why would anyone beat a poor worker nearly to death?"

"I don't know. There's much about today I don't understand." He stared ahead at the wall where an ornamental cloth hung, depicting a scene at the cliff's edge. In the scene, the water rose up, nearly pouring over the cliff and onto land. It was an event that hadn't occurred since the Flicker Men had breached our shores, 150 years ago. Caster took a deep breath, as he stared at the cloth. "Orphos didn't deserve this." Tears burst from his eyes, rolled down his face. "He didn't deserve this."

"Caster . . ." I reached out to him.

He leaned down, buried his face in my hair. I wrapped my arms around him and let my tears fall with his. I thought of Orphos, torn apart. I thought of Porti, lost and alone. Of Shrill, Orphos's innocent beast, dead with him. Of my parents, in cold cells. And of the world, which had changed forever.

SIXTEEN

I LAY IN BED THAT NIGHT UNABLE EVEN TO CLOSE MY eyes. What had Brach and his friend planned to do to me? How many others wished me the same harm? When would they try again? What would happen to Nolan now that he'd exposed himself and the guardsmen knew there was still a Flickerkin in New Heart City? Could I count on Brach's self-interest to keep him from talking about how Nolan had rescued me from their attack? What was Nolan to me, anyway? I could tell the Deputy what had happened, and maybe he could protect me. But if he knew I had seen Nolan and not reported it, he would throw me in jail too. He only cared about my safety so long as he thought me innocent. If he changed his mind, I would have nowhere to run.

I thought back to that moment in the alley. *Flicker!* Nolan had told me. If I had done so, we both would have escaped. But the very thing I was persecuted for, I couldn't do. What if Brach and his friends attacked me again? What if the Deputy found out my secret? How could I protect myself?

The answer was obvious but terrifying. I could flicker. I could disappear and escape just as Nolan had. Despite the entire Guard looking for him, he was still free. But if I learned how to flicker, I could never go back. I would be a Flickerkin—an outlaw, a spy, an enemy of my own people.

If you cause yourself to flicker, the Ability will take control, I heard my mother say. *You will be required to suppress it at every moment.* Her cold blue eyes stared into my five-year-old face. *You must never try to flicker. Do you hear me, Myra?* I would have to be like her, to hold back everything I felt. Strong emotions, a fall from a beast, even hearty laughter might cause me to flicker. I didn't know if I could live that way. But if I didn't learn to, I would be helpless. I couldn't fight Brach and his goons and whoever had attacked the garbage man—and every citizen who had jeered at me—with sharp words and a ladies' boot.

What would my mother say now? Before they took her, she would have told me not to learn. She had let herself be locked up when she could have used the Ability to escape. But now she might be sentenced to Judgment. She had been wrong to submit.

I sat up in bed. I couldn't let myself be a helpless victim again. If I had to control myself, then I would. I was not a weak damsel, crying for a man to save her. I was a rider, and I would have been a champion.

I dug through the chest the Deputy's servants had brought over and found my riding clothes. There would be no ladies' boots for me tonight. Tonight I was taking back my own destiny. The Deputy would think me foolish, and perhaps I was. But I couldn't go another night without a way to escape, should it come to that. I would be back before he found me gone, or I would withstand his shouts. I would withstand his shocks, if he gave them. I wouldn't let him keep me prisoner.

There was no one in the hall or in the courtyard—not strange for the time of night, but strange for me. I was never out this late unless I was at Porti's. The whole city was odd and sinister in the darkness, the streets lit only by widely spaced prezine lamps that shed little light. I saw two guardsmen but slipped out of their sight. Soon I was at the stables, which, for the first time in my experience, were locked. As a beast owner, though, I had a key. I prayed as I turned it that they hadn't changed the lock to keep me out, but my key worked. Inside I went, plagued by the loud creak of the hinges and the crunching of my steps on the turf. I was lucky. No one else had thought to visit the stables for a midnight ride, and Hoof's stall was far enough from the arena to be unaffected by any guard at the blast site.

I slipped into Hoof's stall to find her asleep standing up,

snoring softly. How nice to be blissfully unaware of all that had gone on today.

I patted her back gently as I slipped past her.

"Nolan," I whispered. There was no answer. "Nolan." I kneeled down where I had last seen him and put out my hand. It touched bare skin. I nearly shrieked with surprise—I had expected a shirt—but I stopped myself and touched his back again. "Nolan!"

He stirred.

"Wake up," I said, shaking him.

"Myra!" he whispered, suddenly wide awake. "What are you doing here? What if someone sees you?"

"Well, that's the problem, isn't it?" I said. "I can't be seen, and yet I can't *not* be seen."

"Yes," he said. "That's your problem."

"So you must teach me how to flicker," I said.

He popped into view. It was so dark that I couldn't see the expression on his face, only his bare chest, wide and muscular, and his dark trousers against the light-colored hay.

"I think that's a good idea, Myra," he said. "Those men aren't going to give up. You're one of us—it's not such a bad thing."

"I'm what I am," I said. "A citizen and a mongrel, not one of anyone."

"Myra—"

"No, never mind that," I said. "No self-pity tonight. I just want to learn how to protect myself."

He sat up. "Yes. All right." He patted around the hay pile and found his raggedy once-white shirt. "You can take your clothes with you," he said. "Anything that's touching enough skin. So you can't bring a building or a chair or something, but you can take a wallet or a teapot or a feline."

"A whole cat?" I asked, shocked.

"Sure," he said, buttoning his shirt, "long as you carry it inside your blouse."

I stared at him, unsure what he meant by that, but his expression was matter-of-fact.

"You don't know anything about yourself at all, do you?"

"I did until they took my mother," I said.

"It didn't bother you when they tried to take me?"

"Yes," I said. "But you weren't like me." We sat in silence, both hearing what I hadn't said. He was a worker; I was privileged. He was a Leftie; I had been living as a Plat.

He stood up. "You have a lot to catch up on, then." There was a coldness in his voice, and my heart dropped. I knew now that I had been wrong, but to say so would be hollow, and would be wasting time I didn't have.

"We should go out to the arena," he said. "It can be unsettling, especially if you learn as an adult. You might wake your beast, and who knows, the whole place could be a din of moos."

"All right," I said. I wondered what he meant by *unsettling*, but it didn't matter now. I hadn't given up riding because people were thrown—Hoof had thrown me many times over the years. I didn't give up on calculus because limits made me dizzy, and I wouldn't give up now. The only thing that gave me pause as we climbed over the locked arena fence—right over a brand-new set of sensors that made me shiver but that Nolan didn't react to—was the thought of my mother, who had told me never to do this, who had not done it even to escape. But she had also taught me to take care of myself. Surely she wouldn't want to see me hurt because I had failed to learn.

Lost in thought, I nearly bumped into Nolan when he stopped suddenly.

"This is where the stone throw is held," he said. Sure enough, I recognized the spot where he was standing—a raised patch of short grass. I had watched his throw last year, when things were so different, when I had been stewing over my second-place ribbon. I was about to open my mouth to say that he had deserved the first-place ribbon—any fool could have seen that—but he turned to face me.

"I didn't do it," he said.

"I never thought you did," I replied. "I may not know you well, but I don't see a monster."

"*They've* done it," he whispered, his voice hard and ragged. "So they can blame it on a Flickerkin and occupy the Left Eye.

So they can force our labor and take our prezine. So they can be free of looking at our pale skin. So they can win all the stone throws and feel strong!"

I presumed that by "they" he meant the Council and the Deputy. I didn't believe they had done it—I couldn't believe they would kill Orphos, the son of a Council Member, and put the Deputy's own son in danger. But I saw that Nolan was not rational on this point, and I had no other theories to offer. I couldn't imagine why *anyone* would do such a thing.

"I hope whoever did it is brought to Judgment," I said.

He turned away from me, as if collecting himself, then turned back. "All right. The first thing you must do is block out the rest of the world. You must be able to concentrate on yourself—as if you are the only thing existing in the entire Upland."

I closed my eyes. But I didn't feel alone; I felt like a person with her eyes closed. "How exactly am I supposed to do that? Should I lie down?"

"It's a lot harder to flicker lying down because so much of you is touching the ground. Basically, your body would try to take the whole plateau with you. I flicker before I lie down to go to sleep."

"So you don't have to concentrate to stay invisible?" I asked.

"Not really," he said. "At first you will, but it becomes second nature, like breathing. So yes, you can go to sleep invisible.

But you could be shocked out of it, like if you'd kicked me instead of just touching my back to wake me up. So it's not that safe to sleep. That's why I needed a place to stay where no one would stumble over me."

"Okay," I said. I stood there with my eyes closed, trying to concentrate on myself. But what did that even mean? I felt the same as always.

"Flickering happens as your blood flows through your body," said Nolan. "It looks like it happens all at once, but if you could slow it down like on a photobox player, you'd see that it spreads out from the heart. You tell your heart to start pumping blood with the right structure."

"Heart, start pumping invisible blood," I said.

Nolan laughed. "Right. Except, quietly."

Invisible blood, I thought. But I knew that wasn't what Nolan meant. I was supposed to just feel it. To Flickerkin who grew up in the Eye, it was probably like walking. How would you learn to walk at sixteen? It would be terribly difficult and awkward.

"Maybe I can help," said Nolan. "I'm sorry, this is the first time I've tried to teach anyone. My parents taught me before I can remember." He took my hand and I jumped. "Sorry," he said.

"It's okay." His hand was much bigger than mine, and rough. Much rougher than Caster's. "I'm going to flicker. One, two . . . three."

I opened my eyes and found that I was as solid as ever. Nolan, however, was invisible. He was still holding my hand, though.

"Whatever you were doing just now, I couldn't feel it."

He popped back into view, grinning. "Maybe holding hands wasn't enough."

I pulled my hand away.

He laughed. "I'm just saying. Maybe it will help if, you know, more of our skin is touching."

"Really," I said. But my throat caught. I was glad it was dark, because I could feel my cheeks flushing. I hadn't even touched much of my skin to Caster's yet.

"I found a bucket of water for myself," he said. "So I promise I won't stink too much."

I had noticed earlier. But I wasn't going to say so. "Do you really think it will help?" I asked instead.

"Yes," he said, wiping the grin off his face. "It really might. One time when I was a kid, the guardsmen came through the city with the cuffs—they were testing anyone who looked Leftie. My mother saw them coming and pulled me around a corner into an alley. It was a lot like what had happened to us earlier tonight. Anyway, she flickered, but I was really scared, and I couldn't do it. I just froze. So she wrapped her arms around me, pulled me under her blouse, and I flickered just in time. We would've been deported if they'd tested us, or worse."

"Didn't they come to your parents' shop?" I asked.

"You know how we prepare," he said. "Why do you think I have a triggering rod? But my parents had wanted to spare me. After that, I prepared."

"I'm sorry," I said.

"Must have been nice to have a father on the Council," he said. "If you sit at their table, they keep you on as pale pets."

I wanted to slap him. Instead, I turned my back. Should I walk off in dramatic fashion? Or was he right?

"I'm sorry," he said. "I know it's not your fault you're rich. I wish my parents could have protected me from all this. I'd take it."

"But mine didn't protect me in the end," I said. "They should have taught me how to protect myself."

"We all should have gone back to the Eye. You can live in peace as long as you stay where you belong. Can't work in the prezine mines, though. Too sensitive for potential spies."

I knew nothing about the Eye except for the misty weather and a few words of the language. Nor had I ever cared to learn much more. I knew too little about everything to do with my Leftie half and now felt as ignorant as a baby. If a little inappropriate contact would help me, I would deal with it. "Fine. But I won't be pulling you under my blouse."

He laughed. "Fair enough." He came around in front of me and held up his hands.

I took both his hands. Our fingers wrapped around each other's naturally, as if we had done this a thousand times. He stepped closer, and our arms folded together. Our chests touched. His face was only six inches above mine. It would be so different with Caster, who was so far above me that we had to strain to reach each other. I tried to push the thought away. *Focus,* Myra. *Your life is at stake.*

"From the heart out, Myra," he whispered.

I closed my eyes and felt my heart beat. It was beating fast now. Nolan pressed closer to me, or I pressed closer to him; I wasn't sure which, and I could feel his heart beating. It seemed as if our hearts were beating together.

Our hands gripped tightly, and electricity sizzled through me. It wasn't like being poked with the triggering stick or shocked by the cuffs. It was pinpricks of energy spreading outward from my heart. I didn't open my eyes, and yet I knew.

"You've done it, Myra," Nolan whispered.

"Have I?" I asked. "Or was it you?"

"I can't take a whole human," he said. "But if you need to prove it, step away."

Slowly, I unwrapped my hands from his. I felt one last beat of his heart, and then I took a step back. I opened my eyes, expecting to see no one. But there, floating in front of me, was a shimmer in the air in the shape of a boy. He was see-through and featureless, but he was there.

I giggled. The pinpricks were still flowing through me from fingers to toes. "From fingers to toes from head to nose," I chanted, words from a children's rhyme. "I can see you. You're like a ghost! Am I?" I looked down at my own hands and found that they too shimmered.

"You didn't know?" He laughed.

"When you stuck me, I saw . . ." I held my hand up. I thought I had seen nothing. But I wasn't sure anymore.

"There's a whole world you haven't seen."

"A whole world? Hole in the world! There's a hole!" I made a little hole with my fist. "It's so funny." I looked up at Nolan, unable to stop laughing. "Why is it so funny?"

"There's a lot of new energy inside you," he said. "Maybe you should sit down."

I sat down on the grass. "I'm a ghost! My mother is a ghost. Your parents are ghosts. How many ghosts are there?"

Nolan sat down beside me. "More than the Plats know about," he said.

I was still laughing. But it wasn't funny. There was a whole world out there. A whole life. I didn't know if I liked this feeling.

"Most people don't act drunk when they flicker," said Nolan, though his serious tone broke in the middle of the sentence and he laughed. "You must get used to it, and you'll be fine."

A light went on across the arena, back toward the gate we had come through.

I jumped—a shock flowed through me—and I became visible. I could see my solid legs and hands, and I tried to stand, but my head swam. I stumbled and fell into Nolan, whom I could no longer see.

"Whoa," he whispered. "You're all right."

"The light," I said.

He wrapped both arms around me and pressed my face onto his neck. "Concentrate."

Pinpricks rushed through me. I pressed my face against him. Across the arena, the gate opened, and someone rode out on a beast, his face lost in shadow.

Another rider followed him, shouting "Caster!"

The rider in front—Caster—did not stop. He was nearly upon us, heading straight for where we sat.

"Don't ride away from me!" the Deputy shouted.

Nolan lifted me, his arms still wrapped around me, braced to run, but Caster pulled Monster up short, letting his father catch them.

We stood there, unable to sit down in case they started moving but unable to run in case they heard our footsteps. Nolan held me so tightly that I could hardly breathe, yet I was afraid that if he loosened his grip, I would flicker back into view, so I held on. I almost gasped, seeing the Deputy. If he were to see me . . .

"Hang on," Nolan whispered.

"All right, Father, I've stopped," said Caster. "But why? So you can give me one more lecture? Myra has run off because you insulted her royally. And also threw her parents in jail, can we forget? By the Waters, why would she stay sweetly in bed?"

"Son, you must understand. I am trying to keep that girl safe."

"Are her parents really such a threat? You can't honestly believe Rhondalynn Hailfast is a spy—that she wishes to open our gates to invisible invaders."

"You must learn your history, son," the Deputy said. "This is not a witch hunt or a prezine grab. When the Flicker Men were here, they plotted against the Plateau People and helped the Eye rebel against the government. Their half-blood kin living today continue the cause. There is no reason to believe that Rhondalynn is *not* a spy. Why else would she come to New Heart City and conceal herself?"

I stiffened, and Nolan's strong arms tightened.

"Perhaps she loved Myra's father," Caster said. "Perhaps she was poor in the Eye and wanted to have a grand life in the city. What has she actually done to cast suspicion except be a Leftie? What have the clothmakers done?"

"There is much you don't know," said the Deputy. "There are more Flickerkin here than those we've caught."

"Really? Where's the evidence of this, Father?"

"I am trying to avoid increasing the panic, Caster," said the Deputy. "I can't go telling all of the state's secrets to a boy. But know this. It is not only Flickerkin who are a danger. Ordinary Lefties nurse old grudges, and some would be happy to bring the Flicker Men back across the oceans." He put the heel of his hand to his forehead, the gesture meaning *may the Waters forgive me*. He had spoken of riding on the Waters. "Can't you see my point after what they did today?"

"They killed Orphos because of what *you* have done!" Caster shouted. "You have persecuted them. Tortured them. You tortured *Myra*. You prevented her from riding. There was no reason for it even if you're telling the truth—invisibility wouldn't help anyone win. You acted because of hate, and now they hate *us*."

"We were trying to keep Lefties out of the arena," said the Deputy. "Because we suspected there was a plot."

"And you had to include Myra?" Caster asked. "She's only half, and she's *Myra*."

"Can you listen to yourself for one minute?" the Deputy shouted. "I've told you there is a threat, that they are out there trying to kill us—they came close to killing *you* today—and all you can think about is that Flickerbitch's daughter?"

"Go take a dip, Father," Caster said, and he nudged his beast. He rode straight toward us, and Nolan pulled me out of the way just in time. We landed on the ground, Nolan half on top of me. Monster's hooves pounded on the turf, muffling the sound of our fall, I hoped.

The Deputy pulled his beast around with a jerk—he was riding with a rein, a cruel and amateur practice—and rode back toward the gate.

Slowly, Nolan and I sat up. He kept his arms around me, and I didn't want to pull away, not until the Deputy was long gone. I tried to process what he and Caster had said. They knew I had snuck away. Caster had defended me. The Deputy claimed there were more Flickerkin. He had called my mother a hateful name even as he searched for me, claiming to want to keep me safe. Caster believed the killer was a Flickerkin, like me. But he had fought with his father—the most dangerous man in the Upland—for me, and not for the first time tonight.

"So Caster Ripkin is your boyfriend," said Nolan.

"That's what you took from that conversation?" I asked.

"Well, isn't he?"

"Yes," I said.

Nolan gently pushed me away, and we both stumbled to our feet. I flickered into view without meaning to, and I was suddenly cold.

"I never knew he was different from his father," he said.

"Yes. He's very different."

Nolan became visible as well, and we stood facing each other, just two regular people now. "And you're living with the

Deputy? They were looking for you? After allowing you to just walk out the door?"

"They took my father," I said. "I'm like you now. Except the Deputy to the Waters himself has decided that I'm his responsibility."

"He wishes to keep an eye on you, so you can lead him to other Flickerkin," Nolan said.

"No . . ." But why not? He hadn't taken me in out of kindness. The possibility that he hoped I'd lead him to my mother's supposed friends was very real. If I had slipped up, if anyone had seen me go . . . "I'm sorry," I said. "I didn't think."

Nolan flickered out. "We can't let that stop us," he said.

"I'm sorry," I said again.

"It's all right," he said. His voice was a little cold, but not angry. I wished I could see his face, look into his eyes and apologize again. My stupidity could have killed him.

"Come see me when you can," Nolan said. "I'll be near Hoof—and watching out for you."

"Thank you," I said. But by the time I said it, he was probably already gone.

In the distance, the dark shape of Caster, riding Monster, headed back in my direction. I waved my arms, determined to act as if I had simply come out to see Hoof and take a walk.

"My father is not happy," Caster said, stopping alongside me.

"I suppose not," I said. I thought of what Nolan had said about the Deputy keeping me in order to use me—and how close I had come to getting us both caught. I could only pray that the Waters would convince Caster and his father of the lie I was about to tell. "I wanted to see Hoof," I said. "But she was sleeping so I just . . . I just walked."

"You have a right to walk wherever you like," he said, reaching down a hand.

I had nowhere else to go, certainly nowhere the Deputy couldn't find me—not unless I wished to flicker right here and now, and I wasn't even sure I could. I let Caster help me onto his beast.

"Back to the bear's den, then," he said.

I leaned into his back. "I'm sorry if I worried you," I said.

"You make life interesting," he replied.

I could have retorted that "interesting" was the last thing any of us needed, but I said nothing. I was tired. Flickering had taken something out of me. Perhaps when I got back to my prison I would at least sleep.

SEVENTEEN

I WOKE LATE. THE SUN WAS STREAMING THROUGH THE room's single large window, illuminating the clock on the far wall. My head was groggy at first, as if I had taken liquor, a thing I had done only once and had regretted too much to try ever again. I blinked at the light, trying to recall where I was.

The back of my father's head as he walked away with the guardsmen filled my mind. My mother's hand gripping mine between the bars. Caster's face pressed into my shoulder.

My eyes burned with the aftermath of the day's tears.

The hate reflecting back from Brach's deep brown eyes bored through me, and I pulled my knees into my chest. I was solid now, heavy. Everything was heavy and at the same time, too bright.

Someone knocked on the door.

I didn't answer.

"Myra?" Caster called. "Are you awake?"

I didn't answer.

"Myra, I know you're awake. My father has sent me to retrieve you. Better to get the lecture over with."

I sat up. "All right. I'll come down." I stumbled out of bed, tripped over my feet, and fell back down. I flickered out, then in again. No, I couldn't flicker. I couldn't let this happen. I had triggered it, just as my mother had always warned. I had purposely learned to flicker, and now I might expose myself.

I took a deep breath and stood up again. Pinpricks spread from my heart. I pushed them back. I couldn't risk going downstairs, but I couldn't stay where I was. I had to get control over myself. I waited five minutes, then ten, then fifteen, until the pinpricks were completely gone. I put on a simple dress, wrinkled from being in the trunk, and walked down the stairs with as much grace as I could muster.

I had just reached the dining table, where Caster sat in front of a grand spread, when the Deputy walked into the room. He glared at me, making no move to sit.

"So she still lives," he said.

"I'm sorry," I said. "I was lonely for my beast. She is all I have left." I sat at the table, unable to look the Deputy in the eye but not wanting to seem too demure, too broken.

The Deputy pulled a sweet bread from the pile. "We have one funeral to attend today. Thank the Waters, the garbage man has survived, so there will not be two."

"I must see my parents," I said.

He took a bite of his bread and looked down at me with cold eyes. I thought perhaps he would spit his food back or explode in nasty laughter. But he didn't. "After the funeral, my son will escort you," he said.

I was about to thank him, but the words wouldn't come from my mouth. What would I be thanking him for? Whenever he seemed to show the slightest charity, he could be hoping I would betray my people. Never mind that these supposed hidden Flickerkin were no more my people than were the Flicker Men themselves.

"You will come straight back," he said, not to me but to Caster.

"Fine," Caster said.

The Deputy left the room, leaving me alone with Caster and a feast I didn't wish to eat. I took a muffin and picked off a piece. I hadn't thought about the funeral. I had been to a few funerals, but those were for old people whom I had barely known. This one would be for a friend. Caster, too, sat glumly. His face lacked its usual sparkle; his features in sadness looked more like his father's.

"My father is sitting for an interview," he said after a while. "We might as well hear the worst of it, as ignorance is a sin."

Absently, I put the heel of my hand to my forehead.

Caster turned on the large, ornate radio that sat next to the table. It was decorated with a tracing of an ocean wave made of prezine, a waste of enough of the metal to power a small home.

"... no word on whether the Games will resume," said Sky. "Deputy Ripkin has suspended all contests during the investigation of yesterday's attack. Citizens are reminded that they should remain inside except for urgent business. A strict curfew will be in effect after dark. To update us on the status of the investigation, we are pleased to have Deputy Ripkin himself in the studio. Your Excellency, it's a pleasure to speak with you."

"Thank you, Sky," said the Deputy. His raspy voice was calm and smooth.

"What happened to the sensors?" asked Sky. "They were all over the arena. Did they simply not work?"

"Obviously they were not foolproof," said the Deputy. "This is an issue that we are working quickly to resolve. The sensors are all being equipped with alarms so that if anyone attempts to disable one, we will know about it immediately. Further, our scientists have also been working for some time on a handheld variety, and test versions of these devices will be in the hands of certain officers by nightfall."

Handheld sensors. My blood ran cold. Pinpricks began running through me. *No.* I pushed them back.

"Do you have any information about who caused the explosion?" Sky asked.

"We know this atrocity was perpetrated by an invisible individual," said the Deputy. "We know he used a prezine-based explosive. Obtaining that amount of prezine would have required conspirators in the mines. While we do not yet have a name, rest assured we soon will. To all those who would perpetrate further attacks against the people of the plateau, remember this: we will find you. Your Ability will not keep you safe. You and all those who have conspired with you will be brought to justice."

Pinpricks rushed through me again, stronger this time. I closed my eyes, trying to focus. *Visible blood,* I thought. *Visible.* That was not really how it worked, but I didn't flicker. Caster sat silently, listening.

". . . close watch on all those from the Left Eye," the Deputy was saying. "They will not be in our schools or in the market until this is resolved. This is only a precaution for their safety, due to the unfortunate incident last night."

"Can you give a status for the victim of that attack?" asked Sky.

"The victim is still under medical watch," said the Deputy,

"but he is expected to recover. Let me be clear: no racial violence will be tolerated. These men beat a garbage man who was just doing his job, vitally important work for the health of New Heart City. These men will be prosecuted and jailed like any other criminals."

"Thank you for your time, Your Excellency."

"My pleasure."

"Next, we'll speak with the winner of the women's ride. What does she think of her extraordinary win by forfeit?"

"Turn it off," I said. That was a report I didn't want to hear. Porti had sacrificed everything to take a stand for me, but there was a girl who didn't care, who only wanted her day in the limelight, whether she truly had won or not.

Caster obliged. "I can't believe people still care about who won. It's a game."

But it was more than a game to me, even after everything that had happened. "Before Porti came here, I thought the Game was all I had," I said. I was surprised to hear the words come out of my mouth. I had never thought deeply about why the ride was so important to me.

"All you had?" Caster said. "What about the rest of your life? Your friends?"

I picked another piece of muffin. "Did you see me at the parties before this year?"

He tilted his head as if thinking.

"As soon as Porti arrived, she was invited. And Porti being Porti, she had the power to bring me along, even to make you believe you had invited me yourself."

"Do you think I wasn't your friend?" Caster sat down in his chair. "I found you hard to talk to; it wasn't that I didn't want you there—at parties, or whenever. I would have liked to see you."

"Then why not ask?"

"I don't know," he said. He gazed at me, as if he had never thought about this. He had never stopped to wonder why we hadn't been friends before, or how I might have felt being excluded. He hadn't even realized I *was* excluded. But wasn't that better than for him to have purposely excluded me? I wasn't sure.

"You would have won," he said. "Porti had her day. It's rare for a rider to win two years running."

"Was this my year, then, gone forever?" Perhaps it shouldn't have mattered as much as everything else that had happened, but it did matter. It wasn't fair.

"Perhaps it was her year, then," he said, with a little smile. "Perhaps next year is your year. By then everything will have calmed down, and all you'll have to worry about is what Porti makes you wear to the ball."

I popped another piece of muffin into my mouth. It was a very good muffin. I had never realized that the Deputy's food was even finer than the Council's. But the morsel stuck in my throat.

"You know, I did like you before," Caster said. "There's nothing like a lady who's good at math."

I smiled. I had once overheard Member Solis lecturing Porti on how to find a husband; mathematics was not involved.

"I'm serious," he said. "And of course, you ride. When we were both in the arena, I would watch you training. There's also nothing like a lady with luxuriant hair engaging in athletics."

I tossed a piece of muffin at him.

"And why do you like me?" he asked. "Not because I'm the son of the richest man in the Upland?"

"That helps," I said.

He tossed the piece of muffin back, laughing.

"But that's not all," I said, growing serious. "You are kind to those who aren't rich. I've never heard a mean word from you. Others toss off words against Lefties with no thought, but you—never."

"Strange how basic decency becomes an asset," he said. "I suppose I'm glad of all the boys with asses first."

"How did you come to such decency?" I asked.

"You mean, with the father I have? He wasn't always this way, not before he became Deputy. And my mother was alive then."

"I'm sorry, I didn't mean to bring that up."

"It's all right," he said. "She was very decent. She taught us both." Everyone knew that the Deputy's wife had become ill and died while on a journey around the Upland. She had died at the Top of the Head, far from her family, and had been committed to the Waters with none but strangers to see her off. It had been tremendously sad, but at the same time, as a child, I had wished to see the Top of the Head and had wondered what she must have seen during her last moments. Were all who had previously been committed to the Waters waiting for her?

"I suppose she will greet Orphos," I said.

"By the Waters, yes. I hope she will."

The doorbell rang. A minute later, Koren ushered Porti into the dining room. She was dressed in blue mourning attire and carrying a garment bag.

I jumped up and embraced her. "I tried to come," I said. "Last night, as soon as I could."

"I know. I got the facts out of her," she said. Her eyes were wet, but she didn't let the tears fall. "I brought you something to wear," she said, holding out the bag. "It's not like the gown I had picked for you to wear to the ball, but . . ." She swallowed, unable to continue.

"Thank you," I said quickly. "Let me try it on. I know it's perfect." She didn't want to talk about her loss; I could see that. I didn't wish to speak of mourning fashion, but I would do anything to keep her mind—all of our minds—off the truth.

"I'll meet you ladies in a half hour," Caster said. "You wouldn't mind being my date, would you, Myra?"

"Thank you for pretending I have a choice," I said. "I'd be honored." I took Porti by the arm and led her to my new room.

I unfastened the garment bag and pulled out the gown. It was the deep blue of mourning, with a straight skirt and a cinched waist, and the bust spread out perfectly for my proportions. "Porti, how did you get this?"

"I had to do something last night," she said. "I couldn't sleep. So I altered one of Anga's gowns. For some reason, she has six in this color. See, I took from the skirt, here and . . ." She turned away from me, gasping.

"Porti." I put my hand on her back. "It's all right to be sad. It's the way we should feel."

"He tried to kiss me," she said, sobbing. "Right before the ride. He said 'a kiss for luck,' and he pulled me in, but I stopped him. I was trying to flirt, I guess, playing hard to get. I told him, 'when you win.'" She blew her nose on her handkerchief and caught her breath. "I was going to kiss him after, whether he won or not; of course I was. I was being so stupid. If you like someone, you should kiss him. You might not have another chance."

"Porti, he knew you liked him," I said. "Everyone knew."

"I didn't," she said. "I mean, I did, but I didn't know how much. I didn't know until . . . You should kiss Caster. Go out there right now and kiss him. Wrap your arms around him and don't let go."

"I will," I said.

"I would go back to the first time I ever saw him—it was the day I arrived in New Heart City, the first time I went to the stables. He was there with Shrill." She gave a little sob, remembering the exuberant beast. "With Shrill, and the way he smiled at the beast when he didn't know I was watching. The way he spoke. And then he turned and saw me, and our eyes met. It was like that—we both knew—but I was afraid. I would go back and run into his arms. Why did I not do that?" She sat down on the rug and leaned over her knees, sobbing. "Why did I not do that?"

"He knew, Porti," I said, rubbing her back. "He knew."

She sat up abruptly. "What I am doing crying on the floor? We need to get you ready." She stood and grabbed the blue gown off the bed. "Take that one off."

I followed her orders. Now was not the time to argue.

She pulled the gown over my head. It fit perfectly. Without taking my measurements, she had known exactly.

"I used to make all my own clothes," she said. "If I end up back in the Head, perhaps I can do that instead of beast ranching. I mean, I love beasts, but it's hard work. My back still aches at times, after a year." She wiped her face with both hands.

"Back in the Head?" I said. "No, Porti."

"Well, Member Solis isn't happy with me."

"Because of what you did for me?"

"I'm not hateful enough for this city," she said.

"No, you aren't," I said. "Porti, I don't know what to say. No one has ever done something like that for me, not in my whole life. I will do everything I can to make sure you stay and have everything you've dreamed of."

"Never mind me," she said. "We haven't even spoken of why you are here. Has he done anything more?"

"No," I said. "It's all very civil. He acts as if he cares."

"But Caster must watch you."

"Yes."

"At least it's not an ugly old man who must stay by your side."

We both tried to laugh, and failed.

"Perhaps he can also watch you during the night."

At this, I burst into tears.

Caster knocked on the door. "Hello? Are you ladies decent? Please say no."

At this, I bawled harder.

"We are decent, Caster," Porti said.

He came into the room and, seeing me, came and wrapped his arms around me. "I see you ladies have been having a fine time," he said. "Just like you two to carry on."

"The pre-party is always the best part," said Porti, her voice thick.

Caster reached out an arm and pulled Porti into the hug, and we stood there, the three of us, all bawling.

A moment later, I flickered out.

EIGHTEEN

I DIDN'T REALIZE AT FIRST THAT I HAD FLICKERED. MY friends didn't notice right away, either, so caught up were we all in our sorrow. I couldn't see myself or anything else through my tears. But then the sobs and even the breathing of my two friends stopped.

"Myra," Porti said.

Caster's arms lifted away from me.

My arms now free, I lifted a hand to wipe my eyes. *No!* Pinpricks pulsed through me like a wave. I tried to flicker back, but in my panic, I couldn't. Emotion. Emotion had done it, just as my mother had told me. And I had caused this by learning; I had triggered my curse. *Why* could I not flicker back?

"Myra," Porti said again.

"I'm trying!" I cried, as if she had asked me to flicker, as if she were not horrified and speechless. With one push, I finally flickered back, but I didn't know if I could stay this way.

I was still facing Caster. His face was blank, staring. It was as if he were a statue.

"I'm sorry," I said. "I didn't want to lie to you."

"Lie," Caster said, as if he didn't understand the word.

"It's all right," said Porti. "It's going to be fine."

"Caster, say something," I pleaded. "I couldn't tell you. I couldn't tell anyone."

"Obviously," Porti said. "You're the same person. Nothing has changed. Caster, say it."

"Of course," Caster said, but his face remained blank. He stared at me. "We must leave now, or we'll be late. I'll meet you ladies in the sitting room." He turned for the door.

"Caster, wait!"

But he didn't wait. He escaped through the door as if being chased.

I stared after him.

"He won't tell, Myra," Porti said, behind me. "That isn't like him."

I hadn't thought of that. But of course, he might. I had no idea what he would do. All his support for me depended on the suspicions about me being lies.

"He won't," Porti said again.

I spun around to face her. "We don't know that." I thought

of running after him, but if he was telling, then I should be running the other way.

"It's *Caster*," she said.

I looked at the window. I could go through it if need be, but we were on the second floor. How hard would it be to get down to the street?

"No, Myra," she said. "We can help you here."

"You're not angry?" I asked. I couldn't believe that she was still here, that she hadn't run off as Caster had.

Porti wiped her tear-streaked face. "I know why you hide it," she said. "Of course. There's nothing evil about the Ability. I know that more than most."

"What do you mean?" I asked.

"No one here in the city knows this," she said, "but my father—my adopted father—is a Flickerkin."

Now it was my turn to stare.

"My parents were beast ranchers, but as I've told you, they were killed by their charges when I was seven. I was alone for over a month, afraid to tell a soul of my misfortune. Afraid they would take me away from the beasts. Despite what they had done, I saw them as innocent, helpless without me. I could never blame them. There is really no love greater, is there? Anyway, my father came to sell his feed and found me. He sold his farm and moved to the ranch. As a Flickerkin outside the Eye, he was afraid to have a family of his own."

"Porti, that's amazing," I said.

"I couldn't tell you that part," she said. "I thought you wouldn't understand. I pretended to know nothing of Flicker-kin."

I choked a laugh. "So that's why he doesn't come see you ride."

"Yes. But he taught me everything I know about competition. Before the last round of testing, he did the stone throw."

"Thank you." I embraced her. I had one friend in this world, of that at least I could be sure.

"Ladies, we must go," said Caster from outside the door. I couldn't read his voice.

"She must not go, Caster," said Porti. "Grief made her slip."

"My father insists," he said. "If I leave you, I fear I will be sporting one ear fewer." The joke was typical of him, but his voice was cold. He was forcing his ordinary self. Porti may have been sure he wouldn't reveal me, but I was not. How could I be sure until he faced me? Perhaps if I went with him to the funeral, he would be forced to speak to me. He might see that I was still the same person. And if I didn't go, I would be giving myself away. I would get no more passes from the Deputy.

"Will you be all right?" Porti asked.

"I don't know," I said. "But Caster's right. I can't stay here after last night's foolishness. I have tested the Waters far enough."

"If you do slip, you must stay hidden," she said. "You must run. We will help you if need be."

"Thank you," I said, "but I won't slip. It's past." I did feel as if the pinpricks had receded. At least I was calmer now. Flickering had woken me from my stupor of grief. I felt strangely strong. Perhaps this new strength was the same energy I had felt the night before, when I had erupted in a fit of giggles. Perhaps it was relief that my secret was out and the world had not been besieged by waves. I was not yet in prison, and I would stay free. I would walk out through the gates of the city and up to the cliff's edge and see Orphos off into the Waters, and all would observe that I was as sad and as sorry and as much of a citizen as they were. I pulled the door open.

Caster stood back. "My father's cart is waiting," he said, and he led the way down the stairs. I followed in silence and found a guardsman waiting to escort us.

Now we couldn't speak of what had just happened, and I couldn't dwell on what Caster thought, not if I wished to remain calm. We didn't speak as we climbed into the cart, or as a fine gray workbeast pulled us through the nearly empty streets of the city, or as we reached the south gate, or as we rode through the gate and into the seagrass. Porti took my hand as we rode, and I held on to hers. I tried to cleanse my mind of all thoughts, to focus only on staying present.

It was easy oftentimes to forget that just outside the city

gates lay the high, sharp cliff at the bottom edge of the plateau, called Heart's End, and beyond that, the vast oceans that surrounded us. One could smell the sea air inside the city, of course, but it was one thing to breathe the air and another to see the ocean's vastness. The water was so far below us that it was visible only at the horizon, but it extended beyond sight, vast and mysterious and all-powerful. Each month all those in the city came out to hear a service; for the Council, the Deputy himself led the worship. I supposed the Deputy would perform the funeral service for the son of a Council Member, and sure enough, as we stepped from our cart into the sandy grass, the Deputy was standing near the cliff's edge, facing the ocean, his head bowed.

Perhaps the Waters would take him. Perhaps they were true gods and knew right from wrong. But as we approached the funeral feast, laid out upon a long wooden table a dozen yards back from the cliff, the Deputy turned to face us, and it was clear that the ground he stood on was solid. The Waters were not going to take him; they didn't care what he had done to us.

"Myra, can you see that?" Porti whispered.

"See what?" I asked.

A gust of wind hit us, flattening my skirt against my body. "The ocean is much higher than it was," she said. And she was right. If I hadn't been distracted by the Deputy, I would have seen it right away. The other mourners had noticed it too; they were whispering to one another. The Members of the Council, their close advisors, and their families stood in small groups, all looking out at the waves. We should not have been able to see the surface of the water from where we stood.

"How can it have risen so much?" Porti asked. "Caster, didn't you say it rose a few inches in a month?" She turned from him to me. "At the last service, we had to approach the edge to see the water." It was true. I should have been terrified, but I was numb. I saw the waves. I knew that they shouldn't be visible. But it was as if I were reading about the rising of the ocean in a book.

"The ocean shouldn't be this high," said Caster. He stared out, arms crossed over his chest.

The Deputy waved us all forward. We three were at the back of the group. There were photoboxes set up around the area. The funeral would be broadcast into the homes of ordinary citizens. I didn't see a radio receiver; whatever the Deputy was about to say, only this group and the Waters would hear it.

Why are you rising? I thought. *Will you swallow him up as he stands there? Will you swallow us all? Or will you swallow my family and me and all the Lefties and leave the rest untouched?*

"May the Waters hear me," the Deputy began.

The company bowed their heads. Orphos's mother leaned on his father's shoulder. His sister stood apart, staring straight ahead at the water.

"We have come to Heart's End to commit our beloved son, Orphos Staliamos, to the Waters," the Deputy continued. "Like all the Plateau People, he was born of their choosing, and we return him to their care, that they may love and protect him in death as in life, that they may conduct him to his final home in the vast world beyond this one.

"We all wish that this boy had more time to live among us; we cannot see the next world, and so we do not understand the happiness that awaits him. One day, happiness awaits all of us who return in due course to the Waters. Let us not mourn for Orphos Staliamos, but let us, with our love, assist him in reaching the place where he will live forever."

Four men carried a coffin along the edge of the cliff. Hanging from the back of the coffin was an orange and yellow kite, old and tattered, one we had flown together as children. It was customary for the family of the deceased to send one of his favorite possessions with him to the grave, and the kite was the thing they had chosen. They still saw Orphos as a child, and this itself was sad enough, but sadder still was the fifth man who walked behind the coffin, carrying in his arms the large, sharp white horns of a wetbeast. Shrill's horns.

Porti sobbed next to me. Next to her, Caster still stood wooden. And I couldn't react at all. I couldn't let myself feel even the slightest bit, or I would risk flickering again. Deep in my chest, there was a ball of sorrow that was nearly choking my organs, compressing my stomach, pressing my lungs.

In complete silence, the men lifted the coffin into the propeller, a large wooden contraption powered by prezine that existed solely to commit a body to Waters that were low and far from us, to send the coffin far into the distance, making the journey that much shorter. The Deputy raised a hand, one of the men discreetly pressed a button, and with a loud pop, the coffin shot out. The water was so high that instead of flying over the surface, the coffin skimmed it, leaving a wake, and stopped before it reached the horizon, so that a tiny speck of it remained visible in the distance.

Orphos and part of Shrill and Orphos's kite were floating in the ocean with a wooden coffin. I wished to believe that they were going to the world beyond ours, the perfect world where water and land coexisted, where the oceans were of steady height. I hoped that Orphos would meet Caster's mother and all the others who had died. But I feared he would float out there until he rotted, that the oceans were not gods but ordinary water that would soon overtake us, flow over the seawalls, and wash the city away. If they were true gods, how could they allow Orphos to die? How could they let people be tortured?

As was traditional, the mourners approached the edge of the cliff. Porti, Caster, and I moved forward into the wind, which blew louder and faster than before. I was at the end of the line, to the far right of everyone else. The wind was loud enough to drown out Porti's sobs and anything the Deputy might be saying. I heard only its rush and the crashing of the waves into the cliff wall.

As one, the line of mourners kneeled at the edge of the cliff. I found myself on my knees, staring out at the waves. Orphos's coffin was still visible. The Deputy must be saying something about Orphos's journey, perhaps something to reassure us about the ocean and the wind, some way to try to make it all make sense.

If you are out there, I prayed, *show me why this is happening. Why must my friend die; why must my parents be in jail? Why is my best friend in trouble, my secret out, my ride lost? Why can we not have the lives we wanted? What have we done to deserve this? Why do you let the Deputy speak for you when he tortures your people? Do not the Lefties kneel at the ocean's edge and commit their dead to you in the same way as the Plats? Did you not create them out of the Plateau People and set them high in the Eye so that they could become different? Did you not make them different for a reason?*

It was cold here at the edge of the water—freezing, really. The Deputy must have finished speaking. People were rising from their places, heading back to the tables where the funeral feast was. Porti was still beside me, kneeling, and Caster next to her.

The wind changed. There was a flutter in the light around me, as if the sun were shifting position.

"Caster!" I jumped to my feet and leaped the two steps to him. As I did so, my chest grazed that of a person.

The person—the invisible man—grasped both my shoulders and pushed me aside.

Caster, his knees only inches from the cliff's edge, threw up an arm to block the man's blow. A dagger appeared in thin air above us.

I kicked out a foot, and my ladies' boot connected with the man's knee.

He howled in pain, and Caster grabbed the hand holding the dagger. The two of them wrestled for it, and I kicked again.

"Go!" I yelled at the attacker. I kicked. Pinpricks rushed through my heart.

No, no no no no, I thought. I pressed them back with everything I had. I could not flicker. Not here.

Caster grasped the blade, wrenched the dagger away, and dropped it on the ground, his hand bloody. He jumped to his feet, throwing a punch where the attacker had been. But the man was no longer there. I had not heard him run—it was as if he had truly disappeared, extinguished from existence. The wind returned to normal, screeching around us. I still felt pinpricks, but they were receding. I had hung on.

Caster and I stared down at the dagger. Its handle was

made of fine white wood, a species that grew only in the Left Eye. It looked exactly like my mother's weapon.

"Is that . . ." Porti trailed off.

The Deputy was coming toward us now, and the guardsmen.

Caster bent down slowly and picked up the dagger in his uninjured left hand.

"By the Waters, what was that?" the Deputy asked.

"There was an invisible attacker," said Caster. "But Myra put her ladies' boot to good use. See, they are good for something," he said to me. He didn't smile, though.

"Find him!" the Deputy commanded. The guardsmen were already scattering. Two of them pulled out devices I had never seen before—squares with centers of prezine-looking brown—held them out, and swept them back and forth. The handheld sensors, I presumed. The beam they cast was invisible. I wondered if an invisible person could see those beams as we could see each other or if we could be caught unawares. And hated myself for thinking the word *we*.

"He's gone, Your Excellency," I said. "I didn't know which way to follow."

"She's saved my life, I believe," said Caster, rolling the dagger handle in his palm.

"Does no one care that Caster is bleeding all over the cliff?" Porti asked. She stepped between us and took his injured hand.

She unwound the scarf from her neck and wrapped it around the wound.

"Thank you," said Caster. "Both of you." He looked down at me. Still, he didn't smile.

The Deputy put an arm around his son and pulled him from the cliff's edge. "The feast is over!" he cried, leading us back toward the table. "Take your melon with you! Eat a piece to speed Orphos's journey in your own homes!" He took the dagger from Caster's hand, stopped short, and turned around to face the empty cliff's edge. Porti and I, following, were the only visible people he spoke to.

"You will not survive another war!" he shouted to no one. "You have begun something you can't stop." He held up the dagger. "I will find you. I will hunt each one of you down. You can't hide from me. You will face the Waters and be judged!" He gripped the dagger until his knuckles became white, his features blank and yet distorted. He turned his gaze from one end of the cliff to the other, and as he did so, for a second, his eyes rested on me.

NINETEEN

THE DEPUTY DECIDED THAT IN LIGHT OF WHAT HAD just happened, he could spare two guardsmen to escort Caster and me to the jail. I hadn't been sure the Deputy would keep his word, but as soon as we reached an enclosed carriage, a replacement for our open-air cart, he put his hand on my shoulder.

"Give my best to your parents, Miss Hailfast." He squeezed my shoulder in a fatherly way.

Though I wished to shrug off his hand, I stood there and waited for him to remove it.

"Do not let her out of your sight," he said to Caster. "Nor let him out of yours," he said to me. With that, he gave a very small smile, with no humor in it but possibly a tiny bit of kindness. For helping his son, I supposed. Finally, he let go of me.

I climbed into the carriage, and Caster climbed in after me. Though the guardsmen rode outside, I didn't feel I could speak freely. I wished to apologize to Caster, to force him to say something real instead of hiding behind thin jokes, but I hadn't trusted him with the truth, and I still wasn't sure I could. He was the Deputy's son, closest to the person who had just sworn to hunt down every last one of us. But I didn't have to say anything, because he began.

"We have had many fights," he said. "My father and I. Long before the testing, he told me that you and I should not be friends, that the Waters disapproved of your very existence."

I opened my mouth to speak, but nothing came out, since I didn't know what to say. He held up a hand.

"Let me say this, please. I defended you. I said you were a Plat as much as I was, that you were raised here and loved our city. I told him you intended to take your father's place on the Council someday. Do you remember telling me that, many years ago?"

"Yes." I had gone through a phase as a child in which I told anyone who would listen that I would be on the Council. I had no brother or sister, and I couldn't imagine what might stand in my way.

"He said it would never happen, that no Member would support a Leftie, right of inheritance or no. But I said I would be Deputy someday, and I would support you."

"Caster . . ."

"I just want to know one thing," he said. "Was I wrong? Are you a Plat or aren't you?" He turned to look into my eyes and waited, his jaw set.

"Of course I am," I said. "I'm a Plat as much as you are. I know nothing at all of the Eye." I lowered my voice, in case the carriage walls were thin. "It's an accident of the blood. A fluke. I don't even know how to flicker. If I did, I wouldn't have done it by mistake." I wasn't sure if I spoke the truth. Before the testing, before they took my mother away, before they barred me from the Games, I would have had no doubt at all. But now doubt seemed to be all I had.

"Now I must lie for you," he said.

"If you want me to live."

"My father has killed no one," he said.

Yet. The word hung unspoken between us. I was sure he, too, saw the vision of his father holding the Leftie dagger.

"I'm sorry," I said. "I'm truly sorry. I didn't wish to lie to anyone, especially you."

"How did you know that man was about to attack me?" he asked. "Is it something about you, something you share with him?"

"I felt a change in the wind," I said. "Anyone could have felt it." But I wasn't sure of this either. I remembered the shadows changing. Perhaps I *had* seen a part of him.

"I suppose my father will keep a guard on me now," he said. "We shall be trapped inside the apartment together for some time."

Perhaps he can also watch you during the night, I heard Porti say. I looked up at him, to see if his face would reveal whether he still would think being trapped in an apartment with me a good thing. But he wasn't looking at me now. He stared ahead at the carriage wall.

"I wouldn't mind that," I said. I wished he would put his arm around me, that he would kiss me and make me forget all this for a second, the way I forgot everything when he was kissing me.

"I won't tell anyone," he said. "Your secret is safe."

"Thank you," I said. Perhaps I should have felt relieved, but I didn't. I had only the twisted stomach and the closing throat. This was not the same as having no emotions, as my mother seemed to think possible, but I didn't feel any pinpricks; I was not in danger of flickering. I was perhaps in danger of fainting from lack of air and falling into Caster's lap, whether he would have liked it or not.

The carriage stopped.

"I'll wait here," Caster said. "My father said to give you as long as you like. If they try to cut your visit short, send them to me."

"All right. Thank you." I stepped out of the carriage and let the guardsmen escort me in.

My father was in the cell next to my mother. They could talk, but they couldn't see each other unless both pressed their faces up against the bars. That is how they were standing when I turned the corner.

"Myra!" My father reached through the bars as if he wished to embrace me.

My mother made a great effort to smile.

At once I was in tears again. But I couldn't flicker here. I had to control it. I took a deep breath and wiped my eyes. "The Deputy let me come," I said. "At least there's that."

"How is he treating you?" my mother asked, her eyes ice. I could feel the guardsmen watching me. I couldn't say anything of my flickering, couldn't ask her advice about how to control it.

"I'm safe," I said. "I'm fed."

"Myra, come here," my father said. He reached out his arms, and I clasped his hands in mine. "You look well," he said. "You're a strong girl."

"What's happening?" I asked. "Are they going to have a trial or announce a sentence, or simply lock you up until the Waters let the plateau sink?"

"No one has told us," my father said. "I don't think the

Deputy wants to decide. He knows we're innocent of anything but protecting our family. I have spoken to the full Council about letting us all go to the Eye. They may yet approve it."

"An invisible man attacked Caster," I said, "just now, at Orphos's funeral. The ocean is much higher, high enough to carry ships."

"High enough . . . by the Waters . . ." He shook his head. "Is Caster all right?"

"Yes," I said. "I kicked the attacker in the knee. But he got away. It was as if he didn't have to walk but flew."

"Come here," my mother said.

I let go of my father's hands and took hers. There was something in one of her hands. I couldn't tell what it was as she slipped it to me, her eyes never leaving mine. Her hands were colder than my father's, and her eyes were wet. Her hair was wilder than the last time I had seen her, her cheeks raw as if she had been scratching them. Up close, she did not look well. The emotion in her eyes was unlike her.

"You must go to my mother, Myra," she said. "You must forget about this boy, Caster Ripkin, and your friend Portianna, and even your beast. Nothing is more important than your safety, and you are not safe under that man's roof."

"Momma, I don't like it either, but I'm not leaving you and Poppa. What if they pass sentence and I'm not here?" This could be the last time I saw them. Now my head flared with pain from holding the tears back. But I wouldn't let them fall. I would not give in.

"You *are* strong," she said. "That is why you must leave us. It's time for you to be with your people."

"My people? The Lefties?" I let go of her hands, keeping whatever she had given me balled in my fist. "I don't know them. I've never met your mother. What do they mean to me?" I was nearly shouting. Caster's question replayed in my head. *Are you a Plat or aren't you?*

"They are your family," my mother said.

"So *what*, Momma?" I closed my eyes, breathed deeply. She wished me to curb my emotions, yet once again she provoked them.

"It's that boy, isn't it?" she said. "A *boy*, Myra, *his* son?"

"You seemed happy for me," I said, my eyes still closed.

"That was before I ended up here," she said. "Before he became a target twice over."

"Twice?" I asked.

"Do you think the assassin meant to kill Orphos when he could have killed a Ripkin? *Think*, Myra."

It was true. Caster had been just in front of Orphos. It could have been Monster who landed on the deadly spot. The man who had likely killed Orphos had tried to kill Caster today. And he had gotten away, dissolving into thin air.

"You are in danger on two fronts in that man's home," my mother said.

I opened my eyes to find her looking at me. She raised both eyebrows, trying to say something in silence. I knew she was trying to ask, *Why are you practicing your breathing? What has happened?*

I took another deep breath. "I'm learning to protect myself," I said. "At times my emotions have gotten the better of me, but I didn't embarrass myself in front of anyone except Caster and Porti."

"With my mother, you will not have to worry about any of these issues," she said. I could almost see inside her body, see the twisting and turning that was happening at the same time inside me. I could feel our throats constricting together as she finished her sentence with a slight wheeze. I had never realized what she went through, what it took to be her.

"Do you want me to go?" I looked at my father, hoping to see a disagreement, but he watched me sadly.

"Myra, your mother is right. You must go where you'll be safe. When I get leave for us, we'll join you. We won't be separated for too long." I could tell that my mother didn't share his optimism, but they had agreed she wouldn't say so. I understood that my mother wanted us to say our goodbyes, believing she would be dipped. My father would not entertain the idea, believing the Council Members still to be his friends. He thought the Deputy would keep me safe. He was not sure I should leave yet. But in the many hours together in adjoining cells, they had come up with a plan for what to say to me.

"I can hear all," I said. "You can't hide from me. I will have to make my own choice."

"You must go," my mother said. "Now more than ever." She meant that with my new flickering problem, I was even less safe. That was true, but it was also true that she had survived in New Heart City for almost my entire life and that she had never slipped once, not even in front of my father or me. If she could do it, I could. Though my stomach and my throat and all my organs suffered.

"Momma." I touched her hair, putting a stray back in place. It popped out again. "I need to think. Can we talk about something else?"

She brushed the hair back with her own hand. Her eyes said all she would have said out loud. I was a foolish girl even to think about staying. If she were not behind bars, she would load me into a cart and tie it to two hefty beasts and let them drag me out of the city whether I wished it or not. If my father objected, she would tie him to the cart too. She would do anything to get her way, to remove us from a world where we were not welcome.

I was almost glad she was behind bars.

She didn't say anything. She knew I had heard her.

I told them about the funeral, about Shrill's horns and the way the coffin skimmed along the water, and about the paintings in my new room and the superior pastries and how Porti had hand-altered the dress I wore. My father and I talked about the wind and the rising ocean and who would have won the stone toss and the footraces and the ritual swim. When I left, I hugged each one of them as best I could between the bars, not knowing when I would next see them. My mother's hug was tighter than I thought possible.

"You know what to do," she said. But I didn't.

I rode back to the Deputy's in silence, next to Caster but not touching him. I kept whatever my mother had given me in my hand, not daring to find out what it was.

From *THE BOOK OF THE WATERS*

For what purpose did the Waters create me? This question plagues the minds of all people, and the Waters will answer in their own time.

TWENTY

BY THE TIME WE REACHED "HOME," I HAD COME TO at least one conclusion: I couldn't dismiss my mother's fears. I didn't know if I was a Plat, as I had always believed, or a Leftie, because of the way people now treated me. I didn't know if I would attempt to escape to the Eye. But the Deputy had betrayed my father and tested my mother and acted just as she had predicted in all things. I had to get in contact with my grandmother and find out if there was an escape route for me. I had to go to the beast stalls and find Nolan, and my mind turned over ideas for how I could sneak out of the apartment.

When I entered, I was accosted by the sound of Sky's voice in the sitting room. Through the door, I saw he was physically there, pressing a receiver in Porti's face.

"You must have seen *something*," Sky said.

"It happened very fast," Porti said coldly. "Thank the Waters he didn't succeed."

Caster and I tried to rush by the sitting room, but Sky spotted us. "Ah, citizens, we're in luck! Here are Mr. Ripkin himself and the hero of the hour, Miss Myra Hailfast. Miss Hailfast, please, join us."

Porti rolled her eyes at me.

I walked in slowly. Sky crossed the room to meet me and pushed the receiver into my face.

"We've heard you kicked the attacker. Is that true?"

"I suppose," I said.

"You suppose? Why, the lady is too modest. If not for you, the attacker's blade might have found Mr. Ripkin's heart. Is that not true?"

"I don't know," I said.

"She saved my life," Caster said shortly from behind me. "Now, be so good as to save your own and leave my apartment."

"Ah, Mr. Ripkin, has the brush with death taken some of your good cheer?" asked Sky, making no motion to leave. I recalled that this was the usual time for the Deputy or the Council to speak to the people. The man probably had permission to be here.

Caster turned to the two guardsmen who still followed us. Brach appeared from a hallway but pretended he didn't see me.

Suddenly I had an overwhelming urge to tell the world that I had attacked a Flickerkin and saved a Plat's life. I took the receiver and looked directly at Brach as I spoke.

"I saw the dagger appear in thin air as Caster kneeled before the Waters, mourning our friend," I said. "I kicked where I imagined the man's knee to be, and that gave Caster a chance to grab the weapon. It was a small kick, but I suppose that's all it takes against an invisible coward."

"And where did the man go?" Sky asked.

"Unfortunately, he got away," I said. "But the citizens need not worry. He can be felled by a simple ladies' boot."

Sky took the receiver back. "That was the brave lady Miss Myra Hailfast speaking to us about her heroic action to save the life of Deputy Ripkin's son today during the horrific and brazen attack at the boy's funeral. Thank you, Miss Hailfast. Mr. Ripkin, how did it feel to see the dagger shining above you?"

"Out! Or I'll don a set of ladies' boots and test out Myra's method on your hindparts." Caster grabbed the receiver. "Good day, citizens of New Heart City. I appreciate your support, but as you can imagine, this has been a hard day that is not yet over. May the Waters carry my friend Orphos." With that, he smashed the receiver against the wall.

"That's an expensive piece—" Sky began mildly.

"Has it happened lately that your best friend has exploded

249

in front of your eyes?" Caster said. "I found his entrails to be disturbing. I don't much like daggers shining above me, by the way, but it's better than holding parts of your friend in your arms. Compared to that, I prefer being attacked by floating weapons."

"Mr. Ripkin—"

"Goodbye, Sky," Porti said.

Caster strode out of the room, not looking back.

While Caster was off somewhere stewing and Porti was assisting the guardsmen in ushering the radio man out, I was finally able to escape to my room, open my left fist, and see what my mother had given me. With cramped fingers, I uncurled a sheet of paper that was now damp with sweat. It looked to be a blank end page torn from a book. The black lettering was tiny but readable, in my mother's careful, controlled hand.

Kopan *Myra,*

I have no space for soft words. You cannot live as a Plat. You are a Leftie and a Flickerkin. My mother, Pinwin Urstel, is a leader of the movement to gain back the prezine mines. She will already be near the city. They mean to demonstrate outside the gate and demand rights

*for all Lefties. There is another war brewing, and when it
begins, you will not be safe with Nelston Ripkin or in New
Heart City. You must put aside your Plat love of status
and find Nolan Drachman. He will lead you to your true
friends.*

Here my mother had run out of space, and I had to flip
the paper over. For a minute I was too angry to read it. *My* Plat
love of status? *She* had married a future Council Member. Had
she chosen to collect garbage or serve food? But she was still
Momma. I continued reading. Her print became tinier.

*All of our lives, I have longed to share with you the
beauty of our true selves, the wonder and the joy of
changing from one state to another. You do not know
anything of how the Waters meant for us to be.*

*When I married your father, I resolved that I would
never have children. I thought they would always be in
danger—a sad life. I also feared the Waters, Myra. I
half believed the priests who preached that the Waters
had separated Leftie and Plat. But when I saw you for
the first time, I knew they were all wrong, and I had
been wrong. You are here for a reason. Today, only the*

Waters know. Tomorrow, perhaps the whole Upland will see it. I love you very much, Myra. More than you will probably understand unless you have a daughter of your own.

Momman

Her resolution not to waste space on soft words had dissolved. She believed these would be her last words to me. *I never wanted a child.* I had not realized until this moment that I still took those words so much to heart. And now she admitted she had been wrong. She wanted me.

It was not safe to keep this note. I had to act or I would let emotion destroy me. I ripped it in two. She knew about Nolan. I ripped again. My grandmother was somewhere near— with more Flickerkin. I ripped. There might be a war coming. I ripped again. Not only unrest and oppression and unfairness but more death. I kept ripping until the note was in tiny pieces. I stuffed the pieces in a drawer just as Porti came in.

"That man," she said. "He began asking me about my walk off the field as if he suddenly admires it. I suppose every Leftie must rescue an important Plat, and then things will be all right."

"He'll forget my heroism the next time a light flickers or a beast escapes," I said.

"What happened at the jail?" she asked.

I told her about my ride there with Caster and what my parents had said. But I couldn't tell her about the note. I couldn't reveal all these secrets that weren't mine to tell.

"They want me to go to the Eye," I said.

"That's too much to put on you," she said. "How are you supposed to get there? Just ride out on Hoof alone? It seems safer to stay here with us."

"I know," I said. "I don't understand my mother sometimes. Her fear overwhelms her." I hated to lie to Porti. But I had to see Nolan now. I would fall back on the excuse that had always worked for me.

"I just want to ride," I said. "I can't make a decision in this room. I've been trapped in these walls unable to move."

"The guardsmen have been instructed not to let you out," she said. "I heard the Deputy chastising them before you came."

I couldn't tell Porti about how Brach had attacked me, since it would reveal Nolan. But I stifled a shiver to think that Brach was among those who were supposed to be protecting me or holding me captive, whichever it was. I also couldn't say that perhaps the Deputy's chastisement had been all for show, that he wanted me to leave and lead them straight to the Flickerkin —a hope I now knew was justified. The Deputy might know as much about my grandmother's activities as my mother did, perhaps more. All he needed was her whereabouts.

"That man Brach hates Lefties," I said. "I won't give him a chance to catch me."

"Use your invisibility," she said.

"There are sensors at the door," I said. "And even if I can pass them, invisibility doesn't let me pass through large, hateful men blocking the way."

"There are no sensors there," she said, pointing to the window.

"Nor does the invisibility cushion one's fall."

"We'll use a sheet," Porti said. "I'll lower you down. It will look to the outside as if I'm simply airing a sheet out the window. A very ordinary thing."

"Porti, you are a genius." I smiled, possibly for the first time that day.

"When you need to come up, throw a stone at the window."

"Doesn't Member Solis make you come home?"

Porti shrugged. "She hasn't spoken to me all day. Don't worry, I'll be here when you get back." I should have questioned Porti more on that point; she had given up so much for me. But I couldn't stay in that room another minute with my mother's words burned into my brain. I had to begin to figure out how to escape.

. . .

I felt better once I had flickered—I barely made it to the ground without giggling. I felt not only invisible but light, as if my cares had faded away. *It's only the flicker affecting you*, I thought, recalling how I had felt the first time. But I didn't care. Guardsmen on the street were carrying handheld boxes and swept them this way and that over the sidewalks, but *I could see the beams*. This nearly made me laugh out loud. They were bright green, easy to avoid. *Easy for the murderer to avoid as well*, I thought, but the implications of this floated away. I ducked under a beam to get through the stable gate, and walking light on my feet, I made it to Hoof's stall in no time. All, I was sure, without being followed. Perhaps the Deputy didn't know that I was a Flickerkin after all.

Nolan was there, sitting against the wall, ghostly, next to a half empty bucket of water. He was eating a large roasted fowl leg that must have appeared to float in the air. As I entered, Hoof nuzzled against me.

"So you know me," I said, rubbing her head. "I'm glad." I laughed, finally able to let it out.

"I see you're not used to flickering yet," Nolan said.

"Perhaps," I said. "Or perhaps I'm happy to see a friend who won't judge me."

Hoof mooed softly.

"We're going for a ride," I said.

"Now?" Nolan asked.

"Yes, now," I said. "I've had a note from my mother. She says she knows you. Why didn't you tell me?" I tried to be angry, but I couldn't. I nuzzled my nose against Hoof's.

"I don't know her," he said. "My parents have told me what she wants."

"You saw them?" I asked.

His ghostly mouth twisted. Perhaps he was smiling.

"Never mind, then," I said. "What does she want? I know what she told me, but what did your parents tell you?"

"They want me to help you find your family, if you ask it," he said. "Is that why you're here?" He took another bite of his meat. As the piece entered his mouth, it became invisible too, part of his ghost face. It would be a great trick to play on children, the disappearing fowl leg. What fun it would have been to be invisible as a child. This thought struck me so hard that I nearly fell into Hoof. My unaccountable lightness suddenly shifted to sorrow. I had missed out on so much *fun*. Tears rolled down my face onto Hoof's hairy cheek.

She mooed softly.

"I know, Hoofy," I said. "I'm a mess."

"Focus, Myra," Nolan said. "Do you want to find your family?"

"Yes," I said. I wiped my tears off Hoof's fur. "I'm supposed to find my grandmother, Pinwin Urstel. Do you know where she is?"

"Yes, I know," said Nolan.

"I'm not running away, though," I said. "I'm only going to see her, and then I'll come back."

"Are you sure—"

"Porti is waiting for me," I said.

"And Caster Ripkin?" He tossed the bone into the trash bin with a crash that was too loud to be safe.

"Yes, and Caster," I said. I thought of how he hadn't touched me lately, and it should have made me burst into tears, but my erratic feelings were back on an upswing. I didn't feel sad about it; I felt strangely detached.

"It will be safer to walk," Nolan said. "If we must make it there and back in one night, a ride will be faster, but we risk someone trying to catch Hoof."

"She's the fastest beast in the Upland," I said. I knew that he was right to worry, but my cares were flowing away from me. If this was an effect of the invisibility, I was glad for it.

"Can she carry us both?" he asked.

"I think he wishes to be close to me, Hoofy," I said, laughing. "He has murdered a fowl leg out of jealousy."

"Don't worry, I'll mind my dirty Leftie paws." He made a show of wiping his hands on the sides of his pants.

"I don't think he's dirty just because he sleeps in a beast stall," I said. "Beasts are very clean creatures compared to humans."

There was something I needed to ask Nolan. If he hadn't placed the explosive, then who had? Was the murderer in my grandmother's group? Had they helped him? The thought cut through my giddiness and nearly brought me back to earth. I put my hands on Hoof's back, and her calm breathing steadied me. I was not ready to ask that question.

"Boost me, will you?" I said, keeping my voice light. "Someone has stolen my stepladder. A muck-eating, filthy Plat, I believe."

Nolan laughed, presenting clasped hands for my boot. "But who will boost *me*?"

"A man so strong needs no boost," I said. I landed hard on Hoof's back and grasped her neck. I was not back to myself after all. "There we go. *There* we go."

Nolan clambered on behind me.

"That's the clumsiest mount I've ever seen!" I said.

"Myra, you must be quiet," he whispered. "Hoof is escaping of her own will, recall? Do you need a minute of visibility to steady yourself?"

"Of course not," I whispered. "I must get used to this state. I must learn to control it, mustn't I? You know, I flickered in front of Porti and Caster—let's go, Hoof." We left the stall, entered the passage, and headed for the practice arena.

"What?"

"Don't worry, I didn't tell about you."

"Myra, you aren't safe there."

"Nonsense." We entered the practice arena, and I paced Hoof at a slow warm-up speed walk. "Well, my mother says so, of course. She says they'll never accept me if there's a war. She thinks there's going to be another war. Do you think so?" I suddenly felt Nolan's arms around my waist. They must have been there all along, ever since he'd mounted the beast. They were strong arms, warm. And they were around me, which Caster's were not. I pushed the thought back.

"Maybe there should be," he said. "Head for the door." He pointed to the small gate in the practice arena, the one that led outside the city walls and into the network of training trails. "I don't know anymore," he continued. "First the Council taxed us triple what they took from Plats. Our shop was the best in the city, yet we barely survived. They tested us, and we tortured ourselves. Then they put us through torture we couldn't endure, and now I'm sleeping in a beast stall. What more can we let them take?"

I hadn't known that Nolan's family was barely surviving. I hadn't thought about what the taxes meant. "But war, Nolan. That means death."

"Stop," said Nolan.

We were at the gate that led outside the arena now. I was about to let Hoof push the door open with her horns, as I normally would, but I stopped her.

"Not invisible," he said. "The sensors are thick outside that door. We must flicker in until we pass them."

"Visible," I whispered. "Visible blood." Pinpricks rushed through me. At once I felt exposed, naked in the open air.

Hoof, as if feeling what I felt—and probably actually feeling it, we were so aligned—pushed the door with her horns. It opened outward without any kind of key; one was needed to get back in.

Nolan jumped off Hoof's back and placed a rock at the bottom of the door so that it didn't close all the way. It was a smart move. I hadn't thought that far ahead. The invisibility was still muddling my brain. Nolan's hair was long, falling in his eyes, and his shirt had been torn in the back. He climbed on again, just as clumsily as before. This time, when he wrapped his arms around my waist, I had no trouble feeling them. His chest was hot against my back. I hadn't even realized I was cold.

"Myra, flicker!" he whispered.

I flickered out in an instant, the pinpricks coming when I called them. Green beams spread across my vision. They were all over the front of the door, and only when I looked very carefully could I see the tiny protrusions of the mechanisms that controlled them. They were the smallest sensors I had yet seen, easy to miss.

"Now get us out of the open before someone sees and comes after the errant beast."

We rode toward the trees that began not far from the ocean's edge and covered the sloping landscape away from the city. The forest went for miles, until the trees receded into the plains of the Neck, where most of the Upland's food grew. But among the trees, riders had cut paths, and it was along one of these that I took us, going faster than the simple walk now. It was a little odd to have the extra weight of Nolan with me, but at the same time, it was nice. It gave us a substance I was not sure I had.

"Myra, we need to go south," he said.

"What, toward Heart's End? Have you seen the ocean? It's going to sweep us away, isn't it? All this gone. Never mind whether the Deputy kills our parents, because the Waters will do it." I sped Hoof faster.

"Yes, I've seen it. Breathe, Myra. You're acting drunk again."

"Yes, I am, aren't I? Is that why I don't care about the dip and the End and the water and the Waters? What's the difference, anyway? Is there one? When we drink water, are we ingesting the gods? Don't you find that a bit rude?"

"They say our bodies are water and Waters both," he said. "They're all around us."

"Shall we go to the End then, throw ourselves on their mercy? Let them sweep us away now?" I took a turn in the path, one that led downward, toward Heart's End. We would come out of the trees to the west of where we'd had the funeral. I could feel the sea breeze already.

"No one is getting swept away tonight," he said. "This is where your mother wants me to take you."

"My mother wishes me to run," I said, patting Hoof on the head. "She wishes me to banish myself. To be a Leftie, like you say. I heard there's a lot of mist in the Eye. Is mist holier than non-mist? I suppose it's more water."

"There's a difference of opinion," Nolan said. "My father says it's holier there."

"Your father speaks?" I asked. "That man doesn't speak. He nods." I laughed. This was incredibly funny. I couldn't stop picturing Mr. Drachman nodding, nodding, nodding, holding a pin and nodding at me.

Nolan gave a small laugh, behind me and far away. "He speaks when he has something to say."

Suddenly, I flickered in. There was almost an audible pop. The colors in the woods seemed to change. I forgot for a second where I was. I couldn't see the arms around me. Instinctively, I tried to throw them off.

"Myra, it's all right," Nolan said, holding me tighter.

"Nolan?" I recalled seeing him, his ghost anyway, as I first walked into the stall. The rest was blurring as I tried to remember. "Hoofy? What's going on?"

"You were affected by the flicker," Nolan said. "You would

be drunk one minute and all right the next. But you had several good minutes. Things are improving."

I didn't feel improved. I felt as if I had been knocked over the head with something large and heavy. The night was very cold. I should have brought a coat if I was going to leave the city after dark. I was perfectly visible when I forgot to do that.

"You must get used to it," Nolan said. "Soon it won't affect you this way."

We were at the edge of the forest. The trees were thinning, giving way to grasses. The salt air blew in. The wind was not as strong as it had been earlier, but still it pushed my hair back, blew it out of its ponytail and around my face.

"There may be guardsmen out," he said. "You must flicker again."

"I don't know if I can."

"Of course you can. I'll be here." Almost imperceptibly, he pulled me closer. I wished Caster were here to pull me closer. Only he wouldn't, I remembered. He wouldn't touch me, ever since . . .

"I wish I had never learned to flicker," I said.

"Don't say that." He spoke into my ear. "It's part of who you are. Your parents took that away from you. You just need to practice."

No matter how I felt, I needed to flicker again, to hide in case anyone else was around. "I wish I could take Hoof with us,"

I said. The whole adventure seemed so foolish that I wondered why Nolan had agreed to it. He would have been safer staying in Hoof's stall and leaving me to find my grandmother alone. Why should someone like him help someone like me?

"Myra, if I tell you something, will you swear secrecy?" he asked.

"I'm the best at keeping secrets," I said. "Of course."

"It *is* possible to make a beast invisible, in theory."

"What? But you said I could only take a cat." My mind turned to our battle-of-the-sexes race, to the supposed invisible rider. Even the Deputy hadn't seemed to believe that he was real —but that was before Orphos.

"Just like we interbred with the Flicker Men, the Upland beasts bred with the beasts from beyond the oceans," Nolan said. "The Flicker Men brought many animals with them."

I found myself speechless. What could the world of the Flicker Men be like?

"But they don't flicker on their own—they're said to require a human companion," Nolan continued. "What we know is more rumor than fact."

I thought of Porti's father, the beast rancher. Could he make a wetbeast flicker? Goose bumps sprouted down my neck. No, it couldn't have been Porti's father. The man she believed in could not be a murderer.

"What do you say, Hoof?" I asked. "Shall we find out if the

rumors are true?" My control was returning to me. I wanted to try now. I could hang on to my senses this time, I was sure.

"Perhaps you should lie over her head, like when you race," he said. "As close as you can."

"And you as close to me," I said, poking his chest with my elbow.

"I know the lady has a boyfriend," he said.

"No," I admitted. "I think he's scared of me now that he knows."

"Ah, he isn't so unlike his father."

"He's nothing like his father," I snapped. "He's kept my secret."

"I'm sorry. Never mind that, Myra. Shall we try?" The whole time, his arms had remained around me. I had had many opportunities to shake them off, but I hadn't done so. I wasn't being fair to Caster, perhaps. He had had only one day to get used to the idea.

"All right, Hoofy," I said. I leaned over her head and wrapped my arms around her neck.

Nolan laid his head on my back, his arms still solidly around me.

Pinpricks raced through me. Faster. Prickly. And we were all ghosts, Hoof, Nolan, and I.

"By the Waters, Hoof. May they hear me, Nolan. By the Waters." I couldn't believe it. Hoof was invisible. I giggled.

Hoof mooed softly.

"Myra, you did it!" Nolan was practically jumping behind me.

"Are you surprised?" I found myself puffing with pride. I was at least the second best rider in the Upland, after all.

"No, but Myra—by the Waters—I wasn't even sure it was true. My father can tell a story when you get him going."

"I would like to see that," I said.

"Perhaps you will someday," he said. "When this is all over." He gave a laugh that was perilously close to a giggle. "Myra, you're amazing." He patted Hoof's rump. "You too, Hoof."

Hoof didn't seem bothered by the change in state. I could feel her beneath me as before, her heat, her muscle, and her heartbeat. She was steady as ever, much steadier than I was. But I was feeling a little better. I was still a bit giddy, yes, but that was as much from this turn of events as from my state of being.

"Head for those tents, Myra, can you see them?" Nolan pointed a ghostly finger.

"Tents?" I looked where he pointed. Past the end of the tree line, where the grasses began to turn to sand, only a few yards from the cliff's edge, sat three large, ghostly tents—tents that had not been visible a minute before.

TWENTY-ONE

CLOTHMAKER," I WHISPERED. "YOU MADE THOSE tents."

"Mostly my parents," he said.

"But how? I thought it took life's blood—that's what we learned in school." Horror filled me as I recalled what we had learned about the Flicker Men's invisible ships. Anything not living that flickered was said to be infused with blood.

"There's no human sacrifice involved, if that's what you're thinking," Nolan said. "Plats made that up to spread hate."

I stared at the tents. They were not supposed to be possible, yet to Nolan they were nothing new. Out there was the edge of a world I didn't understand. I felt sober now, a cold return to reality. A dull headache pounded through my skull. I had one more question. I didn't want to face the answer, but I could no longer wait to ask it.

"Nolan, tell me the truth," I said.

Hoof pawed the ground. She didn't like standing still.

"Of course," he said.

"Is the murderer hiding there? Do you know him?"

"*No*," said Nolan. "We don't want to hurt anyone. We don't want Plats to fear us. We want them to see that we aren't a danger to them, that we can live with them and have our shops and our families."

"I want to believe you," I said. And I did. I wanted to believe that neither Nolan nor my mother nor my grandmother nor anyone in the Upland could be capable of murdering an innocent boy, capable of trying to murder someone as good as Caster just because of who his father was. But if these people were truly honest, and we had nothing to fear from them, then why did they hide? Why did they not come to the gate and protest, as my mother had said they would? They would not need to reveal themselves as Flickerkin to demonstrate on behalf of all Lefties.

"If you ride forward, Myra, you'll see what kind of people we are. You'll see that we aren't what the Deputy claims."

"I know that," I said. Of course Flickerkin should be allowed outside the Eye; we were not all dangerous. We lived our lives just like anyone else.

We? I shook my head. I should not identify with these

people, even if we shared the Ability. But I rode forward. It made no sense to turn back, to give up on this quest that I'd already risked leaving the city for. I owed it to my mother to at least see what this other world was like.

As we left the cover of the trees, it was as if we entered a swirling storm. Sand whirled around my feet. The tops of the tents bent in the wind. My ponytail flapped in my face. And the moon hung above the ocean. Water crashed against the cliffs. I couldn't see the waves hitting from this far back; the water wasn't quite high enough for that. But I could see them falling back into the ocean.

Hoof mooed.

"I know," I said. I had thought I would never see the oceans like this, at least not until I was an old lady. But the Waters returned when they willed it—to reward or to punish or simply to join their creations for a moment, nobody knew. Even the Deputy, who was supposed to speak to them, had never claimed to know why they were rising.

We rode up to the tents, and I dismounted. Nolan came after me clumsily, landing hard in the sandy grass. Hoof nudged him with a horn.

"Sorry, girl," he whispered.

Sand whipped into my face, and ocean spray covered me. The tents were looking more and more attractive—anything to get out of this weather.

An insubstantial figure peeked through the tent flap. I couldn't tell much about the person except that he or she was shorter than I was.

"Pinwin, *ponton* Myra," said Nolan.

The figure, my grandmother, stepped outside the tent. The edges of her body seemed less than solid; they flitted this way and that in the wind. I was sure my body was not doing that, and neither was Nolan's.

"*Lopa tartar,*" she whispered. "*Lopa tartar.*" She flitted back through the tent flap. I had no idea what she had said.

"'Come inside,'" Nolan translated.

"Doesn't she speak our language?" I asked.

Nolan stared at me. "Yes, she speaks Plat," he said. "But we're all Lefties."

"I'm sorry," I said. "I've never been among Lefties. I didn't think."

Nolan turned away and patted Hoof's hide. "Don't worry about her. I'll keep her company."

"Stay, Hoof," I said, rubbing her head. I knew I had offended Nolan, but I didn't have time to fix it now. "She's still invisible. Will she stay that way?"

"I don't know," he said, still looking away from me. "If there's a problem, I'll call you."

I didn't like to leave Hoof with Nolan, who probably couldn't restrain her should she take it in her mind to run, but there was nothing to be done. She couldn't have fit inside the tent.

I pushed my way in. The woman stood next to a pile of blankets, baskets of food, and a bag that might have held clothes or other supplies. It was all perfectly visible, shielded somehow by the cloth Nolan had admitted he'd helped make. A small prezine-powered lamp in the center of the tent gave off just enough light to see by.

Pinwin flickered in. She looked younger than I'd imagined. Her hair was part white-blond, part white, as curly as my mother's. Her eyes were light gray-blue, the same as my mother's and Nolan's and those of many Lefties. She was thin, though, without the curves my mother and I had. If you had looked only at her body, you might have seen a short Plat.

"I supposed you're more comfortable this way," she said. Her speech was heavily accented, much more than my mother's. I had to concentrate to understand the words.

I flickered in. Somehow, being visible made me colder. And it made my headache stronger. I wasn't sure how to reply. This was not what I had expected. Perhaps I had thought she would run forward to hug me, or pinch my cheeks, or tell me how much I'd grown, as one expected grandmothers to do.

"So you're my grandmother," I said.

"*Mommanan. Ti.*" She held her hands together, as if she didn't know what to do with them.

We stared at each other. Perhaps she didn't know how to act either.

"It's nice to meet you," I said.

She looked me up and down, her hands twisting. Then her mouth formed into a little smile. "I thought you'd arrive in a gown like a Plat girl."

"I rode here," I said.

"I saw. You've done something very difficult."

"You mean making my beast invisible?"

She nodded approvingly. "A Leftie rider. A champion, if you weren't cheated. One who can change a wetbeast's state."

"I have a terrible headache," I said. "I've just learned to flicker. And I'm only here because my mother wished it." Even as I spoke these words, I kicked myself for being rude to a woman who had just praised me. But I didn't like the way she called me a Leftie. I was only half.

"How is she?" Pinwin asked. Her strong façade cracked, and worry showed through. A mother's worry, much like what I had seen on my own mother's face not long ago.

"She doesn't look well," I said, recalling her wan complexion and messed hair. "She fears the dip."

"That's why we're here at the ocean's edge," Pinwin said. "This is where they'll come when they're ready to have your parents and the Drachmans judged."

"My mother thinks you're here to protest at the city gates."

"That was before the arrests," she said. "Now we can't risk a confrontation. Better to surprise them at Heart's End when they think all is well."

"Will you kill more people?" I asked.

"We didn't plant that explosive," she said. "But yes, if anyone resists our rescue, we have every right. They wish to murder your mother." Her face darkened, anger replacing worry.

I looked away. I too was angry. Some part of me sided with my father, believing against all odds that the Deputy would not dip them. But another part of me was glad that someone was here to rescue the prisoners. I hadn't thought it possible to take action; I had relied on my father convincing the Deputy and the Council not to act. I found pinpricks beginning, emotion overcoming me. Someone was here to help. I was not alone. And yet I didn't trust these Flickerkin. I wasn't convinced they hadn't killed Orphos. They had other reasons for hiding here besides a simple rescue; I knew that in my heart and blood and bones.

And why shouldn't they fight back? I thought. *They are being treated as less than human.*

"*Kopan,* I know it's difficult for you," Pinwin said. "This is all new and strange, but it shouldn't be. You should meet the others, more of your kin."

I nodded, unable to speak. I half wished to run, to climb on Hoof and ride back to the city as fast as her legs would take us. But the words of my mother's letter sat inside me. *You are a Leftie and a Flickerkin.* I still had much doubt, but if this was my mother's wish, I would at least meet them.

Pinwin flickered and left the tent. In a minute, she returned, invisible, and I flickered so that I could see who was with her. She was followed by other shimmering figures—seven more. They were tall and short, wide and thin. For a few seconds, there was silence as we stared at one another, and then they burst into excited whispers—in the Leftie language, so I could understand almost nothing. I heard my name, *"kopan,"* words that I thought were praise. The figures surrounded me. One wrapped her arms around me and pulled me close. She held my cheeks in her hands, just as I had imagined a grandmother would do.

"Kopi," she said. Fine. Or perhaps, pretty. Though how one could tell that while we were all invisible, I didn't know. Men's voices agreed, and there was laughter.

"Come now," said one, "we're scaring the girl."

The others laughed.

"I'm Terta," said the woman who had called me *kopi.* "Your cousin."

"And I'm Groton," said a man. "Your other cousin."

"Cousins?" I asked.

More laughter.

"We're all cousins of a sort," said Pinwin. Her voice was

lighter now. "But yes, Terta is my granddaughter. Groton is once removed."

I didn't know what that meant, only that they were relatives, people my mother had never spoken of.

"I was a miner," said a man's voice. "Or I was until the last round of testing."

"The Plats killed our friend," said another man. "An ordinary Leftie miner, not a bit of Flicker in him. All because he spoke up for our rights." *With a forbidden weapon*, I thought. They had left that part out.

"Toran, leave that for tomorrow," said Terta. "We want Myra to feel welcome."

"How about that beast," said a man.

"A great feat, Myra. Very useful," said Groton.

"Leave that for tomorrow, too," said Terta. She came over to me and put her arm around my shoulders. I wished I could see her face. Her words were kind, but what was behind them?

"I'm not staying," I said. "I came only to meet you."

"Not staying?" said Terta, her arm still around me. "Of course you're staying."

"No, I can't."

"She can't leave," said a man. "She's seen us."

"I've seen nothing except ghostly faces," I said.

Pinwin came toward me, and Terta stepped away. "Give us more time," she said. She touched my face. "*Kopan.* We won't let any harm come to you." And she hugged me. I had to lean down to hug her back, and her body was warm and real, even though invisible, even though still seeming to wisp a little at the edges. She really was my grandmother.

"I can't," I said. "I must return before they find me gone."

The tent filled with silence, and then more whispers in the Leftie language.

"You must not tell anyone about us," said Groton, my new cousin.

"Of course not," I said. I looked at all of them, the ghosts stuffed into the small space, which was now becoming over-warm. "Please answer me one thing, though. The man who killed Orphos, who tried to kill Caster today, he got away from us. There were no footprints. He was there and then he wasn't. Tell me how this could be. I must know in case he goes after Caster again."

I felt their eyes on me.

"Tell me," I said. "I can't fly while in a flicker, can I?"

More silence.

"You really don't know," said Pinwin. She flickered in.

"No, I don't," I said. The tent was pregnant with a secret. And the feeling that I would not be allowed to leave once I knew what it was. I pulled myself up taller, as tall as I could manage. If I wished to leave, they wouldn't stop me. They wouldn't hurt my mother's daughter.

Pinwin flickered again. The edges of her body, already wispy, seemed to float. And then her shape shifted, melted, became round like a tossing stone. But she did not stop changing. The stone shape that had been a woman broke to pieces. Flurries circled around each other, tossing bits of light at the edges, floating up off the floor. The parts of what had been Pinwin floated up and up to the top of the tent and hung there.

The pieces of my grandmother spun as I stood staring, a chill running through me. This was how that man had escaped —by breaking to pieces. He could drop down on us from above anytime he liked. He could jump over the sensors. And it was not right.

"Stop!" I cried.

The others shifted their feet, stared at me.

The pieces came together and the form floated down, becoming woman-shaped again. Pinwin flickered in, and so did I. I didn't wish to be invisible after seeing that. I wished to be human.

"There's nothing to be afraid of," she said. "It's part of what makes us Flickerkin. What makes *you* Flickerkin."

"All right," I said, though it wasn't all right. It was perilously strange. "I won't tell anyone what I saw here." I moved forward, toward the tent flap.

Pinwin stepped in front of me. I prepared to argue, even to

fight for my right to leave, but she wrapped her arms around me again. "*Kopan* Myra. Please return. We are your family, where you belong."

"I must find a way to bring this man to justice," I said. It was true, but it was also an excuse. I needed something to tell her, something besides the fact that she and her faceless friends frightened me. "I'll see you all again." I pushed my way out of the tent, flickering out as I went. I hated that I had to flicker, could not be human for a moment. Pinwin didn't follow.

Nolan was waiting for me, his hand on Hoof's back. His ghostly form was shivering. He had been standing in the wind all this time.

"Boost me," I said, laying my hands on Hoof's hide.

"What happened?" he asked.

"Nolan, *boost me*," I said.

Nolan held his hands under my boot, and I mounted. "Come now or be left in the cold," I said.

He climbed on behind me. His hands and arms were indeed cold. Even Hoof's back was cold beneath us. I rode back toward the cover of the trees, my mind swirling with what I had just seen, rejecting it.

I knew that my mother was right—the citizens of New Heart City didn't see me as a Plat. The story of my heroism today wouldn't change that. I didn't need to be a known Flickerkin to be seen as a Leftie—a suspect, rebellion-fomenting, prezine-hoarding Leftie. I was trapped in the home of a man I hated. But I didn't want to be a Leftie or a Flickerkin. My beast was a ghost beneath me. I didn't wish to ride invisible. I wished to ride in the arena with the crowd around me, cheering us on. I wished to ride to the finish under lights powered by prezine mined in the Eye and go home to an apartment in the State Complex, where my parents were free and where we had a cook and a lady who cleaned for us and I had a school and a future, perhaps, on the Council. I didn't wish to hide here at Heart's End as the Waters rushed in.

I rode into the trees. We were deep among them before either of us spoke.

"What happened in there?" Nolan asked.

"She showed me how the murderer escaped today," I said.

"Ah, you mean she misted?"

"Is that what you call it? Wait—the mist of the Eye, is that made of people?"

"Normally, no," said Nolan, laughing nervously.

"Why aren't you with them?" I asked. "Aren't their tents better than a beast stall?"

"My parents are still in the city," Nolan said. "As are you."

"You don't even know me."

"We're both Flickerkin," he said. "The Waters gave us the same blood."

"I'm not your blood."

"We're all kin of a sort," he said, just as Pinwin had. "But Pinwin and the others, they're the last line of defense in case the Deputy dips our parents. I'm in the city watching what's going on."

"I didn't like the misting," I said. "It was so *not human*."

"It's more than human," he said. "*More,* not less."

"They're probably harboring a murderer. It could have been any of them. They didn't show me their faces."

"I'm looking for him too," Nolan said. "He's giving us all a bad name. First with the pranks—it's as if he wants the Plats to fear us. But that's not what we want, Myra. My parents and your mother and your grandmother, and the ordinary Leftie miners, and all the Flickerkin still in the Eye—we want to be able to live freely, like anyone else."

"You'd kill people," I said. "Like they did before, in the uprising." My mother would have cringed to hear me call it that, but that was what I had learned in school. In the Leftie uprising, Lefties and Flickerkin alike had killed hundreds of Plats. Flickerkin had used their Ability to sneak up on innocents, pulled daggers from invisible sheaths, and left blood on the sand before the Flicker Men had abandoned them with the receding ocean. The old Heart City had been destroyed. Flickerkin were murderous and deceitful, ungrateful descendants of inhuman monsters. As this ran through my head, I realized for the first time how much hate I had learned. And I wasn't sure if it was wrong.

Has it happened lately that your best friend has exploded in front of your eyes? I pictured Caster's back, receding as he stomped from the room. My kin were murderers.

I didn't realize at first that I had stopped, that we were standing on a path in the woods, Hoof pawing the ground, confused, and Nolan sitting silently behind me. The wind from the cliff's edge whistled through the trees. We were perhaps halfway back to the city, but to take another step toward the Deputy's apartment seemed beyond foolish. Nearly as foolish as turning back and going to live with my grandmother and her Flickerkin.

Each option seemed more foolish than the other.

My mother wanted me to go back to Heart's End. My father, though he wouldn't say it, wanted me to go back to the Deputy. Porti waited for me to return, to help me climb back through the window. Caster might not even know if he wished to ever see me again. Whom should I disappoint? What if I were to simply ride north from the city? I didn't need to go to the Eye; I could stop in the Neck, perhaps, and get work as a farmhand. I could go to the upper Head and labor on the beast ranch with Porti's father.

And hear over the radio that my parents had died.

I couldn't go anyplace where I couldn't help them.

"I suppose if I want to survive, I must learn to mist," I said.

"I don't know about tonight, Myra," Nolan said. "You've only just sobered up. The first time will probably knock you out."

"If they take our parents to the End, we must be prepared to help Pinwin and the others save them. We can't allow ourselves to be cuffed with prezine like our parents. Without that, they could float through the bars, couldn't they?"

"They were foolish to let themselves be cuffed," Nolan said.

"Not like you. You knew when to run. You're the only one who isn't a fool."

"Well, yes." He laughed and then turned serious. "If you're sure, Myra."

I had let myself be corralled like a beast into the Deputy's home. Misting, however strange, was one more thing that could help me escape. The murderer and me, both using the same trick.

"I'm sure."

"Then we should dismount. I don't know if a beast can mist, but anyway, we don't want to push you too hard."

On the ground, we stood facing each other.

"Is it going to hurt?"

"No. It's the best thing about being one of us."

"What do you mean?"

"You'll see." He took my hands, and without speaking

about it, we flickered in. The wind blew my hair behind me and his hair forward, so that his eyes were half covered. I tried to find them, their soft blue. They were not quite the same as my mother's and Pinwin's, I saw. They were darker, specked with something.

"It starts like an ordinary flicker," he said. "You'll feel the pricks inside your heart. You'll feel them spreading, changing you. But you don't stop there." He paused. "It's like the flicker in that it's hard to explain." He paused and closed his eyes, but he raised his head as if looking at something far away. All of a sudden I wished for him to wrap his arms around me, to hold me and let me press my face into his chest. Perhaps we could both forget all this for a second. But then he leaned in closer.

"I'll be here with you. The key is, once you've flickered, you don't stop. You don't see the limit. There's no limit."

My stomach tightened. This was more than I could do, more than a human *should* do. This set me further apart from my Plat life, further from ordinary Lefties. If I did this, I would never feel the same again. I would be admitting that I wasn't human, and I would be such forever.

"Are you all right?" he asked.

"Yes," I said. I couldn't be foolish and fail to use all I had to save myself and my family.

He cupped my face in his hand, and it seemed right, so I did the same with his. The pinpricks began. We were only inches from each other, my face approaching his, his face approaching mine. And the pinpricks continued, beyond the flicker, until they were no longer pinpricks, but pure energy. I was not looking at Nolan's face anymore, or where his face would have been. It was as though I could see everything—not only what was before me but also what was behind me. The trees seemed lit as if in sunlight, the stars bright as suns, the moon nearly blinding. The leaves on the trees were bright green, the path cool, shining brown. The wind tickled my skin, flowed through me.

A sudden heat flashed inside me, a burst of blood.

My mind spun; my heart pumped. I didn't feel drunk; instead, everything had become sharper. A colony of ants walked across the floor of the forest. A bird chirped far above me. I thought I was still in one piece, but I wasn't sure. I could see Hoof's features even as she stood ghostly: her eyes and nose and mouth and horns—those glorious, long white horns shining under the blinding moonlight. She was so beautiful—the most beautiful creature I had ever seen.

Another blast of blood burst through me. I gripped Nolan's face with both hands. And then my hands broke into pieces. His arm danced in spots of light. My arms were inside his; his were inside mine. But I didn't pull away. Another burst, and it wasn't just our hands and arms. I could see our bodies breaking, diffusing into fine mist. Yet I didn't feel broken. I felt larger and lighter and more awake. Nolan was around me, and it was like having his arms around me, but it was so much more. As if our arms and legs and all were not only touching but together. He had no more mouth; I had no more head. We had no more hands. We were no longer on the path but above it. We were floating in the air, in the bright light that had overtaken everything. I knew, deep inside, that the stars and the moon were as they had been. But to us, in us, it was not dark at all. We could see everything. I saw what he saw.

I saw myself, fragments that somehow were still obviously me. A piece of an eye, the side of a nose. Strands of my hair every which way. We focused on my hair, me following his vision, and as we did so, a scene formed, and I was in the classroom at school, and the hair floated a little in the winter air, in the static, and I turned my head and spoke to Porti, and Porti said something back, and I leaned my head back and laughed. I saw the forest again, and Nolan's fragments, his eye and his nose, and beyond him, I could see the ocean.

The tents sat next to the cliffs above the roiling water. Grains of sand blew up and were suspended in the air. Back in New Heart City, there was a light in a window of the Deputy's apartment, my window, and Porti was in the room. She lay on my bed, holding a book but not reading it, listening to a radio with a frown on her face. I could hear sounds from the radio, but I couldn't understand the words.

Our vision flashed back to the forest, and I saw the ground coming up to meet us. We fell as one.

I was on the ground, and my head lay in Nolan's solid hand. He lifted my head, his features normal and visible, the sky dark, the wind cold.

"Are you all right?" he asked.

I tried to speak but couldn't.

"Take it easy."

"That . . ."

"I've never misted *with* anyone," he said. "I had no idea that would happen." The corners of his mouth turned down. His eyes crinkled; his brow compressed. "Tell me you aren't going to pass out."

"No." I pushed myself up. "No, I'm fine." My vision blurred and then cleared. I was exhausted, but that was all. Nolan helped me sit against a tree.

"I didn't mean for you to see that," he said.

"What, the bit about you watching my hair as if it were a photobox film?" I tried to laugh, but barely a sound came out.

"Yes, that. You can't blame me for thinking about it. There aren't a lot of Leftie girls our age."

"No, I guess not." I wanted to sleep. But at the same time, I wanted to go back into that place where we were together, where everything was lighter and beautiful and seemed so clear. Nolan was right; it wasn't bad.

"If you break up with Caster Ripkin—you know, if he doesn't come to his senses and see—"

"Stop," I whispered.

"My father doesn't torture people," he said.

"Stop."

"I could throw you farther than he could."

I laughed.

He said nothing.

We sat there.

"It didn't feel bad," I said. "It felt right. Misting. Being with you. Everything." When I saw it from the outside, it had looked wrong, but from the inside, it had felt natural. It felt as right as riding, as if I were born to do it.

"But?"

"But I have to go back. Porti's waiting for me. I don't know what's going to happen with Caster. But I'm not giving up on my life yet."

"Being with me—us, I mean—wouldn't be giving up," he said.

"Yes, it would. You're on the run, and you can't go back. But they don't know about me. If my parents get out and go to the Eye like my father thinks they can, I can go with them, or I can stay, because I'm not illegal, not as far as they know."

"You said it didn't feel bad," he said. "Do you want to give it up—flickering, misting, everything about being you?"

"I don't know." There was so much about being me that had nothing to do with flickering. Everything in my life before the Games.

"Let's go back, then," he said. "I'll be in the stables if you change your mind." He boosted me onto Hoof in silence, and he wrapped his arms around me, and we flickered. I leaned back against him and felt his arms around me and tried not to think about any part of what I'd seen. I tried to let myself feel the ride and his arms and the heat of his breath over my shoulder, tried to pretend that this ride could go on forever and there would be no challenges ahead, no choices I couldn't make.

TWENTY-TWO

AS I CLIMBED UP THE SHEET, MY HANDS AND LEGS felt odd in their solidity. I was as I had always been, but now I felt confined in my own skin. If I were to mist, I could float in through the window effortlessly. In the mist, I hadn't felt the cold of the wind or the pounding of my headache, as I did now. In the mist, I would not now feel the breath in my lungs or the chafing of the sheet against my fingers. Yet the misting had left me exhausted.

Caster's face loomed behind the window curtain as he pulled me up. What would he think of me if he knew that now I could do something even stranger than flickering? If he was cold before, now he would turn away completely. I fell into the room, flickering in as I landed at Caster's feet.

"I'm sorry," he said, holding out a hand to me. "It isn't often

289

that I drag ladies in through the window—unfortunately." His voice was strained and his smile forced. The joke fell flat.

I took his hand and let him lift me. His hand was much smoother than Nolan's, and it wasn't cold. Caster had been inside, safe and warm all this time. He put a hand on my waist to steady me, then pulled it away. I had just flickered in front of him again. I wasn't human.

Porti stood behind him, rocking from one foot to the other. She twisted her closed mouth as she would do when she had something to say but was prevented by etiquette from speaking. I had seen that look often at official dinners and in the schoolroom.

"How was the ride?" Caster asked, not quite looking at me. "You look windblown enough."

"It was nice to be with Hoof," I said. But Hoof wasn't the only one I had been with. Now that I was standing in front of Caster, it was impossible to deny that something had happened between Nolan and me that went beyond friendship. I hadn't set out to do it, but I had, and it was something I had needed, something that had helped me understand myself as I never could have before. I recalled the feeling of Nolan's arms mixing with mine, of our bodies swirling into the same space. I thought of his arms around me, how I had been glad of them.

"Porti and I have been talking," Caster said, taking a step back from me.

"He has an idea," Porti put in. She was nearly jumping with excitement.

"A very good idea," Caster said, smiling at her. Why could he not turn that smile to me?

"An excellent, extremely good idea," said Porti.

"Tell me then, before it bursts from your bosom." I tried to be funny, but my exhaustion was crushing me. I wished for nothing more than to collapse in my bed, to be able to think or, better, to be relieved of thought. I wished for Caster to leave, so I wouldn't have to see the way he didn't quite look at me.

"It might get your parents out of jail," said Porti.

"What?" I sat down on the bed, tried to focus. I wanted more than anything to get my parents out of jail, but my head was pounding.

"Well, who has this invisible man been targeting?" Caster asked.

"Him," Porti said. "He's after Caster."

"Right?" said Caster. "I suppose it's about my father. At times I wish he were a farmer."

"So the way to catch this man—" said Porti.

"And clear your parents of all involvement—" said Caster.

"Wait," I said. "No."

"Yes!" said Porti. "It's the perfect plan!"

"I haven't heard a plan yet," I said. "All I've heard is that you want to use yourself as bait. Am I right, Caster?"

"Of course you are, Miss Hailfast," said Caster.

"You can't do that for me," I said. "Or my parents, or for anyone. It's not worth it."

"It's not for *you*," said Caster. "If I catch him, then he won't kill me. I like that."

"So tell your father your idea," I said. "He can set up the Guard to support you."

"Ah, but here's where you and your Ability come in," said Caster. "Something we can't share with him."

"My . . ."

"Because you can see him," Porti put in.

"True, but he can also see me," I said.

"Yes, but you'll hide. You'll have the advantage," said Porti. "You'll warn Caster."

"And then what?" I asked. "The man might have another dagger. He'll be a Leftie, and that means he'll be stronger than we are."

"Well, my father has the first dagger," Caster said. "The only problem is getting it from him. By the Waters, he follows the law himself. He'll have it locked up out of reach."

"There's a good reason for the law," I said. "People died. A *lot* of people." I thought of my mother's weapon, hidden away in her drawer. I could tell them about it, but then, if someone were hurt, it would be my fault. I would not only be caught and imprisoned; I would deserve the Waters' Judgment.

"Do you think we should let Caster sit and wait to be attacked again?" asked Porti. "And should he be defenseless? Surely it's not a sin to fight a knife with a knife."

I looked away from her. She had a right to feel this way, but I didn't like the idea. I didn't want to see another dagger. A renegade Flickerkin had brought one to the city and had changed nothing about right and wrong.

"We must cuff him with prezine," I said. "That will keep him from flickering."

"But that doesn't solve the problem of strength," said Porti.

"I suppose I can get a kitchen knife from the cook," said Caster. "I'm strong enough to make use of it."

"No," I said. "If he has a blade designed to kill . . ."

I couldn't let Caster walk into danger with only a dull kitchen knife. If it was between Caster and this murderer, I chose Caster. *May the Waters forgive me,* I thought.

"Swear to keep another secret," I said. "By the Waters, both of you."

"We swear," said Porti.

"By all the bath water in the city," said Caster.

"My mother has a dagger," I said. "I can get it—and prezine cuffs too."

They stared at me. For a second, I thought they were going to condemn my mother and me, perhaps run from the room, but then both broke into wide grins.

"Then our plan will work," said Caster.

We spoke of it long into the night. By the time I finally fell into bed, my headache had destroyed my thoughts, a perverse blessing that allowed me to sleep rather than stew.

In the morning, I woke after sleeping nearly fifteen hours to find Porti sitting in the room's only chair with the radio to her ear. When she saw me awake, she turned up the sound.

"What you said yesterday, about holding poor Mr. Staliamos, it touched me," said Sky. "Can you tell the citizens what you're doing to deal with what happened? Perhaps it would help them deal with their own loss."

"I pray for him," said Caster. "I like to go to the fountain and pray to the Waters. Especially when night has fallen and there are few citizens about." There was a fountain in the very center of the city, a place where citizens could worship the Waters without having to go outside the walls. It was not real ocean water, which was considered too holy to move, but fresh water from the Lower Scar River, the source of the city's water for drinking and bathing.

"I feel as if I have a direct line to the Waters when I'm there," Caster went on. "Don't we all?"

"That's wonderful," said Sky. "Really wonderful. I suppose you go with your father?"

"Oh, my father is busy," said Caster. "He's done what he can to speed Orphos's journey and to keep us all safe."

Porti turned the radio off.

I sat up groggily. "So the plan is in motion."

"The beginning of it," she said.

The next part was for the three of us to slip our guards, to convince each man that we were being watched by the others. Putting our confusing statements and conflicting plans in place took the better part of the afternoon. When it grew dark, we headed first to my apartment, which no one had entered since the day of the Games.

The drawer with the dagger wasn't locked; it didn't need to be. The dagger didn't sit in the drawer in full view, but was hidden in its case under a false bottom. I pressed the secret lever and slid the false floor back, and there was the box, exactly as I remembered. I unlocked it with my mother's key—she had not taken it with her—and the dagger gleamed at me. Its handle was white wood. As I pulled it from its sheath, I felt the smoothness of it, the strangeness of this wood that was as pale as my mother, as different from the trees here at the bottom of the world as were the people. Or perhaps, wood was wood. I rolled the dagger between my hands.

Its blade was probably five inches long. In the days of

the war, or the "uprising," daggers like this were used only by Flickerkin, because they were easy to hide in clothing. Plats had had swords then, swords that sliced pale people like my mother to bits.

If I was caught with this, the Deputy and the Council would have no choice but to give me the dip. Even Caster risked severe punishment, though I doubted the Deputy would dip his own son. Caster was supposed to slip the dagger back to me so that I could hide it with my Ability. *Perhaps I'm only strange and abhorrent when I'm not useful,* I thought bitterly, sliding the dagger into the pocket of my riding jacket. I retrieved the cuffs from my father's closet and carried them in their box, careful not to touch them and risk flickering in.

I tried not to look at anything as I made my way back through the sitting room, past the empty couches and the silent radio and the dining table covered in dust. There was a photobox picture of my mother and my father and me on the far wall of the kitchen. I didn't look at it. I slipped out the door and closed it behind me.

At the end of the hall, Caster and Porti were waiting. He spoke into her ear as I approached, and he must have said something funny, because she put her head down and laughed. They looked perfect together, both tall and thin, angled and beautiful. No one would think that someone like Caster Ripkin would choose me over a girl like her, and now she was single. Perhaps

I should let her have him and slip away into the forest, with the Leftie boy where I belonged.

I slid up to Caster. "Here," I whispered, passing the dagger and the box with the cuffs to him.

He slid them under his jacket. "Brilliant, Myra." He squeezed my waist quickly. The touch was as easy as if he could see me. No, I wasn't going to slip away into the forest. Not when he might be getting used to seeing me like this—or not seeing me. Even if it was only because I was useful, it was a change, a small beginning. As we headed for the fountain, I slipped my hand into his.

He froze for a second, then squeezed my hand but let it go again. I couldn't fault him; our plan was for me to zip ahead, to slip around the edges of the square and survey the scene, and then to hide myself while he prayed openly and foolishly alone. But I didn't zip ahead as quickly as I was supposed to. Instead, I waited to hear what Caster and Porti would say.

For a short while, they said nothing.

"Not that you aren't welcome," said Caster, "but why did you stay last night? Is Member Solis still angry with you?"

"Don't tell Myra," she said.

"This can't be good," he said.

"No, it isn't. Member Solis says I've disgraced her. She hasn't yet barred me from the apartment, but she's made it clear that she expects me to leave. Her sponsorship was for a proven winner, she said."

"But you did win!"

"And before, she claimed she would support me if I made the top three. It isn't about whether I won or not. It's about the hate I refuse to carry."

"Well, you can stay with us if you like. My father doesn't have time to care."

"I can't stay forever," she said. "I'll have to go back to the Head sometime."

I thought Caster would make a joke to try to cheer Porti up, or begin planning a scheme to sponsor her at University. But instead, he put his hands in his pockets and continued walking, hunched over a little.

"Tell me something, Porti," he said finally.

"Yes?"

"If you'd known the truth about Myra—the whole truth— would you still have done it, walked off the field?"

"Yes," she said. She didn't tell him why she understood my situation so well. They walked on for a minute. "If you had known, would you have kissed her?"

"I don't know," he said.

My heart ripped into pieces. Pinpricks rushed through me, and I was a hair's breadth from flickering back in again. I should never have eavesdropped, but I couldn't stop.

"She's the same person," Porti said. "It wasn't her visibility you liked, was it?"

"What's a person without a face?" he said. "I can't see her eyes or her smile or . . ."

"Or what?" Porti asked, giving half a smile. But Caster didn't return it.

"It isn't about her feminine assets," Caster said. "It was never about that. It was about a person I thought I knew, who was honest and had a simple way about her and yet was brilliant and athletic and competitive and had a life pulse. And now she's something else, something I can't even see most of the time."

Not most of the time, I thought. *Only sometimes. I'm this way now because you asked me to be.*

"But you'll give her a chance to prove that she's the same, won't you?" Porti asked. "Life is short and the Waters spiteful. They take what you have before you know you have it."

"I'm sorry," Caster said.

"Don't be sorry, but don't let love pass you by. Don't be angry when you should be happy or judge when you could understand."

"You're very wise, aren't you, Miss Vale?" Caster said.

"Now I am," Porti said.

They were approaching the fountain, and I couldn't stay to hear more. I slipped ahead, muffling my footsteps as best I could. There were a couple of people in the square, ordinary citizens sitting on a bench, speaking in soft voices, defying the curfew. As I walked around the square, I saw no Flickerkin. The assassin wasn't here yet. So I stationed myself in the agreed-upon spot, behind the hedge that surrounded the square, in a place where the bushes grew large and I could push my way in among them, making myself less visible even to Flickerkin eyes.

They came into the square. Porti planted herself on an empty bench and bowed her head, pretending to be insensible to the world. Caster walked forward and stood in front of the fountain.

"May the Waters hear me," he said. He wasn't speaking loudly, but in the silence of the night, I could hear every word. "My friend Orphos is with you now. I know you will carry him. He is deserving, and you are just. There is only one thing more that I ask. Advance your justice against the man who has sent him to you before his time. Show me how to find him, so that we may allow him to be judged by you."

The couple on the bench stopped talking and watched Caster. The silence around all of us seemed to grow.

"Grant me the patience to love those who deserve love and judge only those who are against you. Let me not believe lies about your wishes when it is only you who know them."

A ghostly figure came into view on the opposite side of the fountain.

I tossed a small stone into the water—our signal. As it broke the surface, Caster raised his head.

"Grant me strength."

The man came closer. Closer. Closer.

I threw another stone, larger. It missed the water and hit the edge of the fountain, only a foot from Caster's knees.

The invisible man was behind him.

Caster thrust an arm back, and the dagger connected with the man's flesh.

The man howled in pain but didn't retreat. He wrapped his arms around Caster's neck.

"Caster!" Porti ran forward.

I ran forward.

Caster thrust the blade in.

The man flickered, in and out, in and out. And then finally, in.

Just as he became visible, three guardsmen rushed around a hedge into the square.

"Out!" one shouted to the couple. They fled the way the guardsmen had come, looking back in awe.

I could do nothing. I could only stare at the man who now stumbled back from Caster, the white handle of the dagger sticking from his midsection.

Caster pulled the weapon out of the man's flesh and shoved it back into his jacket, spewing droplets of blood.

The man faltered but remained standing. He was nearly the same height as Caster and had the same dark hair and olive skin. I couldn't see his eyes, but I knew them to be dark brown.

I knew his arms to be strong and his voice to be deep. It was Brach, the guardsman. The one who had attacked me and spat at my feet.

Caster pulled the prezine cuffs from his pocket and slapped one on the guardsman's wrist. "You'll not . . ." His voice shook. "Not . . ."

"Did a beast chew out your tongue, Mr. Ripkin?" Brach asked. His jaw clenched. With the arm that wasn't cuffed, he held a hand over his bleeding stomach.

"How . . ." Caster stared at Brach as though the man were a changeling. Which I supposed he must be. How else could a Plat flicker, unless he was no Plat at all?

"Why?" Porti demanded. She stepped between Brach and Caster. "Why Caster? Why Orphos?"

"Porti!" Caster pulled her back.

Brach leaned in.

Two guardsmen stood behind him, each one gripping an arm.

Brach spat. The liquid landed on Porti's neck, just above the line of her modest gown. It spread down until it dropped into her bosom.

Brach smiled.

"Let's go!" one of the guardsmen said.

"I'm sorry," Caster said to the men. "I know you'll take heat for this. But it was the only way."

"You might have clued us in to your plan, Mr. Ripkin," the guardsman said. "Rather than convincing each man that another was with you." His face was twisted with disgust, his eyes wide with horror as he gazed upon his former comrade.

Brach slumped in the guardsmen's grasp, his hand falling from his wound. Blood dripped onto the square.

"I'm sorry," Caster said again. "I'll talk to my father, make him understand it's my fault."

The guardsmen lifted Brach by the feet and shoulders and carried him away, and Porti and Caster went after them. I followed a few feet behind them. A flickering Plat guardsman was the last thing we had expected, and it didn't make any sense. Only Lefties could flicker; it was a solid truth. But there were no changelings. Brach was a Plat and a Flickerkin.

Porti stayed with the guardsmen. "Why did you do it?" she shouted at Brach.

But Brach had passed out; he didn't answer.

"Why? Why?" Porti's cries roused the citizens from their homes. Faces appeared at doors and windows. *"Why?"*

The question lingered in the air.

TWENTY~THREE

T HE GUARDSMEN TOOK BRACH TO THE MEDICAL center, still cuffed with prezine so he couldn't flicker or mist. From the half of the voicebox call we heard between the guardsmen and the Deputy, it seemed that he would survive.

On the way back, Caster had managed to slip me the dagger, and I had found a safe place to flicker in. The story was that I had snuck out to find Caster and Porti. I wasn't supposed to have seen anything, and I had to feign new shock upon learning that the Flickerkin who most likely had murdered Orphos and attempted to murder Caster was a Plat, and not only that, but a Plat guard.

Caster, Porti, and I waited in the sitting room as the Deputy ended his call. The dagger in my pocket was a hard lump against my skin.

"Myra wasn't involved in this," said Caster. "Can you please spare her the flames I see in your eyes?"

"I would like to speak to Miss Hailfast alone," said the Deputy.

"Father, it was my idea," said Caster.

"Yes, you are a right fool," said the Deputy. "Give me the weapon."

"I'm sorry, Father," said Caster. "It was the only way to catch him." He pulled a dull kitchen knife out of his jacket pocket. "One good thrust, and nearly anything will do."

The Deputy took the knife from Caster's hand. "I see you had time to wash the blood off." He shook his head and sighed. "Go. Both of you." He barely looked at Porti.

"It's all right," I said.

"We'll be outside," Caster said. "Scream if you need to." He gave his father a little smile, and he and Porti left the room. Porti looked back at me as if to say, *Say nothing.* But by the Waters, what could I say?

The Deputy pulled a heavy chair from its spot opposite the sofa and sat down, leaning forward so we were eye to eye. He lost the advantage of his great height and yet gained the advantage of close up and personal intimidation. His eyes focused on mine. I braced myself to deny that I had the dagger, to profess my ignorance of where Caster could have obtained the cuffs.

"The man Brach is awake," he said. "He has confessed to the murder of Orphos as well as to causing the disturbances."

I stared at him.

"His exact words were, 'It was meant to be Caster Ripkin.'"

A chill ran through me. We had guessed that already, but it was another thing to hear it confirmed.

"He claims he is in league with no one, that he has acted alone." He paused, waiting for that to sink in. And it dawned on me, finally, what he was saying.

"He has cleared my parents," I said.

The Deputy nodded. "It seems so."

We locked eyes. I didn't see fire in his anymore. Instead, they seemed tired.

"I can't simply take the man's word for it," he said. "Nor is it solely up to me. They are confined by order of the full Council." *We'll get this unpleasant business taken care of.* The Deputy's words and voice burst unbidden into my head, the way he had casually plucked the prezine cuffs from the desk.

I leaned back on the sofa. I could run. I could flicker and run.

"But I believe I can convince them to vote in our favor."

"*Our* favor?"

"Yes, Myra," the Deputy said. "I wish nothing but the best

for you and your parents. I hope you can believe that. I know what I said yesterday in the heat of anger, but I don't wish to destroy all Flickerkin. I wish only for the people of the Upland to sleep safe in their beds."

"Do you intend to release them, then—to restore my father's position, to allow my mother her life back?"

"The Flicker Laws have been in place since long before my time, Myra."

"So that is a no."

"But without the crimes that Brach has confessed to, the penalty of banishment may pass the vote." He attempted to make eye contact with me again, but I wouldn't look at him. I scooted along the couch, leaving myself space in case I should decide to bolt.

"You look as if you want something from me," I said. "But it's in your hands. If you banish them, they'll have to go."

"Because I won't ask the Council to spare your parents unless sparing them will protect New Heart City," he said.

"I don't understand."

"If I release our Flickerkin prisoners, I must be assured that those who support them will leave the city."

"I don't understand," I repeated. My heart took on a life of its own. Blood mixed with pinpricks. What was he saying? What was he hinting that he knew?

"Brach, of course, will get the dip," he said. "We will attach stones to his feet to help the Waters with their Judgment. I will personally tie them on, and I will stand on the cliff and watch him sink."

Goose bumps spread on my skin. I could barely hear the Deputy over my own pulse, barely see the room around me.

"I hope so," I whispered.

"I know you do," said the Deputy. "You are proof that a Flickerkin can be a good citizen."

"I'm not—"

"If you lie to me again, you will regret it. Your film showed three fingers missing, and it is recorded." He looked me in the eyes, his face cold.

The room seemed to spin. I couldn't contain the pinpricks; I flickered out. I tried desperately to become visible, and it seemed to take long minutes. When I finally managed to flicker in, he was still glaring at me. I wiped tears away. If he took me to jail, I must go with dignity. I must make my mother proud.

"You and your friend Miss Vale, even my son, seem to think I'm a fool. Did you think I wouldn't wonder where you got a pair of prezine cuffs or a white dagger? Did your mother think I'd never suspect that you Lefties practice the test? That Flicker—" He stopped short of repeating the insult he'd spoken to Caster that night in the arena.

You weren't smart enough to catch us then, I thought. His

hate dried my tears. I would not go with dignity. I would mist. He would never catch me.

"I wish the best for you, Myra," he said. "And for your parents, because they are both people of the Upland, and they are my responsibility. If you also wish the best for them, you will do what I ask."

"What is that?" I asked. I met his eyes.

"You must take my offer to the Flickerkin who as we speak wait somewhere outside the city."

I could say nothing. I couldn't admit that I knew of them or where they were. Even if I agreed, how could I convince them to leave? My grandmother and her kin barely knew me.

"Tomorrow twilight, your parents and the clothmakers live, Brach dies, and the Flickerkin return to the Eye. That is the offer."

I maintained eye contact, and his eyes bored into me.

"Or we will bring the full force of New Heart City against every Flickerkin and every harborer. We are one state. One Upland. Anyone who threatens that will be stopped."

The Deputy stood and walked a few steps toward the door. Then he turned back to me. "Miss Hailfast, you may not believe that you are the person to accomplish this goal. But you are the only person who can. You stand in the eye of a great storm; you are part of it but not its cause. Sometimes it's hard for those in the swirl of wind to see a way out."

He watched me for a moment as if waiting for a response, but I couldn't speak. He gave me a little nod and then walked out of the sitting room, leaving me alone.

I felt the hard press of the dagger against my stomach. The weapon had given me a way to set my parents free—but only if I could convince people I didn't know to take a deal they might not like. And it wasn't only about my parents. I now knew without a doubt that if I didn't get the Deputy what he wanted, he would be personally attaching stones to my own feet.

TWENTY~FOUR

I COULDN'T TELL CASTER AND PORTI WHAT THE DEPUTY had said to me, could I? I couldn't be sure the Deputy knew that the Flickerkin were waiting at Heart's End in their invisible tents. What if he only suspected their presence and was setting me up to give them away? Perhaps he suggested that I could make peace so he could follow me to the tents and send all the Flickerkin to their watery graves. If that was the case, then I couldn't go there. If I left the apartment, he might have me followed. I couldn't imply in any way that he was right.

But he had offered to set my parents free if I performed this task and threatened to kill them if I didn't. How could I sit in my room and do nothing in the face of that?

Caster had set up Porti in her own room. *I should go to her and confess all,* I thought. She had never failed to support me so far. She would help me figure out what to do.

I must ask that woman, my grandmother, how Brach could be a Flickerkin.

I must get my thoughts together.

I must stand up and do something.

The radio was playing in the background. I thought I heard my name and turned up the volume.

"Well, I don't know about that," said a man whose voice I didn't recognize. "There are Lefties who perform necessary services. Those clothmakers who were revealed as traitors did the best business in the city, and who hasn't wished they were still open?"

"But that's the thing," said another man. "We allowed ourselves to rely on those Lefties, and look where it got us. Imagine if it weren't clothmakers but workers at the prezine refinery who were Flickerkin? The city might be without lights. The city must remove all Lefties from any position of even minor importance. It's a travesty that the Council hasn't done so already."

Apparently, the news of Brach's capture was not out yet.

"As I said, we must think of Lefties like Myra Hailfast," said the first man. "She saved the life of the Deputy's son, did she not? Shouldn't she be allowed to work with prezine if that were her vocation?"

"Myra Hailfast is an anomaly," said the second man. "Her

father is Donray Hailfast, by the Waters. What other Leftie can say that? Her actions mean nothing in the larger context."

"The same Donray Hailfast whom you denounced as a traitor on this very program?"

"Well, he's still a Plat; perhaps he has taught her some of our ways."

"So you agree that a Leftie may be taught to be part of New Heart City society?"

"I am speaking of this one girl. As I said, she means nothing."

I threw the radio across the room. It crashed into the wall, releasing a shower of errant parts. I meant nothing? Partly, I wished it were true. I wished I did not have to do anything, that I could mean nothing back in my own bed with my parents near me.

Caster knocked on the door. "Hello?"

"Come in," I said.

"Ah, you're still in one piece," he said. But he saw how I looked. "Or perhaps not." He glanced at the broken radio.

"He has either given me an opportunity to save my parents or asked me to condemn them," I said.

"The man has confessed," said Caster. "I heard it through my new shadow of a bodyguard. The guardsman's life is staked on me not dodging again."

"Yes." What did it matter if I told Caster? He already knew

enough to sink me. But he didn't know what I knew about Nolan and the other Flickerkin. The Deputy might need that information.

Caster sat next to me on the bed. But he didn't touch me. He left three long inches between us.

I recalled what Porti had told him, about not judging when you could understand. Perhaps that was why he was here. Perhaps I shouldn't judge him. I wanted to trust him, and I still did. Our friendship was real. I had to believe that.

"There is a group of Flickerkin outside the city," I said. "They say they are waiting to rescue my parents and Nolan's parents, should the Council choose to toss the prisoners in. But the Flickerkin are hiding, and I don't know if they tell me the truth. Your father wants me to go to them with a deal: they must leave in exchange for the lives of my parents and the Drachmans, and they must not protest Brach's death. I don't know if your father is being honest with me or if he wants me to reveal their location so that he may kill all of them and then me. He knows I'm a Flickerkin—he said so and frightened me so that I flickered." I had to pause at that and breathe. I still hadn't processed the fact that now I faced the same danger as my parents. "I fear that no one is being honest, but perhaps they all are. Perhaps I am meant to mediate an end to the disturbance in the Eye and all of this. Or perhaps this is my last night alive."

Caster's brow's furrowed. He seemed to be holding his breath, and then exhaled in a long whistle.

"Say something." *Say it's all right. Say you understand why I lied. Tell me what I should do.*

"My father won't kill you."

"I'm sorry I couldn't tell you," I said. "I don't know if I should be telling you now. It's not my secret to reveal, but I don't know what to do. I don't know these Flickerkin. I didn't like what I saw of them. Your father will kill anyone who stands in the way of what he wants, even me."

"No, he won't. If he said that, he was bluffing. Myra, he sees you as a child, like he sees me. I know I've had my conflicts with him, and yes, he believes in separation of Plats and Lefties. The Waters know he hates Flickerkin. But that doesn't mean he wants you dead."

"He said I was the eye of the storm," I said, "able to see what the wind could not."

"It makes sense that someone who is part of both worlds could do some good here," said Caster.

"Then why does he not put me in a cart and ride me out to them, so that we might do this in the open? Why make me travel in secret, wondering how much he knows?"

"Perhaps you're right; perhaps he isn't sure what he'll find there."

"Better to risk a child's life," I said.

Caster said nothing. I feared his silence meant that I was right. The Deputy perhaps did not wish me dead yet, but he would rather risk me than his guardsmen. And he knew that with my parents' lives at stake, I would do anything.

Caster reached his hand across the divide between us and touched my leg. "I will help you. Porti will help you. We're in this together." He leaned closer to me and ran his other hand through my hair.

"Have you lost your mind, Myra?"

I jumped. Who had spoken?

"By the Waters, Nolan Drachman!" Caster exclaimed. Indeed, Nolan stood in the corner of the room, fully visible. He stepped away from the wall.

"What are you doing here?" I demanded.

"What are *you* doing?" he asked. "Revealing us to the Deputy's son?"

"That is not why you've decided to show yourself," I said.

"You think it wise to put our lives in his hands?" Nolan whisper-shouted, coming toward us.

"Good to see you, Nolan," said Caster dryly. "We were all worried."

"Caster has proved that he's trustworthy," I said. "He doesn't go about skulking in corners. Were you perhaps waiting for me to remove my gown?"

"That's unfair! I'm here to speak with you."

"I was here alone for some time," I said. "You could have revealed yourself."

"You see, Myra," said Caster, looking from me to Nolan, "invisibility can be quite creepy. You can't blame me for being put off."

"I see your point," I said. I also saw the outline of Nolan's muscular build beneath his worn garments and recalled the feel of his arms around me. And how it had not felt wrong to see what he saw and feel what he felt. How being together with him was a literal thing in the way it could never be with Caster. I took Caster's hand. "Well, you may speak to me if you wish." I cringed at my own voice. I sounded imperious, like the rich girl from before all that had happened.

"Pinwin has sent me to try to talk sense into you," he said. "You need to go back, as your mother wishes. You can't believe that the Deputy will do any of what he says. Especially if he knows you're a Flickerkin."

"I'll go, but only to pass on the Deputy's message. Then I'm coming back. Or he'll kill my parents."

"Myra—" Nolan began.

"No. It's my decision. You won't make it for me."

"My parents' lives are at stake as well," he said. "We have a better chance of saving them at the End than through an agreement."

"You mean through a fight that will kill more citizens," I said.

"Yes, if it comes to that."

"You weren't friends with Orphos," I said. "You don't understand."

"*I* don't understand?" he asked.

Porti stuck her head into the room. Her eyes widened, and she slipped in, shutting the door swiftly behind her.

Nolan glared at her. "My parents were the first taken; have you forgotten?"

"Yes, but they're alive," I said. "You don't know what death means until it's someone you care for. We can't let people die if it's possible to agree."

"It's not possible," Nolan said.

"We must try," I said. "You can't stop me from trying." During this argument, I had somehow moved closer to Nolan, though I was still holding Caster's hand. And I had realized what I had to do. There is nothing like telling me I can't do something to encourage me to do it. Especially if the person doing the telling is a male who can't seem to comprehend what I find quite simple. Nolan didn't understand that death, anyone's death, must be prevented at all costs.

"Well, you aren't going alone," said Caster.

"Of course not," said Porti. "We'll go with you."

"Nonsense," said Nolan. "You all are Plats. I'll take her."

"Take me?"

"Uh-oh," said Caster.

"Haven't you heard about Plats?" asked Porti. "We're not all quite as solid as we seem."

"You two are solid," said Nolan. "Of that I'm quite sure."

"What, the news about our loyal guardsman doesn't surprise you?" I asked. "You did overhear that during your skulking, didn't you?"

"Of course it surprises me," Nolan said. "I'm sorry you didn't kill him. Would you have objected if *he* had died?"

"Yes, if he died before he confessed," I said. "Now he's given us the opening we need to save our parents without bloodshed."

"Did he say why he did it?" Nolan asked.

"I don't know," I said. "The Deputy didn't tell me that. I thought Brach hated me because he saw me as a Leftie. I don't understand how he even exists."

"What did the Flicker Men look like?" Porti asked.

"What did they *look* like?" Nolan said.

"What I mean is, maybe most Flickerkin look like Lefties because Lefties look like Lefties, but if the Flicker Men looked different—when they were visible—and they had children with Plats, then those Flickerkin children might look like Plats."

"Well . . ." Nolan ran his hand through his hair. I noticed that there was a smudge of dirt on his forehead and dark circles and thick lines under his eyes.

"But the Flicker Men didn't have children with Plats," I said. "My mother and the teachers at school agree on that."

"I don't know what they looked like," said Nolan.

"They obviously *did* have children," said Porti.

"It doesn't matter now," I said. "I must see Pinwin and make the Deputy's offer. If she was telling me the truth and has no other agenda but to save our parents, she should agree. Even if she lied, she'll want to save my mother. And me. I have to convince her that this is the way."

"Fine," said Caster. "Let's go before the night gets colder."

"Caster," I said. I was still holding his hand, and it felt right. "You can't slip your guard again. Nolan is right that you can't come. But, Nolan, you can't come either. I must go alone. That is what the Deputy wants."

"Well, as long as *he* isn't going," said Caster. The tone was joking, but his smile was not.

"You aren't right for her," Nolan said. He waved an arm from Caster's feet to his nose, indicating his height, his skin, his eyes, everything that was supposedly wrong for me. "You can never share what we can share."

"You are a short, creepy, invisible squirrel," said Caster. It was probably the meanest thing I'd ever heard him say. And he said it because Nolan wished to steal me from him. I almost kissed him, but something held me back. Perhaps it was that Porti was watching, eyebrow raised, looking from one boy to the other. I imagined what she would say, perhaps something about a night with two men to watch over me, and I gave her a little smile.

She smiled back. "Well, boys, I guess it's the three of us on sheet duty."

"We can't stop you," said Caster. "But if you aren't back in four hours, then we'll tell my father. He has sent you on this journey. If these Flickerkin do anything to hurt you, or prevent you from leaving, we'll come find you. I'll make sure my father helps you if it costs me all."

"She has a right to stay with her grandmother if she wants to," said Nolan. "And you must not reveal us."

"*Us?*" asked Caster. "You wish me to protect *you?*"

"I won't stay," I said. "And please don't reveal them. I will come back. Four hours." I threw myself into Caster's arms. Then Porti hugged me, too.

"Good luck," she said.

When I turned around, Nolan was gone.

Perhaps it wasn't necessary to sneak out. I might have walked out the front door without anyone stopping me. Yet for some reason the Deputy wished to keep up the façade, so I left the same way as before. Part of me wished I could go back and see my parents again, but part of me was glad I couldn't. I didn't need the two sides feigning agreement, the difference of opinion that would leave me as torn as before. In her letter, my mother told me I was born for a reason, that my life was not contrary to the Waters. Perhaps this was my reason, to prevent any more people from dying.

As I flickered, taking Hoof with me, I recalled the party only a short time ago, Orphos's smile as he helped me lift the broken photobox player. I had always thought of Orphos as Porti's future boyfriend. I hadn't realized that he was a true friend to me, that a hole would appear in my heart when I thought of him. We had flown kites together as children, trained on our beasts together as we grew older, attended Council functions, rolled our eyes at the silliness of our parents and their political squabbles.

If there was another war, hearts across the Upland would be filled with holes. Hearts like mine that didn't know how many souls filled them. As I rode through the trees, I found myself praying. *Sweep the hate from the hearts of all those who wait to shed one another's blood. Make your Deputy see that my mother and my father are both born of you. Let my Flickerkin relatives see that killing even one man will bring only more death.*

The tents were no longer in place. I saw only the expanse of sandy grass at the cliff's edge. The water roiled below it; the wind still blew harshly. Tonight I was wearing a coat, though. I knew a little more of what to expect. And I wasn't going to be deterred because the Flickerkin had moved their camp. I rode out from the trees into the sand and looked both ways. From my far left, where the funeral had been, several ghostly figures came, and I rode to meet them.

I dismounted from Hoof and raised a hand. "I haven't come back to stay," I said. And I relayed the Deputy's message. I told them that he knew about me and he wished for me to make peace, and that he had threatened to kill my parents and the Drachmans unless they accepted that Brach would be executed and left—all by tomorrow twilight. "This shouldn't be a problem, should it?" I asked. "Brach isn't part of your group." I longed to ask them what they knew of how a Plat could be a Flickerkin, of how this man who hated me for being Leftie could also hate the Deputy and wish to strike fear in all the citizens of New Heart City. But I held my tongue.

The Flickerkin didn't seem surprised to learn that Brach was the culprit, but I couldn't see their faces. I couldn't tell if they regarded me with anger or sympathy or any feeling at all.

They huddled together, speaking to each other in the Leftie language. Pinwin, whom I recognized by her height and her strange fluttering at the edges, and a man I believed to be Groton argued sharply. The others voiced their opinions. I understood only scattered words, nothing that would help me piece together what they were saying.

Finally, Pinwin stepped forward again. "*Kopan*, that man should not have involved a child in this."

"My mother involved me in it," I said. "I've been involved since I was born. I just didn't know it."

"We will accept that this man, Brach, must pay for his crimes. But there are many issues we must resolve. We can't simply leave with our mines still under their control, with our people taxed triple, with Flickerkin still banned."

"He will never agree to change all that," I said, my voice rising. "But he *will* agree to spare my mother. Three Flickerkin and my father, who has kept our secret, are in jail, and you can save them." *And me,* I thought. But it was unseemly to beg for myself. My whole approach was not right for an ambassador or a mediator. I thought back to my father's voice, all those nights I had heard him on the voicebox, discussing some issue with another Member of the Council. His voice remained calm. He spoke reason, but he would never waver in his conviction. And he would always remind his adversaries of how little they were giving up.

"The deal is that you return to the Eye," I said. "The Deputy doesn't ask that you give up any rights. He wishes only to bring the criminal to justice while making sure that those whom he mistrusts are safely away. If they leave the city with you and Brach is executed, then the citizens will be satisfied and you can plan your strategy back in the Eye. You may return at some point to press your agenda. He didn't say how long you must stay." Surely the Deputy had meant for them to stay in the Eye forever, but I clung to his exact words.

Pinwin turned back to the others. I wished I could see their faces and know if I was reaching them. They could probably see my expressions, being so much more experienced at invisibility than I was.

Finally, Pinwin spoke again. "How can we be sure that the Deputy is sincere, that he will not apprehend us if we reveal ourselves?"

"You can't," I said. "I don't know how sincere he is. If he has lied to me, then let him answer for it."

Pinwin nodded. "We will be here at the End. We agree to take them and leave."

I nearly gasped with relief. "Thank you, *Mommanan*," I said.

She took one of my hands in both of hers. "And you will come with us, won't you?"

I didn't want to face that question. I didn't know if the Deputy would banish me, too, and even if he didn't, my place was with my parents. I would have to leave Caster and Porti and even Hoof. But we would be free.

"I suppose I will," I said. "I hadn't thought that far."

"Good," she said. "We'll all be together soon." She let my hand go. The others seemed to be nodding toward me, perhaps in acknowledgment. Whether they approved of the agreement or went along grudgingly, I couldn't tell.

As I mounted Hoof and began the journey back to the city, I should have been relieved and happy, but I was numb. I didn't know if the Deputy intended to keep his promise or if my kin intended to keep theirs. I didn't know whether my parents would be free, or whether I would be free, or whether there would be a war. But I had done what the Deputy had asked, and for that, I at least ought to be safe for another night.

From *THE BOOK OF THE WATERS*

Never forget that the Waters, who have created us, may also destroy. When men commit acts that demand Judgment, the Waters will return to wash them from the Plateau. They will suffer only those who are worthy to remain.

But the Waters are merciful in their Judgment. Any who repent will be cleansed and will live forever on the Plateau beyond.

TWENTY~FIVE

CASTER AND PORTI WERE WAITING FOR ME. BEFORE I flickered in, I made sure Nolan wasn't there. I didn't know if I was sorry or glad to find no sign of him. The way I had treated him earlier was not fair, but he had to understand that I couldn't be with him as he wanted. I needed to speak to him, to process what had happened between us, but there was no time for that now. I felt I was barreling toward a future in which we would be thrust together or one in which we would never speak again, and neither possibility was what I wanted. I wanted my own choice, carefully weighed.

"How did it go?" Porti asked.

"They have agreed," I said. I didn't share my doubts.

"Ah." Porti sighed with relief, as I had. She hugged me. "All right. Now that I know, I will let you two alone." She winked at me and scurried out the door.

Caster pulled me into his arms. I wrapped my arms around him and closed my eyes. Touching him caused him to seep into me; my heart melted. I did not want to leave this. I did not want to be confused. *Let me choose this*, I thought. *Let me stay.*

There was a pounding on the door, and the Deputy stomped into the room. When he saw our embrace, his mouth twisted.

Caster pulled away but took my hand. We faced his father together.

"Leave us, son," the Deputy said.

"I'll stay," Caster said. He looked not at me, but at his father. In that moment, both unsmiling, they looked almost exactly alike. The only differences were the Deputy's graying hair and fuller build.

The Deputy shook his head in annoyance. "Tell me," he said.

"They agree," I said.

"They do?" He raised an eyebrow as if surprised.

"If you wished to use their refusal as a reason to kill them, you have lost," I said. I nearly clapped my hand over my mouth, but I didn't. After all, he knew about me. If he was going to reveal me or throw me in jail or have me dipped, he would do it whether I spoke the truth or not.

But he wasn't angry. He shook his head again, this time as if I had saddened him. "Myra, I'm not looking for excuses. I wish to make sure that no one else dies. Until your kin leave, we are all at risk."

"They will leave," I said.

"But she will stay," said Caster. He looked down at me. "If she wants to. She has that right. Father, no one else needs to know the truth. She deserves her place at University. The flickering is an accident of birth. She's no spy."

"If she's telling the truth and the exchange goes as agreed, it will go in her favor," the Deputy said.

Caster squeezed my hand. "She wouldn't lie."

"I hope you're right," the Deputy said. And then to me: "Tomorrow, the Guard will escort you to Heart's End. You may speak with your parents. If you wish to remain here, the choice will be yours." *Unless you have lied. If you have lied, you go with Brach.* I heard the unspoken words loud and clear.

He closed the door behind him quietly. I had not lied, so why was I shaking? Why had I heard only a threat?

Caster pulled me into his arms again. "It's all right," he said. "It's all going to go well."

I couldn't say anything. It was not up to me. Either my kin or the Deputy might betray me.

"I'm so sorry," Caster said. "I know I've been terrible ever since—"

"*I'm* sorry," I said. "I didn't want to lie to you. By the Waters, it's the only thing I've lied about. I had to."

"I know," he said. He released me, only a little. "You won't leave me for the clothmakers' son, will you?" He smiled as he said this, but it was a real question. It made my heart ache.

"Not for him," I said. "But for my parents. They will want me to go with them."

"Is that what you want?"

"I want for all of us to stay in the city," I said. "But that can't happen."

"*You* can stay here," he said. "My father will keep his word. He may walk ass first, but he keeps a bargain. You will have your place at University. Surely your parents would want that for you."

"What you say sounds so . . . normal," I said. "Do you really think I can just have my life back? After my parents were threatened with execution and banished? And I was prevented from riding? And the citizens jeered Porti when she defended me?"

"They cheer you now," he said. "You're the lady who saved the Deputy's son. By the way, I haven't properly thanked you." He drew me into a kiss.

I wiped a tear away. "Is that all?" I asked, trying to smile. "A kiss for a life?"

"I have more to offer," he said. He kissed me again and lifted me clear off the ground. I wrapped my legs around him.

He twirled me, and it was like I was flying, and I laughed. When he set me down, breathless, I didn't want to stop. I wanted to keep kissing him, and forget.

"I should go," he said. "You need your sleep for what comes tomorrow."

"Don't," I said. I stood on my tiptoes and kissed him, and he leaned down to meet me. As good as it had been to have him lift me, it was also good to be on my own feet, to be solid and visible and with him as I truly was, with no more lies. *I do not want to be invisible,* I thought. *I want him to see me.* "Stay the night," I said.

"If my father finds out . . ." He trailed off, smiling.

"There's one more thing I have to tell you," I said. "I lingered to eavesdrop on you and Porti. I heard her say that the Waters are spiteful. They take what you have before you know you have it. She's right, Caster. She wouldn't tell Orphos how she felt, and now he's dead. I will never let that happen. I love you." My face sprouted crimson. I hadn't intended to say that.

"I love you too," he said. He pulled me into a hug. "The way you are. You should never have to hide it."

But I will, I thought. *As long as I stay here. Not from him, though. Maybe that is enough.*

"Help me with these boots," I said, sitting down on the bed. I couldn't stop to think about the future. I wanted to have this time with Caster, whatever would come tomorrow. He kneeled to help me with my riding boots, and I took off my jacket. His eyes went to my bosom, and then he looked away. The tiniest of blushes sprouted on his darker cheeks.

"I'm cold," I said. "Let's get under the covers." Without waiting for an answer, I slipped under the blankets. It was indeed cold in the room, but I found myself sweating. Caster slid into the bed next to me and wrapped his arms around my waist.

"There's nothing better than body heat," he said. He kissed me on the cheek. If Porti knew, she would be giggling, urging me to take full advantage of the situation. I put my hand over Caster's. Having his arms wrapped around me was enough. With him, I felt more solid than I had ever felt before. For the first time since Nolan had triggered me to flicker, I felt as though I was safe in my own body. It would not betray me now, even if I were to suddenly flicker, because Caster knew all there was to know.

"I don't want to leave," I said. I had never wanted to leave; I was only being pushed toward it. I wanted to have Caster as my boyfriend, to ride in the Games, to be a citizen, even to stuff myself into uncomfortable clothes and go to official events.

"I won't let anybody hurt you," he said. "You're safe here."

"We will have to get you some ladies' boots," I said.

He laughed. "If I have to wear them every day, then that's what I'll do."

I closed my eyes and let myself feel his arms around me. If

I could focus on this, then maybe I could get through what was coming. Perhaps the Waters would not be spiteful to us after all.

By morning, news of Brach's capture had leaked, and the Deputy was forced to go on the radio and address it.

"No, we will not begin testing ordinary citizens," the Deputy said, in response to Sky's breathless question. "There is no reason to believe that this man is not a fluke, a sole abomination."

"Of course not," I commented, wiggling into a proper ladies' gown. "When it's Plats who flicker, it's different."

"What evidence supports that conclusion, Your Excellency?" Sky asked.

"He is the only Plateau Person to flicker since the day the Flicker Men breached our shores," said the Deputy. "The explosion at the Games and the attack on my son are proved by investigation to have been the work of a single man. In the early hours of the morning, the Council met, heard the evidence, and voted. Brach Petraguard will be judged by the Waters at twilight tonight. At the same time, we will meet with a delegation from the Left Eye and release the three Flickerkin and the harborer, Member Hailfast, into their custody. Member Hailfast has submitted his resignation this morning. The man responsible for the attacks will be punished, all Flickerkin will be removed from the city and sent back to their legal residence, and we can begin to move on from these tragic events."

"There is talk of continuing protests in the Eye, Your Excellency—"

"Reports have been greatly exaggerated," the Deputy interrupted. "Workers are asking for changes, and the Eye is asking for a greater share of the prezine. But there is enough prezine to go around, and I am confident that we will be able to work out an agreement. Anyone who provided Mr. Petraguard with prezine will be found and punished. There is nothing happening in the Eye that cannot be resolved by rational people working together."

Caster turned off the radio. "Where will he find these rational people, I wonder?"

"If my mother were here, she would say that the Deputy speaks of rationality only to provide cover for future insanity," I said, stuffing my left foot into a ladies' boot. I hated to be cooped up this way again, but I didn't expect to ride Hoof today. The Deputy had made it clear that I was to stay within sight of his guards. He no longer needed me as a secret ambassador and now required me to stay silent.

Caster came up behind me and put his arms around me. "This day will pass," he said. "Your parents will be free, and so will you. To go or stay as you like." He kissed my cheek.

"I hope so," I said.

"But in case something terrible does happen, shouldn't we make the most of the time we have?" He kissed my cheek, then my ear, then my neck.

"We may be doomed," I said.

"The Waters may destroy the city," he said, turning me around.

"Perhaps the whole Upland," I said, kissing him.

"We're all going to die." He kissed me back, and I was forgetting it all again. We were so absorbed in each other that we didn't hear the chanting until it was nearly below our window.

"What's that?" Caster asked. He went to the window and peered between the curtains. "By the Waters," he said. "Look at this."

I went over and stood behind him.

"Test *all!* Test *all!* Test *all!*" the crowd chanted. People were lined up in front of the Deputy's building, holding quickly painted signs. They were mostly workers, ordinary Plats, but I recognized a few kids from school among them, a few parents with ties to the Council.

The main door rattled. We heard the pounding even from my room.

"Where is your father?" I asked.

"The Council is probably meeting," he said. "After he pushed the vote through, he'd have to answer to them."

"Answer how he came to this agreement with people they were unaware of?" I asked.

Caster pulled me close. Our joke about everyone dying now seemed less funny.

"Hello? Are you decent?" Porti's attempt to joke didn't sound very light either.

"Come in," I said.

She came in. Her eyes were red and swollen, as if she had been crying. She didn't make any comment about my night with Caster. Her failure to give me even a wink was unnerving.

"Test *all!* Test *all!*" the crowd chanted.

"Are you all right?" I asked.

She sat down on the bed. "Yes." She stared ahead at the wall.

"Did something else happen?" I sat next to her.

A guardsman pounded on the door. "Miss Hailfast, is Mr. Ripkin in there with you?"

"Yes," I called. "We're all three in here."

"Don't leave this room," he said. "And don't stand near the window."

"I'm fine," Porti said.

"You are not," I said. "Has Member Solis done something?"

"You mean besides informing me that I'm no longer welcome? Besides making her vote for the Deputy's plan conditional on his expelling me from his home?"

"What?" Caster exploded. "He has told you to leave?"

"An hour ago," she said. "I'm to ride tomorrow for the Head. And never to be admitted to University. I'm to shovel beast dung all my life."

"No," Caster said. "He can't do this."

A rock hit the window, shattering it. Glass flew into the room. A shard hit the back of Caster's head. Instead of ducking, as a sensible person would have done, he turned and pressed his face close to the broken glass. "Stop it, you fools!" he shouted. "My father is not here. If you wish to protest, visit the Council!" He plucked the rock off the floor and threw it back. It caught the edge of the window's hole as it flew, shattering more glass.

"I love my beasts," she said. "I do. I love my father. But I was to live here. I was to . . ." She gripped the folds of her skirt with one hand. "I was to be beautiful."

"Porti, you *are* beautiful," I said.

"I was to marry Orphos," she said. "I wouldn't kiss him, but I thought I would marry him."

"We'll figure a way out of this," I said. "We'll find another place for you to stay."

"She has too much power," Porti said.

The chants outside suddenly stopped and devolved into shouts. I joined Caster at the broken window. Below us, guardsmen were pushing citizens away from the building, tearing signs out of their hands. There were more citizens than guards, but the people moved away, shouting back but not fighting—not yet.

"Test! Test! Test!" The chant resumed. But, as Caster had so helpfully suggested, the crowd headed toward the Council building.

"Look on the bright side, Myra," said Caster. "They no longer wish to torture only Lefties."

"Our city is tearing itself apart," I said. "Because they fear people like me."

"Because they fear people like Brach," said Caster, wrapping his arms around me. "Not you."

Porti watched us blankly.

I pulled away from Caster. It didn't seem right to be happy with her sitting there alone. "Porti, we *will* figure this out," I said. "Member Solis is one woman. You have sacrificed your place for me, and I will make it right." I didn't know how I would do it; I had no power. But I had to say something.

"I thought nothing of it," she said. "I thought, I will do the right thing. But the right thing isn't always the right thing, is it?"

"Perhaps Member Solis is a Flickerkin too," said Caster. "Brach was the Plat with the most hate, wasn't he? Perhaps we should take the advice of the citizens and test her first."

"The right thing now is to protect yourself," Porti said. "Take what you have and hold on to it. Because if you do not, the Waters will wash what you have out of your hands." She stared at the window, but her eyes were unseeing. "My beast is not even my own. I will ride back on a workbeast. Member Solis will give Nice Boy to the next girl."

"I will buy her," said Caster.

At this, Porti burst into tears. "You will?"

"Yes, I will," Caster said. He pulled her into a hug. "No one will separate you."

"You haven't left yet," I said. Then I had an idea. "Tonight, let's go all out. Let's wear our gowns for the winners' ball. They'll capture the entire execution on the photobox, won't they? We'll look as beautiful as we were meant to look. Everyone will see it."

"We'll dance over that man's body," Porti said. She straightened a little.

"A little gruesome," Caster said.

"I don't celebrate anyone's death," I said. "But if this is our last night together, then we'll do it in style. We'll have a night to remember."

"No," Porti said. "The winners' ball was the place for that. What brought us together as friends on the day I rode into the city? What was the most important thing in the world to all of us before the world split apart?" She grasped my hands. "I know you feared me. You hated me at first because of this, but it will always be why you are like a sister to me. And, Caster, it is why you understand me, and why you welcomed me when the other children of the Council were unsure. It is why Orphos and I were meant to be and you are meant for each other." She looked from Caster to me. "We will dress for a ride."

So while the citizens of New Heart City threw stones at the Council building, demanding that all citizens be tortured, and while the guardsmen prepared one of their own to be brought down to the ocean and tossed in, Porti and Caster and I donned outfits that the Drachmans had made for us, designed to withstand wind and water and sweat and movement. Porti and I tied our hair back and neglected to powder our faces or file our nails or don the much-joked-about ladies' boots. Caster prevailed upon the guardsmen to escort us to the stables so we could retrieve our beasts, and we rode out to meet the Deputy's carriage: Caster and Monster, Porti and Nice Boy, and Hoof and I. My parents were to be taken in another carriage by another route, and the killer, Brach, by yet another. We rode our own paths, but all of us would reach Heart's End before the sun began its journey down.

TWENTY~SIX

THE CARRIAGE WITH MY PARENTS AND THE DRACH-
mans had arrived first. It sat behind two hefty work-
beasts, who mooed softly as they chomped on the tall
grass. The photoboxes had also arrived—five boxes and five operators. Citizens would see the events up close and with the eye
of a participant. Sky stood to the rear of the carriage, fiddling
with his radio equipment. So the citizens would hear sound
from the execution also. A chill passed through me. *But then,*
I thought, *what sound would there be above the roar of the ocean?*
Even now, people had to shout to be heard.

My parents stood together next to the carriage, their hands
cuffed in front of them. Next to them were Nolan's parents. His
mother leaned against his father's shoulder, her eyes closed.
As we rode in, my father shouted my name. My mother only

watched me. I had no idea what she had been told, or whether she would be happy about my role if she knew. But I guessed that because I had worked with the Deputy, she would be angry.

I held up a hand to wave. I didn't think I would be allowed to approach them until the transfer was done.

I didn't know where my grandmother and her Flickerkin were, and I didn't like the feeling. I couldn't see them because I was trapped in the limitations of a Plat. Hoof's heartbeat flowed into mine; we were in perfect sync. It would take only a small push to send the blood flying outward, to cast both of us into that other state. And I missed it—that feeling that had overwhelmed me and made me giggle or cry now seemed more natural in a way than sitting here on top of a visible beast. What would it be like to ride the course invisible? There was no way of being together like being as one in a great flicker.

Hoof shook her head and mooed.

"I know, Hoofy," I said, patting her head.

There was no way of being together . . . I hadn't seen Nolan since he'd appeared in my bedroom, and after that I had been with Caster, who had finally accepted me the way I truly was. But we hadn't seen inside each other. In her letter, my mother had spoken of *the beauty of our true selves, the wonder and the joy of changing from one state to another.* I doubted that anyone who wasn't a Flickerkin could understand what I'd shared with Nolan. And yet my mother loved my father. She had sacrificed a huge part of her life to be with him, a man with whom she would never share that.

From our left, a carriage came around the edge of the city wall, surrounded by several guardsmen on beasts. The carriage stopped many yards from us, and a guardsman stepped out, followed by Brach, whose hands were bound in front of him with the thickest prezine cuffs I had ever seen. Brach was unshaven and walked carefully. As he emerged from the carriage, his eyes found me. It was as if he had been looking for me alone.

Why? I wondered as I stared back at him. I might get some answers now, or he might simply fall into the ocean and sink, and his hate and his story would sink with him.

Nice Boy reared up on her back hooves.

"Steady," Porti whispered. But the beast wouldn't have reacted that way if she hadn't felt what Porti felt. Monster also pawed the ground.

I was glad it didn't fall to us to bring justice: I didn't want to be the one to do it. But I did want to see it. I hated death, but here was one person whose death would make me, if not happy, then satisfied. My mother's dagger was inside my riding jacket. I had checked to make sure it wasn't visible from the outside, but it took all my energy not to look down and double-check. I hoped to be able to return it to my mother, or if something went wrong, to give it to Caster. I didn't want to have to use it.

The guardsmen pushed Brach forward. He came slowly,

standing straight and trying to hide the pain of his wound. His eyes stayed on me until the men pressed him toward the ocean.

The Deputy emerged from his carriage, followed by Member Solis, Orphos's father, Gregor's father, and the woman and man who rounded out the Council. Since my father had only resigned early this morning, they probably hadn't yet appointed an interim sixth member—a member who would be taking *my* hereditary seat. The unfairness of it burned inside me.

There were no spectators apart from the Council, Caster, Porti, and me. And, of course, the guardsmen, who surrounded Brach and my parents and flanked the Council Members. I counted ten of them. As Member Solis stepped out of the carriage, she glared at us. Perhaps she thought we weren't supposed to be here. I glared back.

Nice Boy growled.

Porti patted her gently on the head, a grim smile on her face.

The Deputy and the Council walked forward, toward the cliffs. We were in the same part of Heart's End where the Flickerkin tents had been. The wind whooshed by my ears. The ladies' gowns were blowing around them. The gentlemen's suits were flattened and the guardsmen's uniforms disarranged. My mother's hair had escaped from its pins and whipped around her face, so that I couldn't see her expression.

Sky came forward with his receiver. The other men carried

their photoboxes. The guardsmen brought Brach in front of the Deputy and the Council, who now stood facing us near the cliff's edge. Brach was still wearing a Guard uniform, stripped of anything to do with rank. It was now simply a dark green suit. His hair was too short to blow in the wind.

The Deputy took the receiver from Sky, who stepped back toward the men with the photoboxes.

"Show yourselves," the Deputy said.

My grandmother appeared next to him. Behind her, four more people appeared, my new cousins Groton and Terta among them. They stood solemnly behind Pinwin, their hair and clothes blowing.

The Deputy didn't flinch. He acted as though he had known where they were standing all along. He was good at faking, I realized. Good at pretending he had control. This thought made me more apprehensive about the near future. If the Deputy himself had to fake his composure, who among us had real strength?

And where were the rest of the Flickerkin? I had counted seven besides Pinwin when we had met before. Perhaps they were hiding in case the Deputy broke his promise, but I didn't like it. The Deputy was sincere. The thought nearly knocked me off Hoof. I couldn't believe that I trusted him in this, but I did. He would allow them to leave. *Let the Waters swallow him if he doesn't.* And let them swallow me, because if I was wrong, I was the Upland's biggest fool.

My grandmother was so much shorter than the Deputy that the sight of them side by side was almost comical, and she was wearing the simple garb of a miner, which contrasted greatly with the Deputy's fancy black suit. She took the receiver from the Deputy's hands and spoke into it. "We are here on behalf of those people of the Left Eye who flicker. From all of us, we are truly sorry for what this man has done. Please know that we offer this murderer no support. With his Judgment, we hope that our peoples may be reconciled, and that we may begin to discuss how to improve all of our lives." She did not look at Brach or at me as she spoke, but out at the photobox operators. She handed the receiver back to the Deputy.

"That is also my hope, Pinwin," he said. It shocked me to hear the Deputy say my grandmother's name, though he surely knew about all the agitators in the Eye.

"Brach Petraguard," the Deputy continued, "you have been charged with treason against State's Guard, the murder of Orphos Staliamos, the attempted murder of Caster Ripkin, possession of weapons, and failing to declare your Flicker blood. Do you have anything to say?" The Deputy handed the receiver to one of the guardsmen, who held it up to Brach's mouth.

"I would like to speak to Myra Hailfast," Brach said.

The Deputy said something I couldn't hear, but it was clearly a refusal.

"Are you not curious about how I came to be?" Brach said. "I would like to unburden myself, that the Waters might show me mercy. But only to Miss Hailfast."

The Deputy's eyes rose to mine. We all wished to know what Brach knew. But he was only attempting to stall his execution. He could lie or merely take the chance to spew more hate. I looked toward my parents. My mother nodded. My father shook his head. They looked at each other, eyes locked in contest. I would get no help there.

"Let her approach me on her great beast," Brach said. "I will stand away from her and shout. You may shock me as much as you like." He held up his cuffs, and I saw that his guards held triggering rods.

The Deputy refused again.

I rode forward.

"Myra!" Caster called, but I wouldn't let him stop me. I didn't care if what Brach said was all lies. I wished to hear something, anything. I wished to understand, if nothing else, how he came to hate me so fiercely.

The Deputy waved me back, but I rode ahead until I was behind the guardsmen who were holding Brach. "I wish to hear what he will say," I said, shouting over the wind. "Hoof and I aren't afraid of a wounded man wearing prezine."

"You will have five minutes," said the Deputy. "But the guardsmen stay. You can accept that or be judged now." He tipped his head sideways, and two guardsmen dragged Brach to my left, out of hearing of the Deputy and the Council.

"Thank you," I said.

The Deputy only glared at me. Pinwin betrayed no expression.

Hoof and I rode up to Brach. I didn't see the need to keep our distance. The man was having trouble standing, was cuffed, and was still held by two guardsmen. I recognized them as those from the jail.

"Tell me why you hate me," I said.

"Is that what matters?" Brach said. He looked as if he would like to spit.

"Answer me," I said.

"You are worse than a Plat," he said. And he did spit. The liquid landed at Hoof's hoof. She lowered her horns and growled softly.

"You *are* a Plat," I said.

"Raised with wealth, living as one of them, abandoning your flicker as if it were a cause of shame," he continued. My heart pounded. The Deputy knew about me, and now his guardsmen had heard me described thus. They didn't react, just held on to Brach.

"So you don't hate Lefties, then? It was all an act?"

"I hate Lefties who aren't Lefties," he said. "You are a Plateau Person with Leftie skin." He spat again, but this time, it fell short, landing at his own feet. He winced in pain. "And I am a Leftie with Plat skin," he said. "Just as there are Lefties in New Heart City, there are Plats in the Eye. Did you think you were the only one of mixed blood?"

I had thought that. My own parents had told me so.

"Well, you're the only mixture of Leftie and Plat." He coughed, as if trying to find more saliva to spit. "I am Plat and Flicker Man. I am from the Left Eye. But above all, I am a Flickerkin, like you." He looked up at me, but I looked away, over his head, out to the water.

"So you hated me because I was rich and happy," I said.

"You abandoned the cause," he said.

"What cause?" I asked. "Murder? What did Orphos do to you? Or Caster?"

"The Deputy's father discovered there were Plats living in the Eye," said Brach. "He believed the races shouldn't mix, so he forced all the Plats to leave. My family settled in the Head, but my parents weren't used to the life there. They couldn't farm the crops they knew. They had to hide their Ability. They became sick and died. My brother and my sister followed. My whole family was dead within a year."

The proper response to such a statement would have been to express sorrow, but I wasn't sorry for him, so I didn't say it.

"I traveled from farm to farm, working for others. Then Nelston Ripkin took his father's place as Deputy. He was no better. In fact, he increased the burden in the Eye, stole even more prezine, began building sensors to catch Flickerkin who weren't harming anyone. He tested his device on his unlucky catches, torturing them until finally he tossed them to the Waters."

My mother believed that this was true. But I wouldn't be sorry for Brach or feel pain for anything he had to say.

"So when the Deputy's wife came to the Head on her imperial journey around the Upland, I poisoned her. Then I came to New Heart City and joined the Guard. I vowed to kill the Deputy's son and then the Deputy. I would destroy Ripkin's family the way he had destroyed mine. I would ensure that the citizens of New Heart City knew they should fear us."

"Because they fear us, I have lost everything," I said.

"You have *gained* your true self," Brach said. He smiled, his eyes bright, and tried to lean toward me. "They torture us because our Ability is so powerful. We will use our strength, and this will be our city. If you join us, it will be your city too."

"Is that why you wished to speak to me? To convince me to carry on this crusade, to kill Caster and his father? How could you think I would do that? It's over, Brach. You will be judged. Take him back," I said to the guards.

"There is one more thing, Miss Hailfast," said Brach.

"No," I said. "This is over."

"We aren't giving you a choice."

Out of the corner of my eye, I saw a change in the light, the same shadows I had seen at Orphos's funeral. I spun Hoof around and felt her hoof knock into something.

Someone leaped onto Hoof's back behind me. I tried to reach into my jacket for the dagger, but the rod stung me, right at the trigger spot at the base of my skull. I flickered, there in front of the Council and all the guardsmen.

TWENTY~SEVEN

HOOF DIDN'T FLICKER WITH ME. I DIDN'T HAVE enough time to concentrate, to form the bond between us that would make it possible. Whoever was behind me held on to me, and I recognized the feel of those arms, their warmth, their strength.

"Let go of me!" I shouted. Nolan fought my attempt to flicker in.

Hoof mooed loudly and reared. She bucked, horns rising up. I held on with my legs, but Nolan didn't know how to stay on a beast. We slid backwards.

"Quiet, Myra," he said.

I thrust back with my elbow, but Nolan was holding me so tightly that I couldn't get any leverage. Ghostly figures stood on either side of Hoof. The Flickerkin Pinwin had hidden.

Hoof bucked again.

Nolan and I flew into the air, but Nolan didn't let go. He hit the ground on his back, still clutching me. I pulled out of his arms and jumped to my feet, flickering in as I did so. I did it without thinking; I only knew that because Nolan wanted me to be invisible, I didn't want to be. Hoof bucked this way and that as if being corralled by unseen hands.

Brach grinned at the scene. The two guardsmen holding him were wild-eyed, but they didn't leave their charge. The Council's guards ran toward us.

I flickered out. I couldn't let myself be caught; I had been exposed. I ran for Hoof and jumped. It was the first time I had tried to leap onto her back in many months, but I was helped by the surge of adrenaline. I landed on top of her and flickered in.

"Now," I said, and we both flickered out. We ran forward, pulling away from grasping hands. They had no hope of holding on to Hoof, and we had the strength and fear to run forever. But my parents were still prisoners. Caster and Porti and my whole life were here. I couldn't leave. *Curse you, Nolan,* I thought. After what we had shared, how could he do this? I stopped and turned Hoof around.

She mooed, giving away our position, but no one came after us. Everyone's attention was on Pinwin, who was floating over the ocean, holding Sky's receiver. Her feet and legs swirled in mist while the rest of her body was solid. "It is time to end the farce that there can ever be peace while Lefties live under Plat rule," she said. "You have tortured our people, stolen our prezine, and controlled our lives. You have denigrated Flickerkin and forced us to hide. But no more. We, the people of the Left Eye, solid and Flickerkin together, declare ourselves independent. As we speak, our people are expelling you from our land. We have regained control of the mines and will no longer supply any prezine outside the Eye. We reject your rule and your laws." Pinwin turned to me, and it seemed that she looked straight into my eyes. "We do not abandon any of our people and will take them all without conditions. If you do not accept our full and unconditional independence, then more Plats will die."

Pinwin dropped the receiver into the water. She raised her arms, and her hands suddenly burst into mist. The pieces of what had been her hands swirled around her arms as they, too, dissolved. Her legs and torso dissolved and swirled, leaving only her face. She stared out at the crowd for a long second, and then she was all mist. She became a churning spiral, spinning above the ocean but unmoved by the wind.

"Arrest these traitors!" the Deputy shouted.

Guardsmen shot green sensor beams at Pinwin, but they passed harmlessly through her mist. The other Flickerkin had become invisible. Their shimmering figures scattered before the sensor beams.

The cuffs fell from Brach's arms, and the two guardsmen

holding him flickered out. Brach followed them a second later. All at once, I understood. The guardsmen from the prison were Plat Flickerkin, and they must have helped Nolan make contact with his parents. Pinwin and her kin had never intended to keep their word and had always supported Brach's campaign of revenge. Pinwin wanted everyone to see her misting, to know that Flickerkin could become impervious to sensors, that they were superior and deadly. She wished to cause terror among the citizens of New Heart City so the Lefties could win their freedom. And it didn't stop there. Brach had said *this will be our city.* The Lefties intended to rule over the Plats as the Plats had ruled over them.

But neither race should rule over the other. That was the truth that almost everyone else failed to see.

Caster and Porti were near each other on their restless beasts, looking on in horror. Beyond them, Nolan's father pushed a guardsman away. He grabbed Nolan's mother, and they ran from the fight.

My mother's cuffs fell off, and then my father's. The Flickerkin freeing them flickered partly in as they touched the prezine and then out again as they dropped the cuffs to the sand. My parents were yelling at each other. A guardsman had hold of my father, and my mother was exhorting my father to fight. I knew he still had faith in the government and didn't want any part of this traitorous rescue. In that moment, a ghostly figure ran the guardsman through with a dagger. My father turned to berate his rescuer, my mother grabbed his hand, and a figure next to her tossed something over his head. He disappeared from view.

A cloth made by the Drachmans.

They're stealing my father, I thought. *And he isn't just my father. He's the only other person who understands that we must all live together. We all need him.*

He and my mother and the other Flickerkin moved toward the Deputy and the Council. Why couldn't they run away as the Drachmans had? Porti and Caster rode toward the Council as well, and they weren't safe even on beasts. As Plats, they were as good as blind.

I owed the Deputy nothing, but he was Caster's father.

And Orphos's father was in danger, too. "Member Staliamos!" I shouted. "To your left!"

He caught a man's ghostly hand just as a dagger appeared in thin air.

"Deputy! They're coming straight for you!" My parents' group was moving toward him.

Caster raced to help his father. Monster ran into an invisible man, and the man stumbled, while Monster mooed in fear. He was a beast built to run, not to fight. The man reached inside his jacket.

"Caster! He has a blade! He goes for Monster!"

Caster wheeled Monster around, and the dagger struck the

thick hide of the beast's shoulder. The beast growled in pain, but he wasn't really hurt. Caster kicked out with his heavy riding boot and struck the man's body. The Flickerkin cried out but held on to his dagger.

How could a man attack a beast? The attack angered me more than all that came before it. I reached into my jacket and pulled out the dagger.

"Momma, get out of the way!" I cried. "Poppa, run!"

The Council Members were all fighting Flickerkin. Gregor's father had suffered a wound to his arm and was perilously close to the cliff's edge. Member Solis raced away from the melee, a Flickerkin in pursuit.

Porti rode toward her. "Anga, get on!" she cried. Kicking out blindly, she struck the pursuer with her riding boot.

Member Solis reached into her coat, pulled out a sensor, and aimed it at the Flickerkin. A green beam sprang from it. The man ducked, barreled into Member Solis's legs, and took both of them down. Member Solis still raised the sensor, and she gave the Flickerkin a shot straight to the belly. He rolled over, visibility spreading from his midsection. He became a strip of torso, clad in the dark, rough garb of a Leftie farmer. He stumbled to his feet.

"On!" Porti shouted. She reached both hands down, and Member Solis deftly climbed onto Nice Boy, gown and ladies' boots and all. She was a former champion herself. As Porti turned Nice Boy away, Member Solis turned the sensor back on the Flickerkin. It struck him across both shoulders, and he became fully visible.

"Anga, forget him," Porti said as she looked back. But then she and Nice Boy pulled up short. "Father!"

The man stumbled backwards, toward the edge of the cliff.

"Father!" Porti jumped off Nice Boy.

"Portianna!" Member Solis shouted, but Porti didn't hear or care. She ran toward her father, who took another step backwards. The waves crashed high on the cliff, much higher than they had been only two days before. Angry wind swirled. Blood dotted the sandy ground.

Porti grabbed her father's arm and pulled him to her. She said something I couldn't hear. He leaned over her, obviously injured. A Leftie, he was barely taller than she was, but much wider. He enveloped her thin frame.

"Portianna, step away from that man!" Member Solis cried. She raised her sensor.

I rode toward them. I couldn't let her do this. By the Waters, Porti had just saved her life.

"Drop the sensor!" I shouted in her ear.

She turned around on the beast and aimed the sensor at me, but before the beam could connect, I pushed her. She waved her arms, trying to keep her balance, but her skirt slowed her movement. I pushed again, and this time she fell off, hitting the ground hard.

"Stay, Hoof." I leaped off and ran to Member Solis, who was attempting to stand. The sensor beam went wild, and I grabbed the thing out of her hand, then turned and threw it toward the sea.

Another Flickerkin came at us. This one I recognized. Perhaps I would recognize him anywhere now. What we had shared meant that I could see him as I could see no one else. He raced for Member Solis's back.

"Nolan, no!"

He stabbed her, right between the shoulder blades. Her eyes met mine as she fell. I could feel her gaze searching and see her confusion. Who was I? Who was this man Porti had saved? Who had stabbed her? It all ran through her eyes until she reached the ground, and her head fell forward, and she lay still.

"You've killed her!" I cried.

"Myra, she would have killed *you*," he said.

"I took her sensor," I said. "I *took* it. She had no weapon!"

"Father, Father," Porti was saying, over and over. He was on the ground now, alive but visible, his breathing heavy.

Nolan and I ran to them. I hated depending on him, but he could help Porti's father. "Porti, Nolan's here. We're going to take him to safety." I put a hand on her shoulder.

"Not without me," she said. She gripped my hand. "Myra, I must go with him."

"You'll be seen," I said. "You'll give away his position."

"I can't *leave* him like this," she said, tears pouring.

"We can take her," Nolan said. "*And* the beast. We have cloth back at the camp."

No, I thought. *She can't leave me.* But I rejected my selfish thought. "All right—Porti, step back," I said. Nolan took her father's shoulders and I his feet, and with Porti's help, we hoisted him on top of Nice Boy.

Porti leaped on in front. "Thank you," she said, wiping her eyes.

I reached out a hand to her, and she grasped it. There was so much I needed to tell her, so many ways to say thank you for everything she had done, but no time to say any of it.

"I'll find you," I said.

She nodded and let go of my hand.

"Follow me!" Nolan cried. He pulled a dagger from his jacket and let it hang visible so she could see him, and then he ran along the cliff's edge, toward where the Flickerkin were now encamped.

TWENTY~EIGHT

NO, NO, NO. I COULDN'T LOSE PORTI. BUT I COULDN'T follow her and leave my parents and Caster behind. Member Solis's body lay face-down near the cliff's edge. Even she didn't deserve this. Her crime was hatred, not murder.

A wave crashed over the edge of the cliff, covering her.

I jumped back. How could the waves have risen this high since Orphos's funeral? Another wave crashed and took Member Solis's body with it as it receded. For a few seconds, I could only stare. We had made the Waters angry, and now they would envelop us.

Hoof nudged me with a horn.

More waves crashed over the cliff's edge. But I didn't care if the Waters were angry. They would not take my parents. They would not take Caster. They wouldn't take anyone else if I could help it.

I had to get my parents out. "All right, Hoof," I said. "Get ready." I stepped back into the puddles left by the waves and took a flying leap onto Hoof's back.

"Poppa!" I cried. "Where are you? Poppa!"

An arm became visible. He had tossed off a piece of the cloth so I could find him.

"Poppa!" I rode to him.

A visible guard grabbed him around the waist.

"Let go!" I called. At that moment, I saw a ghostly figure behind the guardsman raising a dagger. "Behind you!" I cried. The guardsman turned and grabbed the attacker. He still had one arm around my father, but my father broke free and ran toward me.

"Get on!" I reached down a hand.

My father was not an expert rider, but he had ridden beasts before. As he climbed on, the cloth covering him slipped, and his head came into view. It hung in the air, disembodied, until he managed to pull the cloth back.

Suddenly I realized that Brach had to be here somewhere, and he wished to kill Caster. Caster was waving a kitchen knife around wildly. Monster's hooves were in water, getting splashed by each wave. And my mother was here as well, likely on Brach's side.

I didn't want to believe that, but I had to. She had nodded when Brach asked to talk to me. Like the rest of them, she didn't wish to give me a choice. When she was safe, I would disown her.

"Momma! *Momman!* Poppa, where is she?"

I saw the green sensor beam too late. I didn't see who sent it. It hit Hoof in a thin strip from her rump all the way to her shoulder. She screamed and bucked. I clung to her. My father clung to me.

The sensor beam cut again. It hit my father's arm, which shielded me. It didn't hurt him, but it cut a visible strip in the cloth, making us an easy target for sensors. Did my mother not hear me calling? Did she care more for killing Plats than for our family?

I pulled Hoof around. She was still jumpy, mooing in pain.

"Rhonda!" my father cried. "Rhondalynn!" He reached out a hand, and a shimmering outline took it. It must have been my mother, as she truly was.

I leaped off Hoof. "Momma, get on!"

My father pulled her up. She was still a blank, ghostly figure.

"Come, Myra," she said.

"No," I said. "Caster—" As I said his name, I heard him shout. A Flickerkin twisted the knife from his hand. He tottered at the cliff's edge, about to be enveloped by an angry wave.

I raced toward him. I pushed aside a Flickerkin woman. She might have been my grandmother. I didn't care.

The Deputy was fighting for his life. He looked over at Caster just as the invisible man pushed Caster into the roiling water.

"No!" I leaped for him, landing at the edge of the cliff. A wave swirled around me, pushing me back. *No, he doesn't deserve this. I don't deserve this. Do not judge us*, I prayed. I had doubted the Waters many times in recent weeks, but they couldn't be this cruel to us. We were good people. We wanted only to live peacefully and do what was right. We wanted only to love each other. That was not wrong. *We* were not wrong.

Hands grabbed the front of my jacket. "He's gone," said a male voice. Brach's voice.

I squirmed and kicked. "Let go of me!" I screamed. But he pushed me to the ground and held me down.

"This is your last chance, Hailfast," he said. His breath was sour on my face. His hands tightened on my arms. "Are you a Flickerkin or are you a Plat?"

"I am a Plat!" I yelled, and I spat. I had never done such a thing in my life, but my mouth got the job done. The ball of spit landed between Brach's eyes.

He lifted a hand to hit me, a blow surely meant to end my miserable halfsie life, but I was faster. I thrust upward with the dagger. It hit in the same place Caster's blow had landed before.

He screamed, still holding me down with one hand. I twisted the blade. He released me, and he flickered in. He fell on top of me, struggling to lift himself.

I pushed him off, and he rolled onto his back. His face was bruised and bloody; he had been hit by many blows. I still held the dagger. I could have finished him with a single thrust, but he was still human. I didn't want to kill anyone.

The Deputy was beside me, looking down at Brach. "You tried to kill my son," he said.

"I *have* killed your son," said Brach.

The Deputy reached down and lifted Brach up, holding the man against his body. Blood soaked from Brach's midsection into the Deputy's fancy black overcoat.

"Let the Waters judge you," the Deputy said. He stepped to the edge of the cliff and pushed Brach into the water.

A wave crashed into us. Even though the Deputy couldn't see me, he grabbed me and pulled me by my jacket away from the cliff's edge.

"Where is he?" I asked.

The Deputy didn't answer. He wrapped an arm around me and held me close, his grip strong and tight.

"He can swim," I said. "He's an expert at the moat obstacle." But the ocean was roiling. No one could survive out there for long, whether or not he could swim, whether or not he was judged worthy. My renewed faith in the Waters faded. Without help, Caster would drown along with Brach.

"Let me go," I said. "I can save him."

"You will be pulled under," the Deputy said, still holding me.

"I won't," I said. I would use my Ability. *This* was what it was good for.

"Myra, no," he said. "You're only human."

"I'm human," I said, "but I'm also something else. I can save him." I flickered in. I twisted around in his arms. "You knew about me all along. You needed me then, and you need me now."

"I need you to live," he said. "Some of our children have to live."

I flickered and then pushed beyond. I broke into a thousand pieces, slipped from the Deputy's arms, and rose into the air. He grasped for me, grasped through me.

"Myra!" he shouted.

I'm sorry, I thought. But I had lost the power of speech. He ran toward the water, grasping as if I were still solid and within his reach, and a wave washed over him. He shook it off, drenched. "Caster!" he shouted.

I was growing bigger. I saw not only what was directly in front of me, but everything at once. There were solid people,

Plats and wounded Flickerkin. And ghostly people who now took on clearer shapes.

Hoof was farther away than the wounded people, my father still on her back. She mooed loudly. My mother was no longer with them, but where was she? I even saw beyond Hoof, down the cliff's edge to where Nolan and Porti and her father had gone. There were a few Flickerkin down there, and Nice Boy, covered in cloth. Someone was tending Porti's father. Porti was crying, holding on to her father's hand.

Member Solis's body floated atop a wave. The Deputy cried out and reached toward it. But where was Caster? I rose higher, pushed myself out over the ocean. *Focus, Myra,* I told myself. I had to control my vision, find Caster in the waves. He was a strong enough swimmer to have survived this long. He had to be. I propelled myself above the waves, sending my strange long vision over the water, searching. There! A hand, and then a head. Caster spat water, flailing to stay afloat. I flew to him.

He went under, then surfaced again. Without arms, I couldn't grab him. Nor could I just float above him and watch him die. Pinwin had somehow become half solid, so there was a way. I pushed back against the flicker and stopped the mist. One arm became solid, then the other. But I remained invisible.

I grabbed one of Caster's hands.

He looked up.

Caster. I had to make him understand that it was me.

He grabbed my other hand.

I pulled, but I had no strength. I was floating against nothing. I was arms with no leverage. The waves pulled him under again.

I flickered in and dropped like a stone into the water, still holding his hands. I kicked with my feet. A wave crashed over me. This was nothing like swimming in the calm moat. The water seemed to be attacking me from all sides.

Caster clung to me, shaking his head. He tried to speak, but another wave caught us. I flickered without meaning to, then tried to lift my body again, but I wasn't misting. I was invisible, but solid and heavy and vulnerable as before. We were both going to die here. We would find out if there was another plateau beyond this one, with oceans that rose and fell on expected tides. We would find out if Plats and Lefties could be together.

Hands grasped my arms and pulled me up. I could see nothing but a blur and had no idea how they had the strength. I held on to Caster. The misting people, whoever they were, would have to save both of us. We rose above the water. Caster coughed up water, still clinging to me.

I wrapped my arms around his chest. Misting people surrounded us. We flew back to shore, over the Deputy, who stood shouting at us.

The fighting was over. Orphos's father was on his knees, Gregor's father helping him. Another Council Member appeared to be dead. I spotted three dead Flickerkin, their pale faces covered in ocean spray. My new cousin Terta was among them, but my mother wasn't. Perhaps she was among those holding me now.

The misting people dropped us on top of Hoof. Caster listed to the side, but I caught him before he fell. My father was in front of me on Hoof's back. He twisted around and grabbed me, and the three of us teetered there.

The misting people sank to the ground and regained their human shapes. I recognized Nolan. The other two were women.

"*Momman? Mommanan?*" I asked.

"Drop the boy and head for the others," my mother said. She pointed far off, toward Porti and her father.

"No, I'm not leaving him," I said.

"Myra," Caster said, coughing, "leave me. They've all seen you."

"You used the triggering rod on me again," I said to Nolan. "I told you not to do that. I should have turned from you the first time, exposed you to the Guard that moment."

Two guardsmen were approaching us. I saw a few others, but at least three of the ten were missing. Had they been taken by the Waters? Had my so-called kin killed them? The two guardsmen held sensors, but the beams weren't on. The Deputy hobbled behind them, blood streaming from an injured leg.

"Myra." Nolan grabbed my arm, and I broke to pieces. I

fought the misting, but I saw myself through his eyes. I saw my-self turning with my hand to my neck at the moment when I told Hoof I had been stung by bees. I felt us running from the courtyard with Brach in pursuit, my hand in Nolan's, our hearts beating, our faces close as we hid, as he urged me to flicker. And when he let my hand go, left me to go back to my life, I felt how he felt, I felt the emptiness, the unfairness, the anger.

I thrust myself into solidity but remained invisible. I hated to be like him, but I wanted to be able to see everyone.

Hoof mooed and reared. In the distance, Monster mooed back.

Caster laughed, a loud, desperate sound. I felt the same wild relief. Monster was alive. He would help us get through this. Then there was another moo—Nice Boy, calling from far away—and then another. It was not the sound of a workbeast, the kind that would draw a carriage, but that of a purebred. Was it Brach's beast, the one that had spooked us on the practice day that seemed so long ago? It mooed again, a long, heart-wrench-ing wail. The beast somehow knew its rider was dead. At the thought, tears sprang to my eyes. But Nolan must have known about this beast all along. He had pretended ignorance about so many things. They all had.

"Myra, we must go *now*," said my mother. "You aren't safe here. We have done all this to keep you safe." I was sure she believed it. She had lived her life in fear of being discovered and didn't believe there could be another way. But I was no child. I knew right from wrong, and their way was as wrong as the Deputy's.

"*Lopa*," my grandmother said. Come.

Caster let go of me.

"No." I grabbed his arm. "Poppa, you must decide. I wish to stay and work for peace, for a world where Plats and Lefties and Flickerkin can live together. Where there will be no more fights and no more death. You understand this. You can help. Stay here with me."

It was a terrible thing for me to ask. It was a terrible thing the Flickerkin had asked of me. I didn't want them all to be caught; I wanted them to be safe. But I couldn't be with them. They had tried to take away my choice.

The Deputy's guardsmen raised their sensors.

"Leave now," said the Deputy. He pointed at the invisible Flickerkin, and his finger led straight to my mother's nose. "You have saved my son, so I'll give you one minute before they fire."

"I'm staying," I said. My father looked at my mother, but in her invisibility, she couldn't return his gaze. If he stayed with me, he would be breaking with her. All these years of defying custom and even the Waters to be together would end now.

"I gave you my word," said the Deputy. "Donray, if you had no part in this, you too will be safe."

Nolan lunged for the Deputy.

"Watch out!" I cried.

The Deputy raised his arms.

Caster leaped from Hoof's back and landed on top of Nolan.

The guardsmen shot sensor beams that hit Caster harmlessly.

Caster and Nolan wrestled, but Caster didn't have a chance against someone who was stronger, who hadn't been in the ocean drowning.

"Nolan, leave!" I shouted. "I will point you out to them. I will ride over you. I will trample you with these hooves. I will kill you!"

Nolan pushed Caster away and came toward me.

I pulled Hoof around.

Nolan stopped. I could almost see his eyes in the flicker, asking me one last time to forgive him and come, to forget everything he had done.

"You were with Brach!" I cried. "You helped kill Orphos!"

"We fight for our lives!" he shouted back. "Our families, our kin."

"You are as bad as they are!" Tears rolled down my cheeks. I should have seen it from the beginning. It must have been him in that room at Porti's party, terrorizing children to begin the panic, turning the city against all who were like us.

"We aren't the enemy," he said. "You'll see that." He reached out a hand. Did he really believe I would take it after all this?

"I will kill you!" I shouted.

He took one last look at me, and then he ran. My mother and my grandmother had become mist. My mother hovered next to Hoof, a tendril of mist reaching for my father's hand.

"I'm sorry, Rhonda," my father said. "We need peace." He put an arm around me. "Myra and I will work for that."

Another tendril reached out from the mist and touched my face. Tears spilled from my eyes, but I said nothing. I had nothing to say to her but angry words, and I didn't want to say them if she was leaving us.

Her mist rose up into the air and floated along the cliff's edge toward the others. My grandmother went with her. She had not even tried to say goodbye.

"Father!" Caster cried. As I turned to watch, the Deputy collapsed in Caster's arms.

"I'm all right," he said. But he couldn't stand under his own power. Caster gently lowered him to the ground. For the first time, I saw that he was bleeding from his side as well as his leg.

I flickered in and climbed off Hoof. My father followed me, and we both kneeled next to the Deputy.

"I said I'm fine," the Deputy snapped.

I saw Sky out of the corner of my eye, and one man with a photobox. They were coming from the direction of the tree line, where they must have waited out the fight, the cowards.

Caster held up a hand to them and shook his head.

Sky turned the receiver off and took a step back. For the first time, the man was cowed. But the photobox man filmed on.

"We have much work ahead of us," the Deputy said. Even now, after he had tried to save me, his voice was chilling. This was the same man who had tortured me. But I had made my choice to stay here and not join the rebels in the Eye, so I listened.

A guardsman approached, holding a set of prezine cuffs.

"No," the Deputy said. "Let Miss Hailfast be. She and Member Hailfast are under my protection."

The guardsman stepped back, but I didn't feel protected. The Deputy might not have me arrested, but he might trap my father and me in our home. He might demand that we disown my mother, and I wouldn't do that in public, even if I did it inside my heart. I wouldn't hide my true nature, either. It was too late for that, and besides, I was no longer ashamed of my Ability. I had used it for good today, proving it *could* be good. I had helped save Caster; I had protected members of the Council and my parents. I would continue to use the Ability, and to learn everything that I could do. I would not be trapped anywhere.

"I will need both of you to help me," the Deputy said.

"We will not work for you or for Plat rule," I said. "Only for peace."

The Deputy's eyes met mine. There was a part of me that wished he would die and leave us all free of him. But his gaze was strong.

"Peace is a worthy goal," he said. "Above all, no more death." He gripped Caster's hand. "Can we agree on that, son?"

Caster nodded, tears filling his eyes. "We can."

My father put his arm around me. "Agreed," he said.

The Deputy attempted to push himself up, but Caster gently held him down. "Father, please, save your strength," he said. "See, there are carriages coming to help you back." Indeed, behind us, beasts were drawing carriages out of the city gates. Citizens streamed out onto the sand.

I looked up, past the Deputy to the ocean. Waves still lapped the shore. I wondered for what reason the Waters returned, but I was content to wait for that answer, because I had one of the answers I had been seeking. I didn't know whether I was Plat, Leftie, or Flickerkin, but I knew that I had a purpose. I could help reach both sides of this conflict before it became another war. I could prevent more bloodshed. And I would do it openly, as all parts of myself.

Caster and I reached for each other's hands.

I thought of Porti and her father, now far from us. Of my mother and grandmother, chased away. Of those who had died here fighting for the superiority of one race or the other. My existence was proof that the races could live together and love. Caster was proof that one generation's hate could give way to understanding. Together, we would work for the future we believed in.

Let the Waters come.